HIGH HUNT

Susie Drougas

SUSIE DROUGAS

High Hunt

Copyright © 2015 Susie Drougas
All Rights Reserved

Except for brief quotations for purposes of review, no part of this publication may be reproduced in any form or by any means, electronic, mechanical, recording or otherwise, without express written permission from the author.

This is a work of fiction. Any resemblance to persons living or dead is entirely coincidental.

ISBN-13: 978-1519678751
ISBN-10: 1519678754

Layout and design by Katherine Ballasiotes Rowley
Edited by April M. Laine Oostwal and Alice Trego
Cover Photo by Susie Drougas
www.SusieDrougas.com

Published in the United States of America

Pasayten Airstrip, possibly during its construction. Circa 1936.
(Courtesy of John Townsley)

Log cabin currently standing at Pasayten Airstrip

Dusty Rose goes back to the Pasayten Wilderness in September to help his Uncle Bob with his outfit in high hunt camp. The mountains give Dusty a lot of time to think.

Being in a relationship scared the hell out of him. He couldn't think of anything else that put that kind of fear into him. Not having a grizzly pass within feet of him or having to face off a mountain lion and shoot him in the air at mid pounce. No, he shook his head, this was much scarier.

Dusty stood rooted to the floor facing her. Looking at her in earnest, he finally said, "Cassie, I'm not very good at this, but I would like to see you again."

When two of Uncle Bob's top paying clients demand to hunt at the remote Pasayten Airstrip, Dusty and Mike volunteer to guide them. Little did they know the trip would bring them into a collision course with their past and nearly cost them their lives.

Slowly he made his way through the brush and then between the trees and found the small herd of horses grazing—but still no Mike. Dusty snapped a lead on Muley and one on the black quarter horse. "Mike," he called again loudly. Then listened, watching Scout. His dog's ears were forward, but he wasn't moving. Fear clutched Dusty's heart at the thought of something happening to his friend. He knew he needed to remain calm. Maybe Mike had gotten turned around in the snow and darkness. Anything could have happened. He needed to get the horses to camp and then he'd come back out and look.

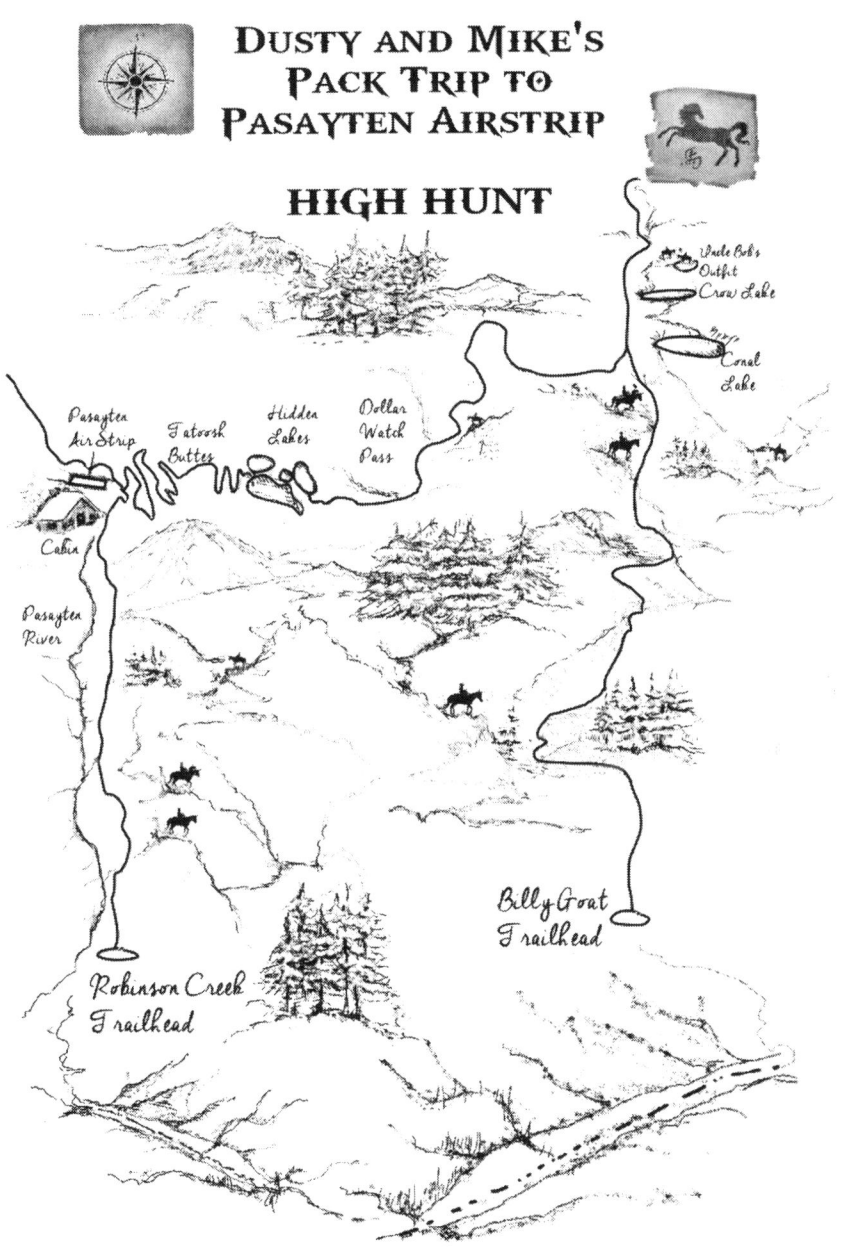

Acknowledgments

I want to thank my Back Country Horsemen friends for all your help and encouragement on this book.

My Yak Writers group for your critiquing, inspiration and keeping me on course. G.K. Kruszka for reading my book and helping me with edits.

Katherine Ballasiotes Rowley, once again, your hours of hard work, artistic talent and graphic design brought this book to life. I can only hope to write a book well enough to fill your cover. Your encouragement and support continue to push me through the slumps of writing and onward to the finish line. It makes me think every day, I'm so glad we buddied up in 2nd grade.

April Laine Oostwal, my dear gifted friend in Amsterdam. You never cease to amaze me with your ability in grammar, punctuation and story. Thank you so much for being my "final eyes" on my books.

Dedication

I want to dedicate this book to horse outfitters. For all the hours you put in the saddle, all the dudes you pack into the mountains, all the fires you cook over, all the planning, packing, cleaning, unpacking you do.

And your horses and mules. For all their saddling and unsaddling. Carrying riders and packs up and down mountains, through snow and rivers. Heavy people, light people, old people and young, knowing their job and doing it willingly, day after day.

You people are a link to our past and our present. People who are in limited physical condition are able to enjoy the backcountry in a way they never could without you.

It fills my heart with joy to see you on the trail. You know what kind of life a packer has—and you choose it.

Thank you,
Susie Drougas.

HIGH HUNT

Chapter One

Dusty Rose drove his F350 Ford truck up the mountain road, the horse trailer rattling behind him. He was deep in thought as he wove through the alpine fir to the Billy Goat trailhead. He loved the Pasayten Wilderness this time of year. *Well, every time of year, but there was something about the breaking of fall into the silence of winter in the wilderness that drew him in. The final closure of autumn into the death of winter, only to be followed by rebirth in the spring.*

He smiled to himself. *Finally getting to be a philosopher. The woods bring it out in me.* He pulled into the parking area at the Billy Goat trailhead. Unlike summer, all the SUVs and compact cars were gone. The parking area was filled with trucks topped with campers and horse trailers. He counted and came up with ten, a full house for this trailhead. Dusty found a spot next to his Uncle Bob's big stock trailer and parked. Scout, his Australian shepherd, looked at him expectantly. "Come on, Boy. You want to do some hunting?"

After setting up camp, Dusty put his rugged-built Appaloosa Muley, and his fine-boned packhorse, Cheyenne, into the wooden corral. His Uncle Bob was an outfitter in the Pasayten Wilderness and had been for years. Bob used the Billy Goat trailhead to launch his riders into the wilderness. When he had a group, they would meet at the trailhead and Uncle Bob and his trail hands would get all the gear laid out and packed. Last Dusty had heard, Bob just let his dudes bring gear to fill half a mule to pack in. Even at that, it was a quite a production. The main thing with outfits was always the food. Fine dining was alive and well in the Pasayten, as well as other wildernesses. No matter where they were—people liked to eat.

The days had become short, even shorter in the high altitudes. Dusty wiped the sweat from his brow after setting things up. The evening chill against his skin cooled his body fast. He shrugged into his Schaefer thermal-lined jacket, went to the back of his trailer and pulled out a couple of horse blankets. Cheyenne and Muley were fine when they were moving, but being in the corral, or even highlined, as they would be later, were less able to keep warm.

Dusty threw the first blanket on Cheyenne. The white horse didn't even look at him and kept on eating. When he went to throw Muley's blanket on him, the horse flattened his ears and menacingly bared his teeth at Dusty. He laughed and just kept right on adjusting the blanket. Muley was once again proving he wasn't a horse for everyone. The blue roan was an intimidator, and even though Dusty had owned him for years and raised him from a two-year-old, the big horse never quit trying. It was almost as if he had to make sure that Dusty was still the right rider for him, and Dusty never let him down. They had a bond that horsemen sought and rarely found. This horse would do anything Dusty asked of him and there was no quit in him. He was, beyond a doubt, the best horse Dusty had ever owned.

After caring for the horses, Dusty gathered some twigs and built a small fire. The sky was completely dark. The winter chill settled around him. He ate dinner and heated some coffee on his stove. Mike, his riding partner, would be meeting him up at Uncle Bob's camp in two days; he had to take care of some things before he left. Dusty had planned to be up here for 10 days. He'd told Bob last summer he'd come back and help out at the outfit during hunting. Dusty chose the high hunt season, which occurs in mid to late September. Despite all the work and cold, Dusty loved hunting camp in the high country. He'd spent his summers in the Pasayten helping his uncle since he was old enough to ride a horse. And his parents had always let him take at least a week off to help Bob in the fall. It brought back fond memories every time he came.

Dusty hunched down in his camp chair and an involuntary shiver passed through him. *Except the last time he was here.*

He flashed back to the unfortunate family he'd met last summer. Even in this day and age, the woods were still an unpredictable environment. You can have your ten essentials for outdoor survival, but that didn't guarantee safe passage. The Ross family had been ambushed by some thugs illegally crossing the Canadian border into the U.S. through the Pasayten Wilderness. Dusty poked the fire. It had ended with the father getting killed, the young girl being taken hostage and the boy saving his sister.

Those kids sure had guts. You didn't see a lot of that anymore. The girl, Sally, said she wanted to work on Uncle Bob's outfit. He hoped that that happened. She was the kind of person that fit in up here. She had sand. He flashed on his all-time favorite movie, *True Grit.* Mattie Ross, the girl in that movie used that phrase. Even today, those were the only kind of women that made it in the wilderness. *Men and women really*, he corrected himself.

His thoughts drifted to Cassie. The attractive young woman arguing passionately for her client in the Seattle courtroom, contrasted by the self-assured horseman he encountered high in the Cascade Mountains; one and the same person. That woman had sand too. Dusty reflected on his homecoming from Cougar Lake a couple weeks ago. The one thing he seemed to be really good at was messing up relationships with women. His marriage wasn't stellar. He'd put 20 years into it and got two great kids. But he knew from his law practice that you had a successful divorce when you realized you were happier single than married. His dating life after that had been pretty much of a disaster. Marrying right out of law school, how was he supposed to know that women didn't like casual flings and expected a commitment pretty much after the first date? Dusty took a drink of coffee. The whole thing was too much drama and way too difficult. Being in a relationship scared the hell out of him. He couldn't think of anything else that put that kind of fear into him. Not having a grizzly pass within feet of him or having to face off a mountain lion and shoot him in the air at mid pounce. No, he shook his head, this was much scarier.

Dusty had driven over to Cassie's house after he got home from Cougar Lake. Scout sat in the front seat with him to lend moral support, or because he was Dusty's dog and it was a truck ride, but he liked to think the former. Cassie's Australian shepherd barked in welcome as Dusty pulled into the driveway. He got out and headed up to the door. It was a very long walk. Cassie stood in the doorway. She had a question in her eyes and a coolness that he understood, but sliced it through his heart anyway.

"What's up?" she asked.

"I—I thought I'd stop by," *he said clumsily. He willed himself to look into her eyes, but his feet were moving in slow motion.*

She looked beautiful. She wore a light-weight plaid shirt with the sleeves rolled up. Her long brown hair lay softly on her shoulders. Her sky blue eyes were guarded, measuring him as he spoke. She remained standing in the doorway.

"Can I come in?"

"Oh," *she hesitated,* "Sure." *She turned and went into the house. Dusty followed. His stomach was knotted in panic. He wanted to leave, jump in his truck and pretend it never happened. He continued to follow her into the house.*

Cassie walked into the kitchen and stopped. She turned to face him and waited. Her face was a combination of confusion and annoyance.

Dusty stood rooted to the floor facing her. Looking at her in earnest, he finally said, "Cassie, I'm not very good at this, but I would like to see you again."

"That wasn't exactly the impression you left me with last time you stopped by," she said flatly.

Dusty felt like he had been physically punched, but what had he expected? That was one of the list of things he respected her for; she called it like she saw it. "I'm sorry about that, but I really mean it. I left last weekend to try to get things straight in my mind. I thought I could just walk away and be myself. Alone." His voice softened as he looked at her, "I couldn't stop thinking about you." He decided to take a chance. Crossing the room, he pulled her into his arms. She came easily, despite anything she may have been thinking. He kissed her and she kissed him back. He felt a dull roar in his ears and his skin burned where it touched hers. He knew he was crossing over into a place he feared to go, but a giant river had him in its current and he let it take him right over the falls.

He picked her up and carried her upstairs to her room. They undressed quickly and were in each other arms. The need to be with her overcame all the reasons he had to stay away.

Dusty's heart pounded like it was going to burst out of his chest. She smelled like faint perfume and the outdoor air. This woman completely consumed him. He burned with passion. Her arms pulled him closer and he had a kaleidoscope of mountains, wild rivers and running horses pounding through his head.

They lay in her bed together, exhausted. Dusty held her. He didn't want to let go of her. Her closeness made him feel complete. A peace enveloped him and he needed it. After being shot a couple weeks ago at Cougar Lake by Roy, an insanely jealous suitor of Cassie's, and knowing he might never see her again, he knew he needed to make it right—or as right as he could.

"You have quite a way of stopping by to say hi," she teased.

Dusty pulled her close and talked into her hair. "I guess I do. You bring it out in me." She turned her head to kiss him and everything started all over again.

Dusty felt the night air settle on his shoulders. His fire had grown small. It was going to be an early morning tomorrow and a long ride in. He banked his fire. "Come on, Boy. Let's hit the hay." They walked to the horse trailer. Dusty had cleaned it out and set up a cot with his sleeping bag. No reason to put up a tent when he was taking off so early. He knew his dreams would keep him warm.

Chapter Two

A heavy frost covered everything the next morning and Dusty could see his breath as he brought hay to his horses. They eagerly tore into it; eating helped them to stay warm. Dusty skipped breakfast and grabbed an energy bar. He heated a cup of coffee on his portable gas stove he set up on the tailgate of his truck. After feeding Scout, Dusty built a small fire to ward off the morning chill while he waited for the horses to finish eating.

Sitting by the fire and drinking his coffee, he reflected. It had been a long time since he had been up here for hunting camp. Remembering back as a kid, he never missed one. Even amidst big arguments with his dad about where he needed to be: a family trip to Europe over Thanksgiving, Hawaii, Mexico, wherever. They could keep it. He wanted to help out Uncle Bob. Now he could. Being single with grown kids, and owning his own law firm had finally put him in a position where he could do what he wanted to do without argument. He knew he wasn't going to be able to part with that ever again. Standing up, he tossed out the rest of his coffee and began preparing his gear to pack into the wilderness.

As Dusty swung into the saddle, the gray clouds were beginning to lift. The sun was starting to shine through the thick cottony sky. He had checked the weather before he left home; it looked like there might be snow sometime this week. That was the thing about the Pasayten, as all the locals in Winthrop, the closest town, would be the first to point out: it had its own weather system.

No one else was on the trail and the muffled footfalls of hooves meeting dirt were all Dusty heard. Muley was stepping out and they were making good time, both of his horses were in excellent shape after a full summer of riding—athletes at their peak. The only difference now was the cold weather. Definitely colder than it had been in Eagleclaw. The animals were used to variation in temperature after all the time spent riding in the mountains.

Scout trotted in front of him, staying out of the way of Muley's hooves. He was already panting. The summer haircut Dusty got him every year was thickening up. There wasn't anything to be done about it. If Scout got his coat trimmed now, he'd freeze sitting around at home.

The trees were thick as the trail ascended up Billy Goat. The Pasayten Wilderness is comprised of 530,000 acres, extending from Winthrop to the Canadian border in Washington state. Last he'd heard, there were four outfitters that ran in the wilderness. With all the regulations, Dusty wasn't sure how long that would last. The trail leveled out and he pushed Muley across a creek. Scout paused and sank down, lapping up water as he went. Dusty smiled, Scout still thought he was a Labrador retriever instead of an Australian shepherd. The dog could not resist water of any kind—he had to plunge in.

After watering, Dusty headed up Three Fools Pass. The trees thinned out and the grass on either side of the trail was still full of lupine. The deep purplish-blue flowers gave off a perfumed fragrance and were one of his favorites. At the top of the pass stood some dead trees bleached white from the sun and wind. Dusty pondered the fate of the trees. Up here it could have been a windstorm or lightning strike. He shuddered to think of the impunity and sudden appearance of the lightning. More than once he'd seen it strike nearby, appearing with very little warning. It was one of the dangers of the backcountry, and if you weren't prepared to encounter it, you had no business coming. None of it stopped Dusty; he still felt at home. If he got lost, it didn't matter. And like Gold Dust Charlie always said, You never get lost, sometimes you just get a little confused. Dusty had been confused, but always found new country to add to his mental list.

It was late afternoon when he crossed the last pass. The trees lessened and views of mountains appeared. The October scenery was spectacular with the larches bursting into fiery gold amidst the solid green pine and fir trees. In a short distance the trees dropped away and large meadows covered the hillside. The surrounding mountains towered above him. The peaks close by were dusted white. They extended into the distance until they became a deep blue. Dusty felt exhilarated just looking at the mountains and breathing in the crisp alpine air. *Good to be back.*

Cresting the hill above Corral Lake, Dusty stopped to let his horses blow. The hillside they had just ascended was deceptive. It looked mild, but the continuous climb was tiring for his stock. The deep blue of the lake lay before him. He drifted back to last summer and his camp there. It was hard to equate the calm serenity of the lake with the life-and-death struggle which had emerged from their "relaxing" pack trip when they encountered the Ross family. He shook his head. What should have been a wonderful bonding experience for the urban family turned into a tragic nightmare. It was always what lay beneath the surface that got you. Things rarely turned out the way they appeared. He should know that by now, but he was a slow learner at times. He glanced over into the thickening of trees, which he knew was Crow Lake. A plume of smoke wound up into the sky and dissipated in the late afternoon. Uncle Bob's outfit. He gave Muley a kick and headed down the trail.

The campfire was blazing and a few men were sitting in camp chairs by the fire.

"Well, I'll be doggoned! Look what the cat dragged in." A slightly stoop-shouldered old man with a well-worn cowboy hat and long gray beard walked up.

"Hi, Gold Dust. Good to see you." Dusty dismounted and they shook hands warmly.

"Glad t' see ya made it back here."

"Me too."

A slightly younger man in his sixties with white hair and gray stubble approached them walking up the hill from the horse area. "Is that my favorite nephew?" Without hesitating, the two men embraced in a big bear hug.

"Good to see you, Uncle Bob."

"So glad you made it." A wide grin split across the outfitter's weathered, suntanned face. Dusty looked at him. Identical deep blue eyes looked back. Dusty always marveled at the fact that he looked more like his uncle than he did his own father. They were bookends; the only difference was age and Dusty's height of 6'2".

"See you still got that ugly old Appy," Bob said jokingly, as he turned his attention to Dusty's horses. "You better get them set up for the night and join us for dinner."

Dusty looked up at the canvas wall tent with the smoke curling out the chimney and the man busily bent over the big Dutch ovens. "Hey, Andy."

The middle-aged man with a white apron, stopped stirring the pot for a minute. "Glad you made it, Dusty. Just about got dinner done here."

"Sounds good. I'll put my horses up." Dusty ignored the "ugly Appy" remark. He knew his uncle well, and with this group that was more a term of endearment than anything else. Muley was a tough horse. And he wasn't what anyone would call beautiful, unless maybe you were a Nez Perce Indian. The horse was a blue roan, which was actually a combination of black and white hairs mixed together, which gave a bluish cast. Muley's head was large and his eyes small and set back. He had a sour attitude toward other horses, kicking and baring his teeth at them. It was no feign either; Muley didn't miss, so Dusty always had to keep an eye on him. That was only the small downside to his horse. The upside more than made up for it. Muley would travel anywhere and never questioned Dusty. He would go all day long. They had a bond that all horsemen dream about; complete trust between man and horse. It made Muley the best horse Dusty had ever owned.

Dusty walked down to the makeshift hitch rail with his horses. Scout trotted along behind.

By the time Dusty got his horses unsaddled, turned out and dragged his own gear up to the main camp, everyone was sitting around the fire with cups in their hands.

"Help yourself," called out Andy from the fire.

Dusty filled up a plate of what looked like chicken, noodles and gravy from the big Dutch oven, grabbed a roll and took some salad. He walked over to the fire and sat down on a log.

"Have a seat," welcomed Bob. "Let me introduce you."

Addressing the rest of the men, "This is Dusty Rose, my nephew." The pride in Bob's voice was evident. Dusty was his boy, as far as he was concerned. His brother Dustin had never taken the time to really get to know his own son, but Bob had. His brother was always working, or chasing women. Dustin may have gotten a lawyer out of his son, but Bob had Dusty's heart.

Dusty and Uncle Bob were cut from the same cloth—packing horses in the high country—and it warmed Bob's heart knowing it. He knew things could have worked out a lot differently for Dusty if he hadn't had his passion for packing and his uncle to stabilize him.

Bob gestured at the young kid in his early 20s, "Down there is Pinto. He's our new wrangler. Jim had to leave right before hunting camp."

The short wiry kid with red hair, freckles and crooked teeth nodded at Dusty, "Pleased to meet you."

"Same to you."

Next to him sat the other wrangler, who was holding a plate and mopping up the gravy with his roll. "You remember Hank from last summer?"

"How's it going, Hank?" Dusty greeted him.

Hank nodded back at him.

"Well, he's not Hank anymore."

Laughter resounded around the campfire.

"His name got changed earlier this fall. It's Wrong Way now."

Hank sheepishly looked down at the ground. "I got a little turned around. It all worked out, though," he quickly added.

"Yeah," agreed Bob, "The only thing is I'm not sure the dudes wanted to stay out until midnight."

Laughter rose up loudly again.

"Next to Wrong Way is Cyrus and Josh."

The heavyset man with a Cabela's Tilley camo hat smiled at Dusty, "Nice to meet you." He looked knowingly at Bob, "We've heard a lot about you."

"Oh, come on now, Cyrus, don't give away all a man's secrets," Bob joked, unabashed.

"It's okay. I know how that is," said Cyrus, "This is my grandson Josh. He's up here for his first backcountry hunting trip." Pride filled the man's voice, Dusty could tell he shared the same paternal pride about his grandson.

"Nice to meet you," said Josh quickly. He was tall, lanky and medium weight, the opposite of his grandfather's compact form. They both shared the easy smile.

"Hi, Josh," said Dusty.

"And over here we have Scott, Randy and Pete, in just that order."

The three men were in their 40s, all had on camo ball caps, camo coats and Sorels. They were obviously three buddies that had come together to go hunting.

"Hey, you guys."

"Hey," they nodded back.

"And you know Gold Dust and Andy."

"Well, I'd say so, only since he was a seed," said Gold Dust.

"Always good to have you, Dusty," said Andy warmly.

Introductions over, the fire felt warm and burned brightly

against the darkness surrounding them. The stars sparkled as they appeared in the big night sky. The moon wasn't up yet, so he couldn't see the surrounding peaks, but Dusty knew they were there and it felt good. He was home.

Chapter Three

Dusty slept soundly. He always did when he rode in. It was a combination of the physical exertion of packing, the long ride, and the effects of the mountain air relaxing him. He had put his bedroll in his uncle's tent. A wood stove burned in the corner. He loved the smell of wood smoke and canvas from the wall tent. He looked over and his uncle's cot was empty. Uncle Bob was always an early riser. He'd have the horses out to graze before the first pot of coffee was on.

A sap-filled log in the black Riley woodstove crackled. Bob must have put another log in before he left. It worked surprisingly well holding the heat inside the tent walls. The square metal box sat on four legs, and a long pipe went out the top of the tent through a specially made stovepipe hole. As Dusty sat on the side of his bed and rubbed his eyes, he was just as warm as if he was at home. Scout had already left. He was probably too hot with his thick winter coat. From the glow of the stove, Dusty switched on the battery-powered lantern and pulled his jeans on over his long johns. It only took him a couple minutes. He put on his Sorels and headed out the tent door, shoving on his cowboy hat as he went.

The stars were starting to fade from the sky as the sun rose. Andy was cooking and he greeted Dusty as he walked up. "Coffee's on. Cups on the table, sugar and fixings if you go that way."

"Thanks, Andy. Black's good for me."

"Great. Do me a favor, if you would, and take that pot over to the fire."

"No problem." Dusty pulled on his lined leather gloves, picked up an empty cup, took the large coffee pot off the stove and walked over to the campfire.

Bob, Gold Dust, Pinto and Wrong Way were sitting by the fire drinking coffee.

"Morning, Dusty, have a seat," invited Bob.

Dusty poured himself a cup of coffee and set the heavy pot down on a rock by the fire.

"We were just discussing plans for the hunt today," said Bob. "Wrong Way is going to take the Boeing Boys up to the Peevy Pass area. There are a lot of whitetail in there. A year or two ago we even saw a doe with twins. It should be good hunting."

Bob took a drink of coffee. "I thought you could take Cyrus and Josh, head east toward the Ashnola River and see what you find down there."

Dusty stared into the fire. "Sounds good."

"And I'm sending Pinto back to the trailhead to pick up two more hunters."

"Too bad we didn't know," said Dusty. "Mike is heading in today or tomorrow and he could have brought them in."

"Well, that works both ways," observed Bob.

"I guess it does." Dusty was embarrassed. Things were so laid back up here, Dusty hadn't thought to let his uncle know the exact day he was coming. He just figured telling him last summer that he'd come was good enough. Dusty smiled to himself. *Funny how quick and easy it was to let go of the appointments and protocols of everyday life when you got back in the woods.* He imagined it wasn't so different for the cowboys in the earlier days before everyone ran on a clock. You gave your word you'd be there. The exact time was another story.

As they talked around the fire, the sun broke over the surrounding peaks. Dusty noticed a thick frost on the grass around them. That happened in the summer up there too. He had awoken to snow in the fall before. The one thing Dusty could count on was the weather could change without a moment's notice. He was comfortable with it and he packed accordingly. The Sorel boots worked well in the snow and thick frost. He couldn't wear his spurs, but he didn't need them on Muley. His horse knew what to do. Although Dusty didn't feel dressed to ride without spurs, he'd take the warmth.

"Good morning." Cyrus walked toward the coffee pot with an empty cup.

"Morning," everyone replied.

"Did you sleep well?" inquired Bob.

"Always do up here," came the older man's quick reply.

"That's a fact," agreed Gold Dust.

Josh walked up a few minutes later with his cup.

"Mornin', Josh," said Bob.

The young man poured his coffee and sat by his grandpa. "Good morning," he returned shyly.

"Hey, Wrong Way, Pinto, you about ready to eat breakfast?" called Andy from the cook tent.

Without wasting a second, the two hands set their coffee cups down and hurried over to the camp kitchen.

"Where's the Boeing Boys?" wondered Gold Dust Charlie. "Think we otter wake 'em up?"

"They were having a pretty good time last night. I'll at least give them a call and see if they want to try hunting," Bob said with a wink as he walked over to their tent.

Gold Dust looked over at Dusty and cocked his head, "So ya stayin' out of trouble?"

The question caught Dusty off guard and a small smile turned up the corners of his mouth as he thought about the past month. "I've been doing okay."

"Huh. Guess mebbe not." The old miner gave him a shrewd look and didn't miss Dusty's body language.

Uncle Bob walked back followed by Pete and Scott. "Coffee's hot. Just grab a cup over from Andy," he directed.

Both men turned and headed over to the cook's table.

When they returned, Dusty noticed they looked a little pale and shaky as they poured their coffee. "Where's your friend?"

"He's still sleeping," replied Pete. He pushed his glasses up and tried a tentative smile at Dusty. "Randy likes to party and have a good time." He hesitated and added, "He's a little better at it than I am."

Dusty smiled understandingly. At moments like this he always felt like someone had just walked over his grave. He had spent a lot of time riding and packing in by himself, knowing all too well the process of getting obliterated the night before and then trying to get well the next morning. He took a deep breath of the ice-cold mountain air. Uncle Bob hadn't see him much then. Dusty avoided people who would be able to see through his drinking. He was glad that he got out of it when he did. There was so much lost time to make up; he was grateful he had the opportunity to do it.

They all had finished eating and were back around the fire by the time Randy walked in. He was over 6'3" and at least 225 pounds. A former football player in high school, he recited play-by-play the same football game at least 15 times the night before. From the way he had been talking, Dusty got the distinct feeling those were the best days of his life. *This morning sure wasn't.* The large man's hand visibly shook as he held the coffee cup and attempted to pour into it. Most of the coffee sloshed over the side. Randy quickly put it down.

"How're you feeling?" asked Dusty in a quiet voice. He couldn't help himself.

Randy turned his bloodshot eyes to Dusty. "Okay." He added quickly, "Takes a while to get adjusted to this high mountain air."

Looking at the red veins and the yellow whites of the man's eyes, Dusty could see this was more than an occasional occurrence. His heart went out to the guy. He knew what it was like. He also knew Randy had to figure it out himself. "We are pretty high up here, right around 7200 feet."

"Andy's got breakfast for you over at the cook tent," offered Bob.

Randy sat down heavily on a log, a shade of green passing over his face. "I think I'll just stick with coffee for now, thanks."

Andy set out the lunch fixings and everyone packed their own. Pinto and Wrong Way had the dudes' horses saddled up and ready to go. Bob and Dusty got their own horses ready.

Bob tied his saddlebags on the back of his saddle. Finishing, he turned to Wrong Way and Pinto, who were just slipping the bridles on their own horses.

"Wrong Way, I want you to take the two Boeing Boys up to Peevy Pass, like we talked about before."

"Will do, Boss," the tall lean, man nodded.

"Pinto, you're going to the trailhead at Billy Goat to pick up two more hunters."

"Wha—aat?" Pinto clearly wasn't expecting to do that.

Hearing the defiance in his tone, Dusty quickly looked up from his saddle. He saw anger light up Pinto's eyes and quickly slide over his face. *Now that was weird.*

Bob obviously was taken aback by his demeanor too, because he did a double take at Pinto. The young man made a visible effort to quell his annoyance and ended up with a plastic half-smile on his face. He exposed a mouthful of crooked, yellow teeth and said, "Whatever you say, Boss. I'll get right on it." He mounted up on the young bay quarter horse and gouged him cruelly with his spurs.

"Take it easy there," cautioned Bob. "That's a good horse and I want to keep him that way."

If Pinto heard him, he didn't indicate it. Bob and Dusty watched his stiff back as he grabbed two of the saddled horses, and took off at a slow canter, the two horses pulling and running into each other to keep up.

"That's different," commented Dusty, watching Pinto and the horses drop over the hill into the gray early morning sky.

"Good help is hard to find up here. That kid seems to do okay for the most part, but he doesn't have the horse experience I would like."

"It appears he thinks he does," observed Dusty. "I guess that's part of being young."

"Yeah. He's got that temper flare-up thing. I don't care for that," said Bob.

"No," said Dusty, thoughtfully.

"But I guess until you're ready to give up that law practice and head up here, I'll have to make do." Bob slapped Dusty on the back playfully. "Let's go."

Dusty helped Josh and Cyrus mount up. He was a little worried about the older man. He seemed easily winded and it was difficult for him to mount his horse. Once he was seated, he smiled slightly embarrassed at Dusty. "Takes me a little while to get my riding skills back in place."

"Don't give it another thought, Cyrus. If I couldn't help out, I guess Uncle Bob would be wasting his money on me."

"Take it easy, Grandpa." said Josh, keeping an attentive eye on the older man.

"I'm fine, Josh. Let's go hunting," said Cyrus, all business now.

Dusty, Cyrus and Josh rode downhill from the camp through the trees. Wrong Way, Pete and Scott already left. Randy went back to bed.

Chapter Four

The three men wove their way through the trees and occasional large rock outcroppings. It was silent except for the horses' muffled hoofbeats on the thick, grassy slope. Josh was a little awkward in the saddle, but his youth made up for it. Cyrus, on the other hand, sat heavy on his horse and it made the animal work twice as hard to keep him balanced. The rifles bounced in their scabbards as the horses went over uneven terrain. Dusty took care to find the smoothest trail with the least amount of obstacles for the men and their mounts.

They rode for about an hour out of camp. The wilderness floor was covered with thick grass. This area was rich with grazing history. Dusty loved to read about the history of the Pasayten. *At one time most of the cattle and sheep were herded into the Methow highlands all the way from the Columbia Basin. Stock driveways were the first routes into a lot of the backcountry here. As early as 1889 cattle were recorded grazing on federal land in the Methow Valley's high country. By the early part of the century both sheep and cattle were wandering the high hills in the summer.*

Dusty checked back on his riders. Cyrus smiled and Josh nodded. "Not much further."

He settled back into the saddle and his thoughts continued. *When the demand for wool skyrocketed during World War I, approximately 75,000 sheep grazed the Sawtooth above the Twisp River. Forest Service records show that somewhere around*

High Hunt

100,000 total sheep pastured in the high country between the Methow and Okanogan valleys. The grazing remained heavy through the 1930s, but decreased through the '40s and '50s. The ranchers would put the animals out as soon as they could, but even at that, it was a relatively short season from snowmelt to snowfall. Some areas in the high country still show the mark on the land of historic sheep trailing. And the names certainly reflect the original use: Sheep Mountain, Sheep Lake and others. The last sheep grazing permit inside the present-day wilderness was converted to a cattle permit in 1949. Dusty had seen a few sheep outside of the wilderness in Harts Pass and further east in Horseshoe Basin country as late as the 1990s, when he was able to help out on Bob's outfit.

The history that composed such a huge wilderness was interesting to Dusty. He mused over it as he rode. They were here for whitetail deer. The count of elk was minimal in the Pasayten. He heard they got eight elk all last season, and that was out of the Sweetwater section. And in a forest this vast, eight was almost nonexistent. Encountering elk probably happened about as often as grizzly up here.

The riders came to a small grassy clearing and silently dismounted. At least deer weren't unnerved by the horses walking by. Dusty was grateful for that fact. They would stop and look, but didn't appear particularly threatened by horses. Deer up here saw people on a much smaller scale than in other more frequented areas, so they were curious. At least at first.

Cyrus stopped his horse. He awkwardly tried to lift his leg over the saddlebags on the back of his saddle while grabbing onto the saddle horn. He started to fall backwards and landed unceremoniously on the ground. Dusty was off his horse and tried to catch him before he went all the way over.

"I need to work on my riding skills, obviously," the old man whispered apologetically as he stood up.

"Everybody has to start somewhere," Dusty said accommodatingly, tying up Muley and then the two dudes' horses.

"Make sure you keep an eye out for each other," he cautioned. Scout sat obediently at his feet.

"Will do," said Cyrus. "Good luck, son," he addressed Josh. Then he turned and headed off through the trees, carrying his rifle pointed downward.

Josh hesitated for a moment. "Don't go too far," cautioned Dusty.

"Nope," said Josh. He veered off in another direction from his grandpa. As he walked toward the trees, his gun pointed in front of him. Then he appeared to self-correct and aimed it at the ground as he continued forward

Dusty sat on a log and waited. Scout laid down at his feet. He stared into the trees, relaxed, and his mind began to wander.

Dusty woke up at some point during the night. He felt really, really good. He checked himself internally for the usual panic that began to rise in his chest if he spent too much time around a woman. Nothing. There was no panic. He could hear Cassie's shallow breathing next to him. Her light brown hair was spread out on the pillow and she had a faint smile on her face. He didn't make it a habit to watch people sleep, but in Cassie's case he couldn't help it. She fascinated him. Her face was smooth—not a care in the world. Once again he felt that catch in his chest. God, she was beautiful.

Cassie must have felt the stare. She opened her eyes. "What's up?" she asked sleepily.

"You're beautiful."

"Just like that?"

"Just like that," he said positively. He pulled her into his arms and kissed her and the heat washed over them like a turbulent river.

Dusty woke later to the smell of bacon and coffee. He could hear the pots and pans banging in the kitchen. The bed next to him was empty. He pulled on his jeans and headed downstairs.

High Hunt

Standing in the kitchen doorway, Dusty watched her cook. Cassie hummed to herself while she flipped the bacon. Sammy lay quietly on the floor watching her and Dusty. She didn't bark—she had already figured out he was no threat. Cassie turned to open the refrigerator with her back still to him. "Good morning," he said.

Cassie let out a little squeak and turned to look at him, wide-eyed. "Oh," she smiled, embarrassed. "You startled me."

"That bad, huh?" Dusty smiled and ran his hand through his hair.

"Oh, no, I didn't mean that at all." She reddened. As he stood in the doorway in his jeans, tanned, toned muscles and perfect hair, she couldn't remember seeing a better-looking guy in her life. There wasn't a huge selection to pick from, she corrected herself, but this definitely was the most handsome man she'd ever seen. Plus, he had gone from being completely annoying to totally attractive. When he smiled at her, which seemed to be often, she felt her blood race. "How do you like your eggs?"

"Dusty. Dusty." Came an insistent whisper.

He must have dozed off. He had moved off the log and now he was sitting with his back against a tree. Josh was shaking him and whispering in a loud voice. "I can't find my grandpa. Have you seen him?"

"No, I haven't. I think I was sleeping." Dusty looked at his watch, ten o'clock. The morning sun was in the sky. All three horses sat tethered to trees and Scout quietly watched him as he lay next to his feet.

Chapter Five

"Why don't you stay here with the horses in case he comes back? I'll go look around," said Dusty, standing up. He was fully awake now.

"Okay." Josh sat his gun down. He looked at Dusty anxiously, "Do you think he's okay?"

"Sure. It's big country, but your grandpa isn't going to get that far. Don't worry, we'll find him." Dusty said reassuringly.

Scout led the way and they headed off through the trees. As he walked he looked around him and caught a glimpse of the surrounding mountains. Dusty could see Bald Mountain in front of him, stretching out like a big lounge chair in the distance. Checking himself with visual points was the best way to keep his bearings. Sure, there was GPS, but he had not let himself go that way. It seemed opposite to the reason that he went into the backcountry. Dusty wanted to get away from civilization, not bring it with him.

Growing up and working in Uncle Bob's outfit, he had learned early the skill of knowing where you were in the wilderness. Before he got to know the country, he always took notice of the mountains around him. He carried a map and compass, and his uncle had shown him how to use it by lining up true north. Dusty would never forget the feeling the first time he'd been disoriented in the forest. He was alone on his horse off the trail. When he looked around, all he saw were endless green trees that all looked exactly alike. He realized then why people got lost and confused in the woods—even when they weren't that far away from camp. In his case he was in the middle of nowhere. He didn't panic. He lined up his coordinates. It got him back to camp in a couple of hours. But better than that, he'd learned he was never lost in the woods, not as long as he could read a map and compass.

The trees were intermittent, and the hill gently sloped down to the Ashnola River. Dusty stopped and listened. It was silent in the trees. The water was too far away to hear yet. As he looked around, he knew that Cyrus couldn't go too far; he wasn't in that good of shape. Dusty figured he'd been out about three hours at this point if they'd gotten there about 7 a.m. He wasn't sure if Cyrus would have continued downhill, the path of least resistance and easier traveling, or been cognizant it would have been all uphill on the way back.

Dusty continued toward the river until he could hear it faintly in the background. He knew if he went north very much farther he would run into Timber Wolf Creek and that seemed too far. Dusty turned and dropped down lower on the hill. He was getting warm with his saddle coat on. He could have left it back with the horses, but he didn't know what he was going to find. Even a short hike could become something much longer in the wilderness. He'd rather be hot than hypothermic.

Walking above the river, the fragrance of fresh pine forest mingled with melted snow filled his nostrils. It helped relax the growing concern he was experiencing looking for Cyrus. Just when he was about to turn around, he saw a rifle laying in the grass. Scout stopped and Dusty picked it up. He was sure the older man wouldn't be that far away. Standing at the spot where the gun was, Dusty slowly scanned the area around him looking for any clothing or disturbance that would lead to Cyrus's location. He could see the white froth of the Ashnola below him, the currents rushing against the rocks.

"Cyrus, are you here?" Dusty shouted.

Silence met his call. He pushed down the feeling of

anxiousness. *This forest was relatively safe, or had been. The confrontation with the thugs last summer and the Ross family crossed his mind, but how many times had that happened? Just once. And yes, there were occasional wolves and grizzlies—but at this point it was just that—occasional.*

"Cyrus," Dusty shouted with a lot more volume this time. He paused and listened.

"Here." It was so faint, Dusty wasn't sure if he'd actually heard the answer, or just wanted to hear it. The forest stood around him silently. He looked at Scout. The dog was looking intently down the hill.

"You see him, Boy?" Scout took off at a trot and Dusty was right behind him, sliding and bounding down the hill. As he got closer to the water, he got his first glimpse of the older man, half laying, half sitting up by a rock. Scout arrived first and poked his furry head against the man.

Cyrus lifted a large wrinkled hand and petted him. "I'm glad to see you two," he said faintly.

Dusty slid in behind Scout. "Are you okay?"

"I think so. But I twisted my ankle, dropped my gun and lost my balance. Just about in that order." The older man reached down and rubbed his ankle gingerly. "I drug myself over to this rock and thought I'd rest up for a while before I tackled climbing that hill."

"Let's take a look at the ankle," said Dusty. He carefully picked up the boot that Cyrus had outstretched in front of him. The older man winced as Dusty touched it.

Dusty had to decide whether to unlace it or leave it tied. Keeping the foot bound would make it difficult to take the boot off later, but it would keep the swelling contained, depending on how badly it was sprained. The ice cold river pounded in the background and an idea came to him, "Let's put your foot in the water for a few minutes to help with the pain." He helped Cyrus get the boot off. His foot was swollen and a purple bruise was beginning to form on the veined ankle. Dusty got under the older man's shoulder and helped him hobble to the river's edge.

"Ahhhh," said Cyrus as he put his foot in the water. "I can't tell whether this feels better or worse," he said through clenched teeth.

"Well, either way, you're probably not going to feel it at all in a couple minutes."

Scout waded in and sat down in an eddy, lapping up water as he went.

"Looks like it's not too cold for him," Cyrus hissed.

"No, he's never been one to let a good body of water go to waste—no matter what time of year," agreed Dusty. Both men laughed.

After a few minutes passed, Cyrus relaxed. "I think it's better now. I can't feel my foot."

"That's a good sign. Let's wrap it back up and head back to Josh. I've got a feeling he's going to be really glad to see you."

Dusty noticed the swelling had gone down perceptively as he helped Cyrus put his sock and boot back on. It wasn't going to stay that way, but at least it would take the bite out of the steepest part of the hill, which was where they were now, right by the river.

"Hang on for second," said Dusty, standing up. He looked around and found what he needed not too far away; a stout stick. Pulling out his knife, he cut off the branches and brought it back to Cyrus. "This ought to help."

"Thanks, Dusty," Cyrus said gratefully. He planted the stick in the ground and took a tentative step. Pausing, he took a few more. Dusty could tell from his face it was painful, but at least now he had something to lean on. The older man walked heavily, leaning on the stick and stepping with a pronounced limp.

Dusty wasn't sure how long it took them to walk back. He could feel his stomach growling, so it was well past noon. Cyrus did his best, but after the initial incline of the hill, he had to take periodic rests—apologizing profusely. Dusty assured him it wasn't his fault and it could have happened to anybody. He really liked Cyrus. He could tell he was a good man and he honestly loved his grandson. *You didn't come across that often enough*, Dusty reflected. When he saw simple honestly in people, it touched him. He had a lot of respect for the older man.

Three sets of pointed ears appeared in the trees. Scout darted ahead. Dusty could see Josh pacing by the horses.

"Grandpa!" The young man raced up to Dusty and Cyrus. "Are you okay?" Without waiting for an answer, he threw his arms around the older man.

"Yes. Yes, I'm fine." Cyrus patted him on the back. "I just got a little sprain is all. I'll be fine."

Josh looked at him, concern mixed with anxiety etched across his face. "Are you sure?"

"Yes, Boy. With the assistance of Dusty here, I'm just fine," he replied, with as much strength as he could muster.

"Let's have some energy bars and head back to camp for lunch," said Dusty, as he helped Cyrus sit down. "I always carry them in my saddlebags."

Dusty learned that as a youth too—even when you plan to be back, always bring food. This was going to just be a morning hunt and they were coming back for lunch, which they would, but it would be a few hours late. Dusty handed out the bars and gave Scout his dog bone. A man never forgot his dog. Scout had done more than his share of work today locating Cyrus. Dusty looked at him fondly as he chewed on his bone. *Best dog I've ever had.*

He smiled as he bit into his bar and the older man recounted his adventures of the morning.

Chapter Six

The autumn sun was low in the sky as they rode into camp, and the evening chill was palpable. Uncle Bob walked up to them. "I thought we were going to have to send out a search party pretty soon," he exclaimed. "Either that or you got an animal."

"I wish," said Cyrus.

"Just took us a little longer. Got any lunch left?" Dusty said abruptly, not wanting to embarrass Cyrus. He dismounted and walked over to help the older man off his horse. Cyrus was still in pain from the sprain. He stiffly dragged his right leg over the saddle. As he put his weight on the ground, Dusty supported him. The older man stiffened and swayed as he put his foot down, appearing to almost collapse.

Josh hadn't missed a thing, keeping a sharp eye on Cyrus. He dismounted and hurried over to his grandpa. "Can I help you get over to the fire?"

"Well, that might be a good idea, Son. Thank you." Taking his arm, the older man leaned heavily into his grandson and they slowly made their way to the gathering area. The fire was dancing and crackling in the dreary afternoon. With the unpredictable temperatures from freezing cold to fall-like coolness, if the camp was occupied, a fire was going. A seemingly never-ending stack of wood sat next to the blaze. The wranglers' job was to keep it full, and Bob made sure they did. Gold Dust Charlie's voice boomed out in welcome to the men as they approached.

Dusty grabbed the three horses' reins and took them off to unsaddle. Bob walked over to the fire to see about getting his guests comfortable.

The horse area was kept just below the camp on the hill. Bob had lashed together old logs for a makeshift corral. It served as a temporary holding pen for the horses waiting to be saddled or turned out. Dusty tied the stock to the hitch rail and pulled the saddles off. He threw them up on the saddle racks, also fashioned from logs lashed together, putting the blankets on top to air out. A tarp covered them to keep the animals away. The porcupines, deer and small rodents, among others, were attracted to the salt. More than once Dusty had repaired chewed-up leather while working on the outfit. Covering them, for the most part, was a good deterrent.

He brushed down the horses and turned them out. The smell of horse sweat and mud filled his nostrils as he worked. The fall air was brisk, with a hint of snow in it. Dusty felt like he was two people—the man he was now and the guy wearing a suit in the courtroom. He'd be lying if he said he didn't enjoy the mental gymnastics of the law. How to find exactly the right case and use it in exactly the right way to come out victorious for his client. The adrenaline rush of winning.

But all of that was nothing compared to how he felt up here in the mountains. He did what he had to do for now, but he knew at some point he'd be walking away from his law practice for good. Dusty needed to set himself up financially first, and that was going to take a while yet. He put the horses into the corral and walked back up to camp. Scout trotted behind him.

The fall sunlight had faded and been replaced by a heavy gray fog that seemed to settle in the hills around them. As Dusty walked past the cook tent, he could feel the chill against his face.

Andy, the cook, was undeterred by the weather. He had just finished putting the lid on a large Dutch oven and setting it on the coals.

He had a smaller cooking fire and he heated his ovens with

charcoal briquettes, or a huge gas stove, depending on what he was cooking. The briquettes made judging the heat easy. Dusty had seen it done plenty of times and even tried cooking with them himself. He knew the rule of thumb was briquettes spaced two inches apart on the top and on the bottom of the Dutch oven equated to about 350 degrees. You put more or less, depending on the ambient temperature and the cooking heat you wanted. It was hard to mess something up cooking with Dutch ovens, and the fresh outdoor air made people extra hungry. But there were still some people that had a special knack for it and Uncle Bob's cook was one of them. He had a reputation that extended over the whole Pasayten Wilderness and beyond. Dusty heard he had even published a cookbook on cooking with Dutch ovens.

Dusty stopped for a minute and asked, "What are you making tonight, Andy?"

"I got barbeque beef brisket that I marinated all night, carrot salad, cornbread and caramel apple crisp." Andy piled some coals on top of the large oven and stood up.

"That sounds amazing." Dusty's mouth watered. He was hungrier than he thought. Looking for Cyrus had taken his mind off food, and the energy bars weren't much.

Andy smiled at him. "That's my job."

"And you're really, really good at it." Andy flashed a big grin and Dusty turned toward the fire. Besides good horses, good trails and good camps, a big staple of an outfit was good food and lots of it. He corrected himself—food and eating was the biggest part of the camp. As hard as he'd worked in the summer on the outfit, he couldn't remember ever losing any weight. All the cooks that Uncle Bob employed over the years were good, but Andy was the best.

Cyrus had his foot propped up on a log as he sat in a lawn chair next to the fire, his grandson next to him. They each had a mug in their hand and tortilla chips on paper plates. Gold Dust was regaling them with a tall tale from the past and Cyrus had a big smile on his face.

At the other end of the fire ring sat the three Boeing workers. From the flush on his cheeks, Dusty assumed that Randy had started getting "tuned up" again. He was in an animated conversation with Scott and Pete, who sat stoically listening. They all held blue enamel coffee mugs in their hands, which Dusty assumed probably had something stronger than coffee in them.

A large stump by the fire pit held the tortilla chips and a large bottle of Jack Daniels sat next to it, with more metal cups. He picked one up and went to the fire, pouring from the ever-present large coffee pot. Sitting down by Bob he asked, "Anybody do any good?"

"Not so far," said Bob.

"We got off a couple shots out at Peevy Pass," said Wrong Way, "but they missed. Those deer always seem to know when it's hunting season."

"I guess that's part of the challenge," agreed Dusty.

"Did you ever see that deal on the internet they had with the hunters and the deer?" said the wrangler. "I think it was a video or something. The hunters were standing in this grassy area looking for this deer. The deer actually got down on his belly and crawled away from them in the grass."

"Really? No, I haven't, but I believe it. It seems like in the summer you can't get rid of them, but as soon as hunting season hits, they become amazingly scarce." Dusty took a drink of coffee.

"Pinto should be coming in any time now," said Bob, looking expectantly at the trail leading into the fog. "He's got two more hunters with him."

"You've got a full house, huh?" said Dusty.

"Hopefully they all get along in camp." Bob stared into the fire. "We'll take out separate hunting parties, of course, so no problem there. And Gold Dust is a great crowd manager," he added.

The three men looked across the fire and the old miner was winding up with another story. He never seemed to have a shortage of them. Cyrus and Josh's faces were all smiles.

Randy seemed to have recovered from his morning hangover.

His cheeks were flushed and he was animatedly talking to Scott and Pete. Dusty glanced over at him. Randy was well into another drunk evening. Watching him, Dusty felt a pull of compassion in his stomach. He knew exactly how Randy felt—he'd been there too. Bob and Pete smiled good-naturedly at Randy as he got louder and they all laughed and appeared to be having a good time. Although he'd spent a good deal of his time at home drinking at the end, Dusty remembered earlier times where he would basically tailor the trips around drinking. He shuddered at the thought of it now. He hadn't been there for his family and later, his dog or his horses. What would have happened if one of the horses had gotten hung up in the middle of the night on the highline? He wouldn't have been there to help them, laying passed out dead-drunk in his tent.

Dusty shook his head to clear it. That was a long time ago now, and he'd had eight years of sobriety to get over it. He knew he'd forgiven himself, but he'd never forget it either. Uncle Bob stood up. "I think they're coming in now."

Four horsemen emerged through the foggy gray light into camp. The horse's long hair was matted with sweat and their breath was coming out in steamy puffs. Pinto was on the lead horse, a young bay horse. The wrangler wore a cowboy hat and wild rag tied close to his neck. His expression was even more disgusted than when he'd started the very long ride out that morning. His lips were tightly clamped together like he'd bitten into a sour lemon.

Behind him sat another man in his early 40s. He wore top-of-the line hunting gear and boots, and a Rolex shown out from the sleeve of his camo coat and leather gloves. If he was in any discomfort, it didn't show. His arrogant attitude of self-entitlement was so thick Dusty sensed it even before he spoke. It seemed a good bet a major part of Pinto's problem lay with that rider.

Uncle Bob didn't let it stop him. "Welcome to the outfit," he said, sticking his hand out to shake the man's. "You must be Reginald Flynn?"

"Yes, Reggie is fine. Nice to meet you finally," he said, with emphasis on the last word, dismounting. He smoothly shook Bob's hand.

"Come on over to the fire while we get your gear unpacked," gestured Bob, as he walked up to the second man in the string. "And you are Clifford?"

"Yes, nice to meet you. You can call me Cliff." He awkwardly got off his horse. His clothing was on the same par as Reggie's—very expensively decked out. They were obviously set for roughing it for a few days. Their appearance left Uncle Bob undeterred. Working with dudes was part of his business, and they came in all different forms. Most people were excited to experience the backcountry. How well they chose to blend in after they got there was a different story. Sometimes less was more, but they didn't all see it that way.

The last rider sat quietly on his horse with an amused grin on his face. "Good to see you, Mike," said Bob, walking up to him and firmly shaking his hand. Mike returned the handshake from the back of his horse.

"Great to be here again." Mike dismounted and picked up Cliff's horse's reins along with his horse and his packhorse's. "I'll help Pinto get these horses squared away for the night."

"I appreciate that," said Bob.

"I'll help," Dusty said, walking over and picking up Reggie's horse's reins while Pinto took his packhorse.

"Okay, then. Dinner should be shortly." Bob turned back to the fire to make his new guests welcome.

The three men made short work of unsaddling the horses and putting the tack away. They put away all the saddles, blankets and bridles for the night. They secured everything, tucking the edges of the tarp underneath the equipment. The big job now was turning out the herd. They belled the lead mare and hobbled all the horses in the remuda and turned them loose. The clanging of the bell signaled the location of the stock as they walked away, heads down and ripping off tufts of grass. They had been silent as they went about their work. Dusty walked alongside Mike as they hauled bags up to the camp area.

"So how did you end up riding in with those guys?" asked Dusty.

"I met the lawyers at the trailhead last night. We shared a campfire and found out we were headed to the same place."

"*The lawyers?*" Dusty asked.

"Oh, yeah. Just wait—it's their favorite topic."

"You didn't say anything about me, right?" Dusty asked, the feeling of no escape quickly ascending on him.

"Are you kidding? Geez, Dusty, come on. I've known you how long? I know you hate that."

"Good." Dusty felt instant relief flood over him.

Mike took his pack bag over to set up his tent. Dusty set the bags he was carrying inside the remaining wall tent. There were two cots inside and a lantern hanging from the ceiling. Uncle Bob put a tarp on the floor. It was clean and roomy. As Dusty turned to walk out, he just about bumped into Pinto.

"How's it going?" Dusty asked, watching Pinto dump the bags on the floor.

"That guy is one asshole," Pinto hissed, appearing to be relieved to finally just say it.

Dusty looked at the younger man; he knew it was Reggie without being told. The man had grated on his nerves and he'd only barely met him. "You know, you're going to meet all kinds of people up here. This is the job you hired on to do. You're going to have to put your personal feelings aside and take care of business." He was protective of his Uncle Bob and the outfit. One bad wrangler could severely impact both.

Pinto's face was cold and angry. Dusty's words seemed to have bounced right off him.

"Did you hear me?"

"I heard," the smaller man said curtly.

Dusty looked more closely at him. He knew that wranglers could be hard to find and he wondered how much his uncle had interviewed this guy. He was okay with horses, but there seemed to be something off about him. He was going to have to talk to Uncle Bob about this kid. Somebody else should be guiding the lawyers.

"Okay, then. Let's go get some dinner." Dusty threw a quick arm around the younger man's shoulders to ease the tension. The younger man immediately hunched up. *Well, that was awkward.* Dusty quickly let go. Mike walked up just in time to witness the scene—silently he rolled his eyes. Dusty shot him a pained look, and the three of them walked up to the cook tent in silence.

Chapter Seven

Dusty settled around the fog as they walked to the camp kitchen. Two lanterns hung from ropes tied around the trees to light the area. Andy stood behind them ready to serve the sliced brisket. The ovens sat open on a metal table elevating them to serving level. The food smelled wonderful. The second oven held golden cornbread. It was cut in big chunks with melted butter dripping over it. Andy never was one to minimize helpings. Dusty already knew how good and moist the cornbread was; he was sure it would be completely gone in no time.

"Help yourself to butter and salad," Andy said, gesturing at the small table next to the ovens. The salad was set out with napkins and silverware. There were two log picnic tables in front of the cook tent. Both sat empty.

Dusty could hear talking by the fire. In the summer the tables would be full with dudes eating dinner, but in the colder weather usually everyone elected to take their plates to the warmth and light of the fire. He poured some lemonade into a tin cup, picked up his plate and headed over. Scout trotted behind him.

The heat hit Dusty in the face as soon as he got close. Uncle Bob had his hunting camp fire in full blaze. To help mitigate the colder temperatures, bigger logs were used for the evening. The wood measured a good 12 to 15 inches in diameter and the fire ring itself was four to six feet in length and at least three feet wide.

The heat flowed over him. Dusty felt like taking his jacket off as he sat on a log and set his cup down. The men were all eating and talking. They sat in the groups they had come with, the wranglers mixing in. Uncle Bob sat with Reggie and Cliff. He was always good with the more difficult guests. Wrong Way ate by the Boeing Boys, Randy, Pete and Scott. Gold Dust Charlie continued his stories with wild gesticulations in between mouthfuls of food with Cyrus and Josh. Mike joined Dusty and left the spot at the far end of the fire by Wrong Way open for Pinto. Dusty figured keeping the most space between Pinto and the new arrivals was a good plan. Scout, instead of laying at Dusty's feet, went around behind him. His winter coat caused the dog to overheat easily, so he put as much space between himself and the fire as possible, still keeping Dusty close.

Mike dug into his food.

"Got your camp all set up?" Dusty asked.

"Yup," Mike answered. Dusty observed he was unusually quiet tonight. The ride in must have tired him out. It was either that or the dudes. And after witnessing the new arrivals, Dusty figured it was both.

Dusty took a bite of the beef brisket. It melted in his mouth. As he chewed he listened to Bob and Reggie or, more aptly, Reggie. The lawyer talked about big-game hunting safaris in Africa, elephants charging at his Jeep. Other trips in Alaska, with a pack of wolves boiling out of the woods and, at the last minute, having to shoot or be killed. The nasal aristocratic tone of his voice grated on Dusty's nerves. Cliff, sitting next to Reggie, laughed in agreement and urged his friend on in the stories, apparently having participated in a good many of the trips.

Uncle Bob never broke his composure. He sat calmly, nodded and appeared interested. Dusty tuned Reggie out and ate. Dinner plates emptied and were replaced by dessert. The men ploughed through the still warm caramel apple crisp with whipped cream and Dusty was sure the oven would be empty.

As dinner finished, Dusty helped gather up plates to take over to Andy. Everybody handed him their dessert bowls and nodded, except of course Reggie, who didn't bother to take a breath or look at Dusty as he thrust out his bowl and continued talking.

"I'm going to go check on the horses," said Dusty.

"I'll give you a hand." Mike followed Dusty into the night.

The fog had settled into the hillside around the lake. The added darkness cast an eerie effect. The trees appeared shrouded in grayish-white. The moon was a yellowish-gray and the sky was starless. Dusty, Scout and Mike walked a little ways below camp and stopped to listen. A faint clanging of the bell on the lead mare could be heard in the distance.

"Dang, it sounds like they took quite a walk," said Dusty.

"I'm surprised. I thought they'd stick closer," said Mike.

"It's a good thing we came out when we did," Dusty said. He was glad he knew this area, the contour of the land, even some of the tree patterns. It was going to be difficult enough to locate the horses in the dark and fog without trying to find the way back.

As they walked through the trees, a howling sounded in the distance. Dusty stopped to listen, and it seemed to get closer. Barking followed and then more long, low-pitched howls. Even though he knew they were wolves, the primal depth of the noise and the proximity made him nervous.

Scout stood staring intently through the trees. "Easy, Boy. You don't want to go there," cautioned Dusty.

"I never get used to that," Mike said, rubbing his neck.

"We better get to the stock before they do," said Dusty.

"Good point," Mike agreed, and they walked at a faster pace toward the horses.

Dusty snapped his rope on the bell mare. He took off her hobbles. Mike unhobbled his two horses and clipped their lead ropes on. As they walked back to camp the rest of the horses hopped and leaped in their hobbles to keep up. Dusty was glad he had on his insulated Sorel boots. The ground was wet, still in between the night freeze and the afternoon thaw. He and Mike squished through the mud and damp grass as they made the uphill climb back to camp. Scout trotted along next to him. Every once in a while he darted out to nip at a horse and Dusty would call him back. It always amazed him the dog would get his head right into the heels of a horse he'd never seen before and nip on the heel. How he didn't get his head kicked in was beyond Dusty. Even Muley, who'd bite and kick anything that moved, left Scout alone.

Pausing a couple of times to rest on the hill, Mike panted behind him, "Sometimes I wonder if I'm getting too old for this."

Dusty took a second to catch his breath. "That runs through my mind too occasionally. But it never lasts more than a couple of seconds."

As they approached the corral, Pinto and Wrong Way walked up.

"So you doing our job?" asked Wrong Way, holding the gate open.

"Just helping out," said Dusty.

"We saved you a big after dinner walk," Mike added.

"Well, I appreciate that," smiled Wrong Way.

"No problems here," added Pinto.

They had all the hobbles off the horses in no time, stored them under the tarp, and walked back up to camp.

As he passed the cook tent, Dusty noticed Andy had buttoned everything down for the night. The dishes were neatly stacked and dishrags folded on the table. The fire was still blazing and Dusty grabbed a cup off the stump. As he did, he noticed the bottle of Jack Daniels was empty. Bending by the fire to pour some coffee, he could see Randy was full-blown drunk. His eyes were glazed and his face bright red. His stories were loud and he kept repeating himself. If Randy's friends noticed anything, they didn't show it. Scott and Pete's cheeks were flushed and both had a slightly buzzed look as they listened tolerantly while he loudly stumbled through his story.

Cyrus and Josh looked sleepy as they listened to Charlie. Uncle

Bob had a polite smile on his face as Reggie, having recited all his big-game hunts, was into his amazing wins in trial court. Dusty and Mike sat down again by Bob. Pinto and Wrong Way resumed their seats by the Boeing guys.

Staring into the yellow-reddish flames, Dusty got a weird feeling. He glanced up and caught a malevolent look boring into him from across the fire. He felt an immediate adrenaline rush. *What the heck?* Pinto's small face was screwed up into a mask of hate. Dusty felt it was aimed directly at him. When he caught the younger man's eye, Pinto shifted his glance to Reggie. The hair on the back of Dusty's neck rose. The feeling something was really wrong with that kid coursed through him. As Dusty watched Pinto, the wrangler pointedly ignored him, instead took another drink from his cup and said something to Wrong Way.

Dusty was going to be talking to Uncle Bob about this kid tomorrow. He'd thought originally the anger was directed toward Reggie, which he could understand. All the man did was talk about how great he was. He annoyed Dusty too. But now he wasn't so sure. It looked for a minute that Pinto's real focus was him. Dusty knew one thing; he was going to find out what that kid's problem was.

Chapter Eight

The minute his head hit the pillow, Dusty passed out. Sometime in the night he began to dream.

Sitting at Cassie's kitchen table watching her cook, Dusty watched her and couldn't remember a more attractive view. She loaded his plate with eggs, bacon and hash browns and put it on the table in front of him. He watched her as she sat down across from him.

"Are you going to eat?" she asked puzzled. Her hair was still tousled from the night before and he couldn't help but notice the top couple buttons of her shirt weren't snapped.

He smiled lazily. "Oh, yeah." And picked up his fork.

The bacon was cooked just the way he liked it and the eggs melted in his mouth. "I really admire a woman who can shoot and cook... Kind of a scarce commodity these days."

Cassie blushed. "I spent a lot of time cooking when I was young. I watched a lot of westerns and I figured if I could cook and sew, I'd have it made."

"Sewing too, huh?"

"I baked bread. Sewed all my own clothes. I had a lot of dreams about living in the 1800s. They were so vivid, I could see my high-buttoned shoes, long skirts. Even the muddy streets and horse-drawn wagons. At times I wondered if I had only dreamed it, or actually been there."

Dusty felt a surge of disbelief shoot through him. He reflected *on his own pull to the Old West. The hours he'd spent reading history of the 1800s and always felt so at home with it. This woman never ceased to amaze him. He wouldn't have thought it possible to be more attracted to her.*

"So where does the shooting come in?" Dusty asked, thoughtfully chewing on a piece of bacon.

"Honestly? Cooking and sewing are boring." She took a drink of orange juice. "I love the Old West, horses and guns. To quote one of my favorite characters, 'I can't think of nothing better than to ride a fine horse into new country.'"

"Gus in Lonesome Dove. My favorite too." agreed Dusty, grinning. He couldn't stop himself from smiling. It occurred to him he'd been doing it ever since he got here.

They finished breakfast and Dusty helped carry the dishes to the sink. "I've got to get going."

Cassie looked disappointed as he put on his coat. "I guess it is a work day."

Standing in the doorway of her house, he wrapped his arms around her. She was tall; her head came just below his chin. Desire surged through him as he buried his face in her hair and inhaled the smell of wood smoke. The scent was so real he swore he could even hear the logs in the fire crack and pop.

Dusty rolled over in his cot, slowly awakening. The Riley stove in the corner of the wall tent was burning brightly. Scout was gone. Dusty dressed in the warmth of the tent, pulled on his coat, shoved his hat down on his head and headed out the door.

The gray light of morning was just filtering through the thick fog. The sun looked as if it might actually break through later. Bob sat by the fire with a cup of coffee warming his hands.

"Mornin'," said Dusty, as he sat down.

"How'd you sleep?" Bob inquired.

"Like a rock," said Dusty. *Except for maybe in his dreams this morning.* "What's the plan today?"

"I was just thinking that over," the older man said slowly. "I'll go out with Reggie and Cliff. We'll try down by Quartz Lake." He set his coffee cup on the log. "Pinto and Wrong Way can take out the Boeing group. Maybe hunt down in the lowland behind Corral Lake."

"How's Cyrus doing this morning with his ankle?" asked Dusty. "It looked pretty stiff yesterday."

"I'm thinking he's going to spend the day in camp today. That's okay, though, Gold Dust Charlie will keep him entertained."

Dusty chuckled, "That old guy never seems to run out of stories."

"Hey, did I hear my name?" A gruff voice called out as the old prospector walked into the fire ring. He shot them an appraising glance drawing his brushy gray brows together, then bent down and filled up his coffee cup.

"Just getting the details laid out, Charlie. No worries," Bob soothed.

"Mornin', Gold Dust," Dusty greeted.

"Mornin' to you, Dusty." The old man sat down heavily. "We'll see what yer uncle's got figured out for me to do t'day."

"Charlie, I figured you could stick around camp and keep Cyrus entertained while he nurses his bum ankle."

"I'd be honored to do that fer ya. I like that old man." Dusty thought he saw relief pass across Gold Dust's face. It had to be tough. He didn't know how old Charlie was, but he had to be in his late seventies. Dusty hoped to be as spry as Gold Dust when he was that age. It was at least 20 miles into the base camp, and the old man rode it, pulling his packhorse, with no problem.

"Okay. So that just leaves Josh." Dusty looked back at Uncle Bob. "How about you and Mike take him out toward Sheep Lake and see what you can come up with?"

"Sounds good to me," Dusty said.

The tinny sound of Andy ringing the breakfast triangle chimed out. "Come and get it!"

The dudes were just emerging from their tents. Bob, Charlie and

Dusty headed over to eat ahead of the guests so they could get the horses ready.

Dusty's group was the first to leave. He pulled along Cheyenne, who carried Utah panniers, open on the top so the leak-proof game bags would fit in them. They were ready if they got an animal. Dusty led the way, with Josh behind him and Mike riding drag. Dusty had offered him the lead but, as always, Mike turned it down. He said he'd rather keep an eye on Dusty's back. It was a joke between them.

Josh had been reluctant to leave his grandfather, but Cyrus urged him to go. It made Dusty wonder if the young man was out here for his grandpa or himself. But after a conversation with the older man, he loaded his rifle, grabbed a lunch, and mounted his horse. As they left camp, Cyrus and Gold Dust had resumed their positions by the fire, Charlie waving his arms and talking animatedly.

The trail wove away from camp and continued down the hillside to Sheep Lake. Dusty couldn't help but think about the last time he was down this trail. *He found young Scott Ross not so far from here. Crazy to think it was only this past summer.* Dusty was glad time wasn't passing too terribly fast—he had a lot of riding yet to do.

"We don't need to ride all the way to Sheep Lake, Josh. Once the trail drops down by the Ashnola it gets more forested. We may have some luck in there, catch them coming down for water." Dusty said.

"Sounds good," said Josh. He was pretty quiet when his grandfather was there, now even more so. The silence didn't bother Dusty and Mike at all. They would ride for hours and say nothing.

The morning was also silent. Unlike some denser parts of the forest, the birds in the arid hills were limited to the occasional scream of a hawk overhead circling its prey. The horseshoes made muted thuds as they walked down the trail, and occasionally a buckle would jingle. Dusty inhaled deeply. He could smell the fresh pines—interspersed with something else. He took another deep breath. He smelled snow. The one thing you could depend on in the Pasayten Wilderness, the weather was completely unpredictable. Sun one minute, snow the next, torrential downpour, thunder and lightning. Dusty had awoken more than once in the middle of August with snow covering his tent. This was October, so the chances of snow had increased exponentially. He glanced around at the peaks surrounding him; the tops were laden with white. Scout trotted along next to Muley and as they came to a stream, the dog took his usual bath and drink. His thick winter coat billowed around him in the water.

Dusty felt clear-headed and alive up here. It was like being in a different world—which it was. He knew his life in Eagleclaw existed; it just didn't hold a lot of relevance. Dusty always carried what he needed on his horse. If he got stuck and needed to spend the night, he was ready. He felt completely free and at home in the wilderness.

The trail switchbacked down to the river, which flowed at a good rate. Not as fast as spring, but with the snowfall it was consistent. As they came down to the bottom of the hill, they stopped and watered the horses. Directly across from them was a three-sided shelter.

"We'll tie up the horses over there," he said, gesturing towards the split-wood structure. A fire ring sat in front of it. The Ashnola was one of the few remaining shelters in the Pasayten. In years past it was standard for hikers to rely on shelters intermittently throughout the wilderness, but now with the *Leave No Trace* program emphasized so much in the back woods, they were few and far between. The Forest Service had dismantled most of them. The old trapper cabins that remained were taken over for the backcountry rangers.

Dusty preferred to stay in his own tent, rather than stay in the shelters. Mice, beetles, spiders and other unpleasant inhabitants made their homes in the lean-tos, enjoying the occasional leftovers from hikers. He supposed they served a purpose when you needed them.

Dusty looked up at the slate gray sky. The hint of sun had disappeared. A distinct smell of snow burned his nostrils. He hunched deeper into his Schaefer coat and gave Muley a kick.

Chapter Nine

Dusty and Mike tied up the horses to stout trees and loosened their cinches.

"So have you got your bearings, Josh?" Dusty asked. "We don't want another repeat of yesterday."

Josh pulled out his GPS. "I downloaded the map before we left. I've got the trail marked."

"Okay. You're ahead of me with that thing," Dusty said, shaking his head. It wasn't that he couldn't learn it, he just didn't want to. He still hung onto the idea that the backcountry was primitive. And although he understood the use of the GPS for location and trail marking, he wanted to do it himself. He knew that the times were quickly changing and he hoped that people would still want to experience the backcountry in its primitive state.

Uncle Bob's outfit had taken a brief downturn for a few years, but seemed to be doing okay now. Hunting camp was fully booked. The high costs of insurance and Forest Service permitting made it tough on the outfitters. They had to raise the rates dramatically on their clients in order to clear all the costs and still make a profit. Dusty hoped it would continue to work out, both for Uncle Bob's sake, but also for the outfitter industry in general. He knew it served a far greater purpose than simply a living for the outfitters. It allowed people who would never be able to make it into the backcountry on their own two feet a chance to experience God's handiwork at its finest.

Dusty turned back to Josh. "You got your energy bars and water, just in case, right?"

Josh patted his pocket. "Right here."

"Okay, then. Good luck. We'll start a small fire while we're waiting. That way, in case your thingamajig doesn't work, you'll be able to locate us the old-fashioned way."

Josh smiled. "Okay. Thanks a lot, Dusty."

Mike watched the interplay. "He's probably got extra batteries."

Dusty looked crestfallen. "Oh, I hadn't thought of that."

Josh quickly said, "I'll look for the smoke, thanks." He shouldered his rifle and headed into the trees.

Scout lay on the ground, his thick fur still damp from his bath in the creek, and watched Josh intently as he walked away.

"I'll get some wood," said Mike.

Dusty stared after the retreating younger man, "Good idea."

In no time at all they had a small blaze. Dusty shivered involuntarily. The early morning air was chilly, in spite of the thermal long johns and thick wool shirt he wore. The heat from the fire felt good. Dusty knew it was probably the mental sense of well-being a fire brought, as well as the actual heat.

Neither man spoke as they stared at the snapping and crackling of the small twigs bursting into flames.

A warm feeling coursed up Dusty's spine and his shoulders relaxed. All he had to do were the basics up here. It made life simple. He knew that's why he craved it so much. His mind was clear. The physical exercise of caring for the horses and riding made him feel alive. The mental overload of his law practice was gone. He knew he was going to choose this life as soon as he could swing it financially.

"Did you get everything taken care of in town?" Dusty asked.

"Pretty much."

Dusty waited. He wasn't sure what Mike had been doing. He was pretty sure it wasn't anything for him. There weren't any big cases on his desk when he left. The Wolfe divorce had been the major one a couple weeks ago, and the arrest of Paul Wolfe had pretty much ended it—as far as investigation—Dusty corrected himself. They would still need to sort out the paperwork for the dissolution. Julie, Paul's wife, would need to reassume possession of her family's business.

Mike sat quietly staring into the fire. He didn't seem like he was going to add to the answer, when finally he spoke. "I went over to Terri's."

"Really?" Dusty had a hard time keeping the surprise from of his voice. He knew Mike had gone riding with her, but she must mean something to him. Dusty couldn't remember Mike ever doing more than occasionally riding horses with a woman.

"So how did that go?"

"Good."

"Okay. Well, I wouldn't want you to give out too many details, or anything," said Dusty with mock seriousness.

"Yeah," said Mike shortly, not going for the bait. "How's it going with Cassie, anyway?" he asked innocently.

Dusty thought about it. If Mike was seeing Terri, she sure liked to talk. He wondered if Mike knew more about what Cassie thought than he did.

"What do you know about that, anyway?" Dusty cut to the point.

Mike looked up at him, amused. "Nothing. Well, I should correct that. It is felt that Cassie likes you. End of story. Terri said Cassie does not talk about men. Period."

Dusty broke into a big white-toothed grin. He felt relief wash over him. He didn't realize how much he wanted to hear that. He was bad enough at trying to go out with her. He didn't want to hear anyone else talk about it or possibly laugh at his expense. "Huh, I knew I liked her for a reason."

"Oh, turns out you do." Mike looked at him. "I knew it."

They stared into the fire lost in thought. Scout stretched out enjoying the warmth and they waited for Josh.

A shot split the forest air. Scout stood up and faced its direction in the trees. As Mike and Dusty rose, a second and then third shot rang out. They walked briskly through the trees in the direction of the gunfire to see if Josh had gotten an animal. Scout knew the drill and trotted ahead of them. Dusty was a little surprised. He wasn't sure if the young man would actually kill a deer. He knew that's what he was here for. When it came down to the kill, people sometimes just couldn't do it. Dusty wondered which kind of person Josh was.

As they entered a small clearing, Josh knelt down on one knee over the carcass of a whitetail deer.

Mike whistled, "Holy smokes! That's a three-point," he exclaimed. "Way to go, Josh!"

Dusty stood next to Mike. "That's a nice animal," he said admiringly.

Josh blushed standing up. "Thanks."

Looking down at the deer, Dusty could see it was also an excellent shot. Josh had hit the deer right in the shoulder. "Nice shot too."

"I missed the first two. I really lucked out hitting him on the third. He bolted and it was a lucky shot."

"Doesn't look lucky to me," said Mike.

"You guys dress him out and I'll go get Cheyenne," said Dusty.

Josh and Mike went to work.

As Dusty walked back alone to get his packhorse, he had an uneasy feeling. He was starting to doubt himself. This seemed to be happening often lately. He knew it could be an animal, but he felt he was being watched. Coming back to the shelter, the small fire burned low. Their gear was right where they left it. Four pairs of equine eyes were fastened on him and Scout. Dusty could hear a low throated nicker of recognition as he walked up to the horses. He tightened Cheyenne's packsaddle and headed back through the trees pulling the horse behind him.

The back of Dusty's neck felt tight and he rubbed it. The hair on the back of his neck stood up. Dusty heard the metal slide of a rifle bolt being cocked through the trees over the rustle of brush and thuds of Cheyenne's hooves hitting the earth. Dusty came to an abrupt halt. *Did he hear that or was that his imagination?* Scout stopped and turned to look at Dusty inquisitively. Not getting anything from his dog, he looked at Cheyenne. The big white Appalaoosa stared back at him. The horse was a little antsy because he wanted to be back with his herd, but other than that, no reaction. Neither dog nor horse was looking in any particular direction. Dusty shook his head. He must have imaged it. He continued toward the clearing, the hair on his neck still standing.

Chapter Ten

They got the deer loaded and headed back to camp. It was late morning and the golden autumn sun was high above them. Cheyenne was loaded down with deer meat, and the rack was tied on the pack saddle. Josh had a huge smile on his face. Dusty could see that he had highly underestimated the younger man. He was tough.

People could be funny that way. Dusty had mistaken Josh's kindness and caring towards his grandfather as weakness. He'd been around long enough. He should have known the difference. Josh had completely gotten that past him. He smiled to himself and looked at the mountain peaks around him as they rode. A rush of crisp fall air felt frigid on his face. He could smell the fir and something else—snow.

"Smelled like snow" was a phrase that didn't really make sense to Dusty. How could a person smell frozen water? But there it was. The scent reminded him of when he was growing up and skiing at Crystal Mountain. He used to take the ski lift up to the highest point at Green Valley and he and his friends would launch right off the top, racing down like they weren't supposed to, leaping over moguls and weaving in and out of slower skiers. The snow whooshing up behind their skis as they cut through it—and that smell of snow filled his nostrils.

The hillside they rode along dipped in and out. Occasionally small wooden bridges rose up above the streams. There was a time that Dusty would have taken the bridges for granted as being something the Forest Service put there. He now knew from personal experience that hard work and sweat went into building the structures. Packing in tools and planks, hacking and digging on the ground to set the stringers, and nailing on the planks to withstand time. Dusty also knew that it was all volunteer work. Since the logging had been done away with, for the most part, the Forest Service—once wealthy from the sales of timber—now had to rely on grants and volunteer work to get trail work done. He knew that's why the Back Country Horsemen were so important. The volunteer hours they spent on the trail were tallied up and traded for grant money for further projects and helped to employ summer hands.

As the trail turned, Crow Lake appeared below. The blue of the lake contrasted sharply with the dark green pines around it. Smoke curled up from the fire and Dusty could see activity in the camp below. The three horsemen wound their way down the hill, the heavily laden packhorse trotting behind.

As they rode into camp, Gold Dust Charlie approached, followed by Cyrus, who was limping at a fast pace, trying his best to keep up.

"How'd ya do?" Inquired Charlie, eyeing Cheyenne's load.

Before Dusty could answer, Cyrus exclaimed excitedly, "Josh, you got your deer!" His face was filled with pride.

Josh blushed and smiled, "Yes, Grandpa."

"Well, isn't that something? A three-point too, by the looks of it." Cyrus limped in closer to examine Cheyenne's load.

"That there's a mighty fine deer ya got there," Charlie agreed enthusiastically.

"It surely is," agreed Cyrus.

"We better get these horses unloaded and get that meat hung," said Dusty, turning Muley toward the corral.

Cyrus couldn't contain himself. "Well done, Son!" He beamed at his grandson.

"Thanks, Grandpa," Josh said modestly, and followed Dusty down to unload.

Gold Dust slapped the older man on the back, "Ya got yerself some kind of young man there, all right. A reg'lar hunter."

"Yes, I believe I do," agreed Cyrus, delight etched across his face. They turned and walked back to the fire.

Dusty and Mike got the horses unloaded and turned out. They hung the deer on the meat pole by camp, set up high to discourage unwanted animals. Uncle Bob liked to get it into town and refrigerated as soon as possible, so it would be taken out in the morning. The meat could be left hanging in camp for a while, but that would be banking on the temperatures staying cold, and Dusty knew his uncle didn't want to risk other people's money on the weather. Good meat could go bad in a hurry. As they walked up to camp, Josh was sitting with his grandpa and Charlie.

"Anyone else back yet?" asked Dusty.

"Nope, not yet," said Charlie. "I thought I heared a coupla shots down Whistler Basin a ways, but I cain't be sure."

"Shouldn't be too much longer then. The deer seem to settle down in the afternoon and don't get active again until dusk." Dusty grabbed a cup and helped himself to the coffee pot. "There shouldn't be too much action going on."

Andy walked into the fire area. "I got sandwiches made up, chips and cookies, if you want to help yourself to lunch."

"Sounds great," said Mike. They headed to the kitchen area.

Bob rode in a short while later with Reggie and Cliff. Dusty noted Bob's packhorse was empty. Reggie seemed undaunted and continued to talk about himself. Cliff had a perennial smile on his face and Uncle Bob just appeared amused.

"How did you do?" Bob greeted them.

"Josh got one. A three-point."

"Nice," said Bob.

That halted Reggie for a minute. He looked over at the meat

hanging and saw the antlers next to it. Dusty was amazed. It actually shut him up for a minute.

Then Reggie said dismissively, "Beginner's luck." He turned back to Cliff and continued talking.

Dusty felt heat course up his back and willed himself to calm down. It was the one thing about bringing dudes out here—you couldn't take the city out of them. He'd seen plenty of Reggies in the courtroom. They were excellent winners and poor losers. Everything was a competition. To congratulate the other side was next to impossible. He stopped himself. He refused to think about it anymore. "I'll give you a hand unsaddling." He followed them down to the corral.

By mid-afternoon everyone had returned from hunting. Josh was the only one who had gotten an animal. The Boeing Boys were seated comfortably by the fire and Randy was well into his afternoon drunk. Lots of stories were circulating about the one they almost got, and all the circumstances that weren't their fault that prevented it. Laughter and talking rose above the crackling of the fire.

Mike, Dusty and Bob were sitting together. "I'm going to need to get that deer out of here tomorrow morning and into the freezer in town," said Bob. "I'm going to send Wrong Way with it this time."

"Pinto didn't seem too excited on his last trip," observed Dusty.

"I don't know if that had to do with the 40-mile ride or his traveling companions," agreed Bob.

"Maybe a little of both," offered Mike.

"Yeah," said Bob. "I don't really know what to make of him yet. He's an okay hand with the stock, but not the best I've ever had, for sure."

Bob took a drink of coffee. "He seems to have kind of a chip on his shoulder. I just haven't quite placed what his problem is 'yet'." Bob said "yet," Dusty knew, because he was an excellent judge of character. He didn't work an outfit for years without getting really familiar with people and their quirks and personalities. It had saved him more than once from a bad decision, whether it be sizing up a man or woman to ride an animal, or taking them on a trail they couldn't handle. Bob watched and learned a lot without even talking.

Dusty looked across the fire at Pinto. He seemed to be involved in a conversation with the three men from Boeing. Having rode with them that day, they seemed to get along pretty well. That was a relief, since he was unable to contain his anger at Reggie and Cliff earlier.

"He does seem a little thin-skinned," observed Dusty.

"I've seen that too," said Bob. "Kind of a tough thing when I've got to set my dudes up with the right stock, and now I've got to watch out and set them up with the right wrangler too."

"Always something," Mike agreed.

The three of them sat there for a while enjoying the fire and the talk. Reggie stood up and walked over to them.

"Bob, Cliff and I have been talking. Have you heard of the Pasayten Airstrip?"

"Well, sure," answered Bob.

"How far is that from here?" the middle-aged man asked.

Bob looked at him questioningly, "It's a long day's ride from here. You'd go down through Dollar Watch Pass and past Hidden Lakes."

"Cliff and I would like to do it," he said with finality. "A good friend of mine's great grandfather flew into it in the 1940s. I've always been curious to see it."

Bob looked perturbed, "I would have to see if I could get ahold of the outfitter over there and get permission. That's out of my guide area," he said hesitantly.

Reggie, in his usual style, replied, "Okay, then." He turned on his heel and walked back to Cliff on the other side of the fire.

"Well, don't that beat all," Bob said, scratching his head.

"Kind of unusual," said Dusty.

"I believe that's the first time I've had someone do that, and if not the first time, the first time in quite that way."

"Can you do it?" asked Mike.

"I just don't know. I guess I better get on the radio and see what I can find out. I've known the outfitter over there for years; I may be able to make a trade with him. Territory's just not something we like to give up easily." Bob got up and walked to his tent to begin the process.

"What do you think of that?" said Mike.

"I want to go," replied Dusty.

Mike smiled at him. "I figured you'd say that. Me too. I've never seen that country."

"It's been a very long time for me. Uncle Bob doesn't guide in that part of the Pasayten, so I just did it on my own years ago. As I remember, the trail can be very challenging going out of Hidden Lakes to Tatoosh Buttes."

Mike rubbed his hands together. "This is sounding better all the time."

Chapter Eleven

The sky was dark as Dusty walked down to turn the horses out. He had a long ride ahead of him. It was amazing how Bob could pull it off, but he did. He made a deal via backcountry radio with the outfitter out of Robinson Creek. He and Mike were going to take Cliff and Reggie over to the Pasayten Airstrip. He watched the horses crowd and push to get out of the corral.

"Just calm down, everybody. You'll get breakfast as soon as you get your hobbles on."

Dusty grabbed a bunch of the leather straps and bent down to put them on the horses' front legs. He took the older horses that would stand quietly first. The younger ones got excited, pushing and snorting around the corral.

As he finished buckling hobbles on one horse and turned to the next horse, Dusty heard voices near the corral. Mike and Wrong Way approached, their breath shooting out in icy puffs.

"Mornin'," called Dusty from under the horse.

"You're up early today," observed Mike.

"We've got a long ways to go, so I thought I'd let the horses get a head start on breakfast."

"Let's do it." Mike and the wrangler picked up hobbles and began putting them on horses. Soon the three men stood outside the open corral watching the herd hopping out through the mountain grass on the hillside. Steam blew from their noses as they gathered up on their hind legs and propelled themselves forward on their bound forelegs, resembling big rabbits. The older horses followed along, seasoned in having their front legs bound by the hobbles, they took little measured steps and seemed to cover as much territory with less exertion.

Dusty drank in the moment. The peaks were becoming more defined in the gray morning light. The grass was icy with the overnight frost. The morning air had a bite to it. Dusty felt it now after working. The three men stood for a few minutes, making sure all the horses got out.

"Where are you riding today, Wrong Way?" asked Mike.

"I'm not sure what Bob's got planned for me. He may want me to ride out with the old guy and his grandson. Pinto wasn't too friendly on his last trip in with the lawyers."

Dusty listened, but didn't say anything. He wondered what Wrong Way thought about Pinto. He knew the older wrangler kept his opinions to himself, for the most part. It pretty much came with the territory working on an outfit. When you had a small number of people it always worked best to keep to yourself.

"He seems like he's got a little bit of an edge to him at times," Mike said evenly.

Wrong Way didn't offer a reply.

Dusty waited for a couple of minutes and then said, "Guess we'd better see if Andy's got the coffee done."

"Boy, I hope so," Mike agreed. He turned and led the way up the hill to camp.

The fire was roaring as they walked up and the big coffee pot sat on its rock. Gold Dust Charlie and Bob were talking, blue metal cups in their hands. Dusty and Mike got breakfast and worked with Andy on supplies.

"I always keep a stash for times like this," said Andy, digging through his storage boxes. "You making a base camp at the airstrip then?"

"Yeah," affirmed Dusty, "that's what the plan is. I guess we'll be hunting by braille over there, since we've never scouted it."

"If the airstrip hasn't changed much since I've been there,

there's lots of graze on the strip. Ought to be plenty of animals around. I even ran into some riders one time that saw a moose over there," said Andy, as he bent down and put cans in the pack box.

"That would be cool to see," said Mike, standing by Dusty and watching the progress.

"You don't hear of many of them around here," agreed Dusty.

"Just don't piss them off and you'll be fine." Andy stiffly stood up and rubbed the small of his back.

"No worries there," said Dusty, chuckling. "We'll get loaded and bring the horses up for the boxes in a little bit."

"I'll be ready for you," said Andy.

Mike and Dusty walked down to the stock area. "I hope Bob's got the sleeping beauties ready to ride this morning."

"We can leave that to him," Dusty said ruefully. He was trying not to think about spending time with Reggie and Cliff. Since they made it into base camp and were still ready to ride farther, he was sure they had the stamina for it. Dusty came to the mountains to forget about his "other life" in the courtroom, and Reggie seemed to want to talk about it constantly. He was just going to have to practice his tune-out skills. Dusty threw a pack saddle on the horse. The horse bounced up a little, cold-backed in the early morning air, then relaxed.

"Easy, Boy," he said reassuringly, straightening out the latigos and cinching him up.

The sun warmed overhead, and the fog evaporated. Wrong Way had the deer packed and Josh and Cyrus were ready to ride out. The older man and his grandson stood by the fire when Dusty walked up to them.

"You've got quite a hunter in Josh. I hope to see you guys again."

"Thanks, Dusty," Cyrus beamed. "We've been talking about next year. Your Uncle Bob runs an excellent outfit."

Josh piped in, "I couldn't have done it without your expert guiding, Dusty."

"Thanks, Josh. You're one heck of a shot." Dusty slapped him on the back.

Josh reddened, "Beginner's luck."

"Hey, do you think we can finish with all the thank you's and hit the trail?" Reggie cut in rudely. "You've got other paying customers here and it's a long ride, I'm told." He stood impatiently next to Cliff, his arms folded across his chest.

Dusty felt heat course up his back. This seemed to happen a lot when he was around Reggie. With a determined glint in his eye, he willed himself to ignore the remark and smiled warmly at Cyrus and Josh.

"Hope to see you next year." Then he turned and walked slowly to mount up, not acknowledging Reggie or Cliff. It was going to be a long day.

Chapter Twelve

The horses' hooves methodically thudded on the dirt and the mountains towered around them. Dusty's irritation dissipated as the sights and smells of the high country penetrated into his being. He led on Muley, pulling Cheyenne, his packhorse, with Reggie and Cliff in the middle. And Mike followed on Toby pulling Duke and two other pack animals. They had two for their camp and one with food that they could shift around if they needed to load on game. The lawyers talked occasionally among themselves and Dusty was glad. He just wanted to think. The high country brought that out in him. He could pull his thoughts out, get them straight and put them away. Then he could ride without thinking, letting the mountain scenery wash over him and cleanse his soul.

The sun flashed light on the rocks and the larches were bright orange, interspersed with an occasional green pine or fir tree. The creeks babbled and as he stopped to water his horse, Scout plunged his face into the sparkling water. Dusty always marveled at how clear the water was. You could see every little stone in the bottom, the small green aqua plants fanning as the water flowed through them.

"What time do you think we'll get to camp?" asked Reggie impatiently.

Dusty had been deep in thought. By the tone of his voice, it sounded like it wasn't the first time the question was asked. He shook his head, "Hopefully we make it by dark. At the pace we're going, we ought to, as long as we don't get too slow on the climb out of Hidden Lakes."

Reggie frowned like it hadn't been the right answer. Irritated, he said, "All right, then. Let's move."

"The stock has got to drink. We're going to climb hard and there's not a lot of water up on top. We don't want any animals tying up on us." Dusty purposely spoke in a calm measured voice.

"That means they get one big stomachache from overexertion," Mike added quickly in explanation. "If that happens we won't be going anywhere for a while."

"Horses first," said Dusty, to reaffirm it.

"Okay, Boss," Reggie said sarcastically.

Dusty let Muley drink, maybe a little longer than necessary, and then moved him forward, leaving room for the next horse to drink.

They hadn't gone much farther after watering the horses when Mike turned in his saddle and called out, "Easy there, Duke." He was pulling his regular packhorse, with two of Bob's horses behind him. The additional horses were tied together by breakaways, thin pieces of rope that broke if too much weight was put on them. It kept the horses together, but if something dangerous occurred, the horse could break away—hence the name. They usually worked.

Mike had a black horse behind Duke and a sorrel behind that one. The black snorted as his pack began to list. The sorrel wanted none of it and sat back on his breakaway—it didn't break. The black, unable to rid himself of the boxes, began to buck, and kept kicking. Mike held onto the bunch as long as he could, but when the flying hooves reversed directions and the black, dragging the sorrel, came after Duke—who had just tried to stay out of the way of the rodeo—Mike had to let go.

The four horsemen stopped on the trail and watched the rodeo, both horses bucking like broncos. The black's pack boxes went airborne, careening down the gully on the side of the trail, bouncing end-over-end, opening and scattering food as they plummeted downward. The boxes came to a rest just inches from dumping into the stream at the bottom. The black stopped bucking and stood shaking, ropes and mantie tarp hung over him, his front legs through it. Mike, off his horse in a flash, spoke quietly to the horse and removed the rope before there was another explosion. He checked for burns.

The sorrel stood nearby. The breakaway finally worked, but not before he was able to send his pack skyward and down the gully. The contents burst open about halfway down.

Dusty noticed Reggie and Cliff staring open-mouthed at the packhorses and the scattered gear. Dusty felt a rush of happiness at the fact that something had actually shut Reggie up.

Dusty quickly dismounted from Muley, dropped the rein, dallied Cheyenne's lead around his saddle horn and hurried over to the sorrel, who stood quivering. They were going to have to start from scratch and repack the horses. Duke was still fully packed, and stood quietly by Toby, as if nothing had happened. At least that saved one horse to repack.

"Make yourselves comfortable, boys. It's going to be a while," Dusty called over his shoulder as he walked down the side of the gully to pick up their supplies and pack boxes.

"What in the hell got into those horses?" sputtered Reggie.

"Hard saying. Could be something or it could be nothing," said Mike, gently stroking the black horse on the neck.

Cliff interjected, "There's a whole lot to be said about ATVs."

Reggie gave him a withering look, "In the wilderness?"

His friend quickly deflated and added, "Just saying."

A small spikey form caught their attention at the bottom of the creek bed where all their supplies lay scattered. A porcupine was crawling out of the draw, apparently disturbed by all the ruckus. His steps were slow and purposeful, and the quills on his head bounced haughtily. He clearly looked like he'd had enough and was moving out. As Dusty and Mike began to collect their gear, the little animal didn't even look back, just continued purposefully up the hill.

"I guess we ruined someone else's day too," said Mike.

"Yup, guess so." Dusty picked up a pack box and righted it.

Dusty and Mike worked quickly and efficiently as a team. They'd packed lots of horses. The food wasn't damaged, the pots and pans had a couple more dings, but the coffee pot was untouched. Dusty always wrapped it in dishtowels and bagged food so, well-insulated, the pot took less of a beating.

Dusty was thankful for the cool weather. It made their work a lot easier than sweating in the summer sun. In less than an hour Dusty was tying off the last knot.

Cliff and Reggie had dismounted and sat staring glumly ahead, their plans temporarily on hold. Dusty shook his head. Wrecks and packing were pretty much synonymous; you pack enough, you're going to have wrecks. It was really the nature of the beast. Knowing your stock, your trail and your loads went a long ways to reducing them—but it was the unforeseen that could get you every time.

In this particular incident, Dusty figured it had a lot to do with Mike pulling the two horses behind Duke, a strange horse. That set things off kilter right off the bat, and once one horse went, there goes the string. Horses were very particular about the order they traveled.

"You guys ready to mount up?" asked Dusty as he gathered up Cheyenne's lead rope and swung into the saddle.

The men hurriedly got to their feet and followed suit.

Mike sat quietly at the end. This time he had the black right behind him, followed by Duke and then the sorrel. He knew, if nothing else, Duke would help keep order in the string, and the black wouldn't be kicking the sorrel anymore.

The autumn sun had broken through and was well in the sky by the time they resumed riding. Dusty figured they would have to stop somewhere tonight in order to avoid climbing the steep trail out of Hidden Lakes in the darkness. He'd wait and see what their progress was at that point. Each man had a lunch, so they didn't need to stop. It was usually better not to when you were pulling packhorses—gave them less of a chance to get in trouble. Judging by the hurry that Reggie was in, Dusty was sure he'd rather keep going, anyway.

The trail dropped down through Whistler Pass and then began the climb through trees to Dollar Watch Pass. As Dusty led through the forest, his mind began to wander.

Chapter Thirteen

The look of disappointment on Cassie's face replayed in his mind. Her long light brown hair lay tousled against her shoulders, and her cheeks were flushed. She leaned against the front door, arms crossed. The white T-shirt she wore contrasted with her tan. A tiny gold locket around her neck twinkled in the sun.

"So you're going up to your Uncle Bob's hunting camp?" she repeated, even though he'd just said it.

"Yes. I told him I'd be up to help out this fall," Dusty said patiently as he stood on the pathway leading out to his truck. He couldn't believe how much he was drawn to her. Good sense told him he was already late for his 9 a.m. appointment, but if Cassie wanted to talk to him, he was compelled to listen.

"Okay," her voice trailed off.

"I'll be back in two weeks," Dusty reiterated. He was still rooted to the ground.

"Doesn't look like you're making much progress," she laughed.

He blushed, "That obvious, huh?" With a herculean effort, he turned to his truck. As the door creaked open, he heard a voice.

"Wait," Cassie called again. She ran out to the truck and threw her arms around him. For the second time he thought about carrying her into the house and forgetting the appointment. The way he felt scared him. He could easily forget about everything else but her. Finally, he wrapped his arms around her, kissed her on the top of the head and said, "I'll call you when I get back."

As he backed out of her driveway, she'd stood there with her arms folded across her chest and the edges of her lips turned up into a funny little smile.

A fallen tree blocked the trail in front of them. He turned Muley and they made their way around the obstacle. As he looked behind him, everyone followed in silence. Mike's new lineup of packhorses seemed to be working. There were no more disagreements among them. The trail stretched out in front of Dusty and he rode with the distinct feeling he was missing something.

The weather began to change. It had been foggy in the morning and the sun had come out by the middle of the day. As they rode on and Hidden Lakes got closer, the sun had completely disappeared. In place of the humming of fall insects and birds, there was silence. Dusty looked up at the sky. An ominous sheet of slate gray descended over them. Little bits of rain, then sleet began pounding down on them.

"Oh, great," he thought sarcastically. "This is the icing on the cake for a perfect trip with the hunting party."

Reggie and Cliff said nothing. Reggie hunkered down in his camo coat and pulled his collar up. The precipitation wasn't too bad yet, but it could go either way in a hurry up here. The good thing about October was it was a little late for the lightning storms, and Dusty was pretty sure he hated that the most. He had tried looking up where it would be best to pitch a tent in event of lightning. From what he could tell—nowhere. He quit looking.

"What do you guys say we make camp at Hidden Lakes tonight and then do the climb out to Tatoosh Buttes early in the morning?" Dusty asked, turning in his saddle and facing the group.

"Sounds good to me," agreed Mike. Dusty loved that about Mike—rainstorm or sunshine, he was always on an even keel.

He turned to Reggie. Clearly miserable, but not about to show it, he finally gave up.

"With the late start we got and now this weather, looks like that might have to be the way we do it," the lawyer acquiesced slowly.

Dusty had to hand it to him; he still maintained control of himself. Cliff nodded in agreement. He was shivering. Dusty stopped, "Did you want to pull another sweater out?"

Cliff stopped and seemed to consider it for the first time. He turned in his saddle and quickly began opening and pawing through a saddlebag to locate a wool sweater. The sleet had picked up a good rhythm and didn't seem like it would stop any time soon. After Cliff got his extra sweater and coat back on, they continued down the trail.

As they dropped down some switchbacks, a patch of gray water appeared through the fall-colored trees. Usually the lakes would have been blue, but reflecting the sky color, they were gray now. The trail followed one side of the lake and Dusty kept an eye out for a camp in the forest. It didn't take him long and he led the group into a horse camp. The trees helped take some of the bite out of the sleet and there was even an old makeshift corral. A fire ring stood in the clearing, built up with rocks, and someone had taken the time to build log benches around it.

Dusty and Mike tied up the stock and dropped the packs as Reggie and Cliff took a short hike down to check out the lake. They could see the mountain they would be ascending the next day. The top was covered with puffs of clouds as the icy rain continued to beat down.

In record time they got the tents erected and a tarp lashed up over what would be the cooking area. It covered part of the fire ring. Mike set out collecting wood. Since the rain was relatively new, there was still dry wood underneath the foliage and next to the bottoms of trees.

As he bent and lit the kindling, Dusty thought that there was something about the warmth of a fire. No matter how miserable the conditions might be, it gave a kind of hominess to the place. The dry twigs caught, and a small flame glowed. Reggie and Cliff moved into their tents and the rain flies, coated nylon tarps, were holding so far against the storm.

Mike hobbled the horses in the grassy area behind them. He put a bell on Muley. Once the fire was steady, Dusty walked down to the lake and filled a big pot with water to get some coffee going. Then he opened a few cans of soup and put them in a pan with a lid over on another part of the fire. Satisfied, he turned to organize his own gear and put up his tent.

Reggie and Cliff came back and sat by the fire, engrossed in some big case they were working on.

Dusty was glad, because he didn't feel like talking. Setting up camps for dudes was something he'd done since he was young. Granted, it didn't happen all that often anymore. While he surely wasn't the cook Andy was, he was still a capable hand at it.

By the time the coffee was boiling, the sleet had let up. "You think the storm is over now?" asked Reggie, pausing from his trial strategy discussion long enough to wonder.

"For now. It's really hard to predict the weather up here, though. It can vary from any weather report you have. The locals always say the Pasayten has its own weather."

"I've heard that too," conceded Reggie. "The locals? So what is it you do if you're not a local?"

Dusty immediately regretted having said that. This was not the conversation he wanted to have.

Mike walked into the fire ring area and threw his soaked gloves down on the log next to him. "He works for me."

"Really?" said Reggie, looking at Mike appraisingly and not being sold.

Dusty shot Mike an interested look and waited.

"Doing what?"

"Well," said Mike, "I run an investigation business and Dusty works with me a lot."

His shoulders immediately relaxed. *Well, that wasn't completely untrue. He did work with Mike a lot.*

"So what do you investigate?" asked Cliff, his interest now piqued.

"Whatever I'm asked to investigate. Anywhere from people wanting more information on someone they've met from an online dating service to people filing for divorce, wanting to get dirt on their mate, or prove infidelity. I also do business investigations. Just whatever."

"Well, I guess you just don't know who's outfitting you anymore." Reggie shook his head. "How does that make you so good with a horse and a pack?"

"This is my sport. This is actually what I do, and my job gives me the money to pursue it." Mike lifted the lid on the coffee pot. The water was at a rolling boil. "Water's ready."

Dusty opened up the pack box and fished out the coffee. He scooped out a cup and dropped it into the roiling water. "We'll just let that sit a minute or two and then set it off to the side," he commented to no one in particular. It just seemed like if he said something, it might move the conversation about what he did farther on down the line.

Dusty pulled out some camp bread that Andy had made up. It was a bread that was somewhere between actual bread and a biscuit. Once heated and covered with butter and honey, you really didn't care what it was. He wrapped the bread in aluminum foil and set that on a rock to warm next to the soup pot.

The fire was blazing and the sky had faded to black. The early evenings of fall were upon them, and Dusty was glad that everyone had agreed not to press on. He wasn't sure what the weather held for them. He'd been smelling snow. A storm was always a possibility this time of year—actually, any time of year, he corrected himself. As the soup boiled, Dusty said, "Looks like dinner."

After dinner, the fire was roaring and crackling. The smell of wood smoke and hot coffee was in the air. The tents were set up and their futures looked brighter. Dusty always appreciated that transformation from sitting on a wet horse in the freezing cold, wondering where you were going to end up—to sitting with a hot cup of coffee in your hand. The fire crackled and roared in front of him, the heat warm on his cheeks. The smell of campfire smoke permeated the air and a feeling of well-being centered him. It wasn't a perfect world, but things were shaping up a lot better than they had for a long, long time.

Mike sat his cup down. "I'll go get the horses."

Dusty stood up too. "I'll give you a hand." The two men walked through the pitch black, with Scout following along. They stopped and could hear Muley's bell clanging in the distance.

"Sounds like they went a ways," said Mike.

"They always do when you wish they wouldn't." Dusty pulled out his flashlight and continued through the trees and brush. Mike followed with his light.

Amazingly, it didn't take them as long as Dusty thought. Once again it was the black quarter horse that was leading them out. For sure he was going to talk to Uncle Bob about that horse. Not only was he a troublemaker, but he'd led the herd away on hobbles. Not a good thing to have a "bunch quitter" as Uncle Bob would say.

As Dusty approached Muley, Scout stopped and began to growl. The hair was sticking straight up on the ruff of his neck and he started barking. "Easy, Boy," said Dusty, trying to see what alerted his dog. He flashed the light and just the horses stood, necks down in grass pulling and munching. Only Muley stood with his head held high looking haughtily at Dusty. His expression was, *How dare you interrupt us.*

"I don't see anything," Mike said, pointing his flashlight around. "Maybe it's an animal, or something."

"Maybe," said Dusty uneasily. He was tired and there was nothing else he could do tonight. He snapped the lead on Muley and unbuckled the hobbles and turned to the next horse. Between the two men, they freed the horses in no time and turned to head back to camp, the herd following Muley.

Scout finally stopped barking and left it at a growl in the back of his throat. He took one last look back and followed Dusty through the brush.

Chapter Fourteen

Reggie and Cliff had gone to bed by the time they got the horses back. Dusty sat down for one last cup of coffee. He knew that he was in a small population of people, but coffee actually relaxed him at night. It woke him up in the morning, but not in the evening.

Scout lay at his feet. His high alert had passed, but he kept a wary eye on the woods behind the camp. Dusty reached down and scratched his head. "It's okay, Boy." The woods were dark and the fire was the only light. Scout had different levels of barking, and he knew his dog. The last round of barking seemed to indicate something different than animal, but only Scout knew for sure. Still, Dusty felt unease in the pit of his stomach. Creeping around hunters' camps didn't seem like a very intelligent thing to do, but he'd done enough criminal law over the years to know intelligence wasn't a prerequisite.

Dusty poked the fire; it crackled and the flame rose high momentarily. Mike walked up and sat down.

"So what did the weather say before you rode in?" Dusty asked.

"Don't know. I checked it before I left and it didn't show any big storms coming. For what it's worth," he added.

"Yeah," said Dusty. "Guess that just adds to the excitement." He stared into the fire and let his mind go free. "Oh, and thanks." Dusty never wanted to divulge what he did for a living, especially to people in the same profession. That's why he came to the wilderness. The earlier conversation with Reggie and Cliff had come perilously close.

Mike knew right away what he was talking about. "You don't have to thank me. I know the rules," he joked, as he stirred the fire with a stick and watched the coals glow in the dark.

Scout was steaming as he lay next to the fire by Dusty. His fur had soaked up water from the underbrush and he was basking in the heat.

Dusty took another drink of coffee. "You ever think about her?"

A big smile crossed Mike's face. "Maybe."

"Thought so." Tossing out the rest of his coffee, Dusty stood up. "I'm going to hit the hay. We've got a big ride tomorrow."

"That's the best kind of day there is," Mike said happily. "I'll take care of the fire."

Walking over to his tent, Dusty threw the flap open and entered. Scout trotted in behind.

Dusty took his boots off and climbed into his sleeping bag fully clothed. He could see his breath and it felt twice as cold now that he left the fire. The smell of camper cloth and his sleeping bag made him feel at home. He dozed off as soon as his head hit the pillow.

Dusty felt Scout's wet nose in his face. Half asleep, he wasn't sure what time it was, but Scout wasn't one to give up. The Australian shepherd nosed him again and sat back and waited. Groggily, Dusty looked at his watch, 5:30 a.m. "Good job, Scout. Looks like it's about time to get up."

A fire crackled outside and Dusty knew Mike was already up. He chuckled to himself. He wasn't sure that guy ever slept. He reached over and unzipped the tent. Scout bounded out. Dusty pulled himself up and slipped his legs out of his sleeping bag. He quickly tied his boots, shrugged into his coat and shoved his hat on his head, grabbing his gloves as he ducked under the tent flap.

Walking to the fire he noticed the ground was white with a heavy frost. The sky was slate gray and without cloud breaks. Dusty couldn't really decide what kind of day it was going to be yet—besides cold. The sky could change, but right now his breath was coming out in puffs of steam. Mike had the water boiling on the fire.

"Just put the coffee in, so about seven more minutes," said Mike. "I let the horses out about a half hour ago."

"Wow, Suzy Homemaker. What's for breakfast?"

"That's where I draw the line," said Mike.

"Oh, is that right?" Dusty said with mock dismay.

"Well, maybe not the line," Mike relented. "I just didn't think you'd want me to ruin all your food."

"It's really pretty easy. It's a hunting trip, right? So it's bacon, more bacon, and then a little more bacon," Dusty said, looking for his frying pan to get started.

"Perfect."

Reggie walked into the fire area carrying his rifle. He sat stiffly on the log.

"Doing some hunting this morning?" asked Mike.

"No, but I wanted to be ready when we get there. I wish I'd have gotten a moose tag. I got a bear, and deer of course, but I never thought about a moose."

"It's probably not going to be a problem," said Dusty. "I've only heard tell of one moose. There's a lot more griz than there is moose through there."

"Oh, really?" Reggie sat up. "Grizzlies?"

"It's not that long of a walk from the Selkirks and they pretty much go where they've a mind to," added Mike.

"Dang!"

"What's up?" Cliff asked as he came to the fire.

"I just found out there's griz up here and nobody bothered to tell us," said Reggie petulantly.

"It's not like that," said Dusty. "It's not official, so I'm not really sure you can get a tag for an area that they're not officially in."

"Figures," said Cliff.

"What time we heading out?" said Reggie impatiently.

"Soon as we can get breakfast done and everything packed up," answered Dusty.

"Let's do it," the lawyer snapped as he poured himself a cup of coffee.

Always the senior partner. Dusty got the bacon out of the cooler.

The lakes got smaller and smaller as they climbed out of the basin. The trail was full of switchbacks and poorly maintained. At times it seemed to make a faint slash into the hillside and then fade away to nothing. It wasn't the best place to take a packhorse, but Dusty and Mike didn't mind. Reggie and Cliff, on the other hand, Dusty noticed, spent a great deal of time "pulling leather" as the old timers would call it. They grabbed onto their saddle horns as the horses negotiated some of the sheer drop-offs. Dusty wasn't sure, but he thought he saw Reggie's face turn white on a few corners. Maybe it was his imagination, but the thought was pleasing to him.

Dusty was glad that they hadn't pushed on last night. It would have been an adventure for him and Mike, but since his first responsibility was to get the dudes in and out safely, it would not have been a good idea. The sky still resembled a dark gray basement as they crested the top of the hill and began riding along Tatoosh Buttes. This was wide-open country, no trees. Dusty loved the feeling of the space. You could see for miles and the land graduated from tundra into snow-capped peaks in the not so distance. He noticed they seemed pretty heavy with snow, and wondered if that had been added to in the storm yesterday.

It had been years since he'd been up in this part of the Pasayten. He'd made camp on the top of Tatoosh Buttes. There were carpets of wild flowers everywhere. The smell and color filled his mind. Now in October, the ground cover had turned to burnt reds, greens and yellows. Still beautiful, but in a different way. He looked carefully; he knew there was a hidden creek up here. As he rode, he found it—actually, Muley found it. The big blue roan plunged his nose into the small pool. Reggie and Cliff's horses quickly followed suit. Mike went off trail with the packhorses and watered below them so they wouldn't get hung up and cause another wreck.

The path was wet and muddy as they continued down the Tatoosh Buttes Trail. It wove down a steep hill with young trees replacing those lost in a burn a few years back. The trees were just tall enough that Dusty was only able to get a snatch of the scenery in front of him every so often as he descended the hill. He could see the white-topped mountain peaks. These were more like foothills—Frosty Pass, the Parks. So the snow level was definitely dropping, Dusty mused. Not surprising, but something to keep an eye on.

At the bottom of the hill he turned in his saddle, "Not much farther now to the airport."

"About time," Reggie said begrudgingly.

He never gave up on his attitude. Once again Dusty patted himself on the back for deciding to work in a small town rather than going to Seattle and possibly having to work under somebody like Reggie.

Chapter Fifteen

Muley didn't seem to miss a beat, despite the ground that he'd covered. Scout ran alongside with his tongue hanging out. They breezed into the airstrip late afternoon. The name was misleading in the fact planes were no longer flying in and out. It was now a large grassy swath, originally built in 1931 by the Works Progress Administration. From 1931 to 1968 the Pasayten Airstrip was listed on the annual facilities inventory for the Pasayten—at that time the Winthrop Ranger District of the Okanogan National Forest. Dusty had done the research a long time ago. The idea of airstrip and wilderness was a conundrum to him, and he loved history. He even knew the first aircraft landed there in 1932 from a neighboring airfield.

The Pasayten Airstrip had been used fairly consistently through the years, mostly for fire suppression. The field itself was depicted as a single 3,400-foot sod north/south runway. Dusty looked around. Today the airstrip still had lots of grass growing, despite the freezes. A weathered log cabin, appearing in good repair, stood silently at the end of the field in some trees.

A camp sat in the trees just past the cabin. Dusty rode over and investigated. A large rock-ringed fire pit lay in a clearing. Riding a little farther back, Dusty saw a corral lashed together with white weather-beaten logs.

"Not bad." Mike rode up next to him looking at the corral.

"I didn't know what to expect. Let's drop our packs and set up camp."

Reggie and Cliff had already dismounted, eager to look around. Dusty walked up to them leading Muley. The lawyers quickly handed him their reins and walked toward the cabin. As he and Mike were dropping the packs, a wind whipped the trees. Dusty zipped his Schaefer coat a little higher.

Mike rubbed his hands together. "Hope it's just wind."

"Probably ought to get our camp up as soon as possible," observed Dusty.

They unloaded the tents and dropped them where they'd put them up and then figured out an area for the kitchen next to the fire ring. They hobbled the horses and turned them out to eat, belling Muley, since he was the lead horse now. The animals didn't hesitate and bounded toward the green grass of the landing strip.

They set up a tarp over the kitchen area and included the fire ring. Even though it wasn't raining now, the weather could change quickly. The temperature was dropping as darkness approached. Dusty and Mike hurried to finish getting their camp in place.

The fire had just began to crackle and the coffee pot was on when Reggie and Cliff returned, beaming. "This is even better than I'd imagined," said Reggie gleefully. "I'll bet that log cabin was built in the early '40s for the airport command post."

"You can practically see those planes coming in," agreed Cliff.

"It's been a while since it's been used, to my understanding," said Dusty cautiously.

"They probably still air-evac people out of there. It's a nice landing spot," offered Mike.

"Probably so," agreed Dusty.

"I tried the door on the log cabin and it's locked," said Reggie ruefully.

"The Forest Service has commandeered most of these old cabins up here and made them layovers for their help when they're in the area. Probably don't get a lot of use. Last I heard there were only two rangers roaming the entire area of the Pasayten," Dusty said, as he pulled pots out of the pack boxes for dinner.

"And one of them got married," added Mike.

"I'd sure like to get in there," Reggie said again, looking wistfully at the cabin.

Dusty was annoyed. Once again, even understated, the undisguised message came through that it needed to happen. His stomach tightened. *He was in the woods, for crying out loud. That kind of behavior could go on in the city, but there was no call for it here.*

"Huh," he grunted and started dinner.

Seeing he wasn't getting anywhere, Reggie sat down and warmed his hands by the fire. Cliff joined him.

"Hey, you guys have anything to drink besides coffee?" Reggie asked. "I mean a real drink."

Oh, great. Here we go. Dusty hated this part about the outfit. Drinking wasn't something he supported. He felt a little bit of antagonism towards it, actually, since it came pretty close to destroying his life. On an outfit a guest was a guest. If they wanted a drink around the fire, it was up to Dusty to provide it. He checked the box and found that Andy had packed a bottle. "Got some Black Jack. Will that do?"

"Kind of prefer Canadian Club on the rocks, but since we are roughing it, that will have to do. More ice?" Reggie asked pragmatically, holding out his cup.

"I do." Amazingly, Andy had put some in the ice chest. He was resourceful. He'd leave fresh water out and let it freeze overnight, then pack it into a cooler until they needed it. *You could sure tell he'd been working on outfits for a while.* Dusty placed two half-full glasses with the amber liquid on ice on the log in front of the men.

"Now we're talking," said Reggie. Raising his glass to Cliff, he said, "To tomorrow's hunt!"

"Cheers," agreed Cliff, touching his glass to Reggie's. The lawyers downed the drinks in one gulp and held out their glasses for more.

Dusty placed the bottle on the log. "Here's the Jack and here's the ice. Help yourselves. Dinner will be done shortly."

He turned and opened a couple of large cans of stew, dumping them into a Dutch oven pan. Putting the heavy anodized lid on top, he positioned it next to the fire. He mixed up some Bisquick and water for dumplings to put on top once it boiled. *Nothing like stew and dumplings to stick to your ribs on a cold winter night—at least that's what Uncle Bob would say.*

The cooking had taken Dusty's mind off the weather. Straightening up, he looked around. It was snowing. Very faintly, but snowing for sure.

"Mike, you think you could grab up the horses? It's been about an hour."

Looking out at the airstrip, Mike agreed. "I was beginning to think about that too—probably a good time to bring them back." He walked over and took some lead lines from the makeshift corral and headed into the darkness with small flakes of snow swirling around him.

Dusty rotated the Dutch oven in the fire, set down his tongs and poured himself a cup of coffee. "You boys interested in any coffee?"

"I'm fine," replied Reggie dismissively, annoyed. He was once again in the middle of some amazing legal strategy with Cliff playing the devil's advocate. Their eyes were beginning to droop and their voices were slurred. Dusty looked over at the fifth and made note of the fact it was only a quarter full. He'd better get some dinner in them or they were not going to feel very well on their first hunting day at the Pasayten Airstrip.

Lifting the lid up, Dusty dropped some Bisquick on top. "Should be ready in about 10 minutes," he announced. The lawyers didn't even hesitate in their discussion, so Dusty figured the food would have to speak for itself. He walked over to the edge of the airfield and peered into the darkness. Scout followed him and looked out as well. "See anything, Boy?" Dusty only heard silence. He wasn't sure how far Muley could have gone, but what made it worse was that black quarter horse seemed to lead the whole herd astray. Next time they were going to have to triple hobble him. To triple hobble a horse you tied both the front and back legs together and then extend a third hobble to the back legs. It had been rare, but he had seen a horse run with those. The standard was it slowed them down a lot.

Dusty thought he heard a faint jingle in the distance, but he wasn't sure. He hesitated, unsure what to do. He could get dinner served up and then head out to find Mike and the horses, or he could wait a while longer and see if he came back. The snow had now accumulated to several inches on the ground. It didn't show signs of stopping anytime soon. Dusty made a decision. He walked back into camp. "Dinner's ready, boys." He dished up the stew and biscuits. He went into his tent and put on his insulated Sorel boots and came out tying a wild rag around his neck. "I'll be back in a little bit. I've got to find Mike and the horses."

"Go right ahead," Reggie slurred. "We'll watch the fire." Then he laughed a drunken laugh. As if on cue, Cliff joined in guffawing.

Dusty left the two of them in their amusement and headed out across the airfield, Scout trotting alongside through the snow. The dog would walk and then stop and listen for a while. At first Dusty heard only silence—then the gentle swishing of the snow falling. He strained to hear a bell. He thought he heard a faint jingle. The problem was Dusty wasn't sure he could hear it because he wanted to so badly, or because it was really there. He stopped and looked behind him at the firelight. It was really easy to get turned around in the pitch blackness and snow, so he made sure to keep the fire behind him.

"Mike. Mike," he called, and then stopped and listened. He looked down at Scout. The dog's ears were perked forward. "Do you see something, Boy?"

Scout took off like a shot. Dusty loped behind him. The dog tracks were easy enough to follow, but Dusty hoped they weren't going to get too far off course. At the far end of the airfield Scout had stopped. Dusty almost ran over the top of him. The jingle of the bell was now audible. *Strange, but no Mike.* Dusty looked around frantically.

Slowly he made his way through the brush and then between the trees and found the small herd of horses grazing—but still no Mike. Dusty snapped a lead on Muley and one on the black quarter horse. "Mike," he called again loudly, then listened, watching Scout. His dog's ears were forward, but he wasn't moving.

Fear clutched Dusty's heart at the thought of something happening to his friend. He knew he needed to remain calm. Maybe Mike had gotten turned around in the snow and darkness. Anything could have happened.

He needed to get the horses to camp and then he'd come back out and look.

Chapter Sixteen

Reggie and Cliff had all but polished off the Jack Daniels when Dusty returned. Their plates sat barely touched. Dusty felt a flash from days gone past, followed quickly by, *thank God it's not me*. He elected not to say anything about Mike—or the lack thereof. At the moment the two lawyers were in a spirited drunken argument about a case.

Dusty put the horses in the wood corral and securely tied the gate. The snow was coming down a little harder. He headed back out into the night and quickened his pace. Scout trotted next to him, bounding over the larger chunks of snow. They retraced their steps to the horses. Their prior footprints were still faintly visible in the snow, but quickly filling in.

"MI-IKE," called Dusty loudly. He stopped to listen. Nothing. Scout and he made their way across the airfield, pausing occasionally to look back at the position of the fire. The white ground covering made finding directions more difficult to determine. Reaching the end of the field, they stopped at the thickening underbrush.

"Mike," Dusty called again. He heard a faint moan. Stopping, he looked at Scout. The Aussie was focused on a snow-covered clump right in front of them. Hurrying over, Dusty fell on his hands and knees, pawing in the snow, looking for anything resembling his friend. "Mike, buddy, are you in here?" His chest tightened as he waited for the response. The fear of hypothermia setting in and possible injury raced through his brain as he dug in the snow.

"Uggh," the sound again. On all fours Dusty crawled over to a white stump in the bushes. The dog was nosing what appeared to be a form in the snow next to it. It was hard to distinguish in the darkness. Digging through the fresh snow, Dusty hit clothing.

It was Mike.

Wiping the snow from his face, he could see Mike's eyes were closed. He faintly moaned when Dusty shined his flashlight in his face. He felt Mike's head. It was cool. Reaching around in the back, Dusty's hand came back covered in blood.

"What the heck? What happened?" His friend didn't respond.

Dusty knew he shouldn't pick Mike up with a head injury, but what else could he do? If he left him out in the snow, he'd die for sure from hypothermia. He couldn't rely on any help from camp; those guys could barely stand up on their own.

Dusty kneeled in front of Mike. Very carefully he pulled Mike's arms over his shoulders and slowly stood up, bending forward. With a mighty heave, Dusty lifted him. He staggered and slipped in the snow. Mike wasn't small, but thank God he wasn't huge either. Dusty threw all his weight forward and, as gently as he could, carried Mike back to camp.

Walking through the airfield, he could see the now faint light of the fire still flickering in the distance. An occasional drunken laugh would carry on the wind. The snow fell silently around him as his breath came out in labored puffs. The quiet serenity of the snow-covered landscape warred with the fear he felt inside for Mike.

The wound looked deep, but he calmed himself with the knowledge that head wounds always bled a lot. Still, the thought of losing his best friend pushed up a darkness inside of him that he usually managed to keep at bay. He grew cold inside and put one foot in front of the other resolutely. Mike would be okay—he would see to it.

It seemed like hours, but Dusty figured it was only a short

distance to camp. He brought Mike in and laid him down by the fire. This got the lawyers' attention.

"Waaht happened to himmm?" slurred Reggie.

"Is heehurtbaaad?" managed Cliff.

"That's what I'm hoping to find out," said Dusty. He got a lantern and put it right by Mike's head. Getting the first aid kit out, he cleaned the wound. Mike had a large bump on the back of his head that was swelling at a pretty good rate. The force split his scalp open. "We were lucky we found him," said Dusty.

"Weee?" said Reggie, confused.

"Scout and I," said Dusty, annoyed. Scout sat right next to Mike and offered him his best moral support—body heat. He laid his furry head on Mike's chest.

Dusty took more ice, put it in a bag with snow and laid it on the bump. He opened Mike's eyes and looked. One eye appeared sluggish. Dusty feared it was a concussion. If that were true, he knew he couldn't let Mike sleep—he'd have to keep him awake. Well, maybe he'd have to get him awake first.

As Dusty thought it over, Mike moaned and tried to sit up. "Take it easy there. You've got quite a head wound," cautioned Dusty, lightly holding him down. Mike looked confused, but didn't speak. "Just take it easy for a little while."

"I feel dizzy," Mike finally said, so softly Dusty could barely hear him.

"No doubt. Do you remember anything?" asked Dusty.

"Just walking to get the horses. I heard Muley's bell and I headed toward him. The last thing I remember is walking into the trees at the end of the airstrip," Mike frowned, confused.

"Don't stress yourself," Dusty cautioned him. "You're back safe. I've got all the horses put away. You just need to take it easy for a while. Don't go to sleep. That's a big mistake with a head injury."

"Head injury, huh? Great," said Mike.

"You're going to be fine," Dusty reassured him.

The excitement over, the lawyers staggered off to their tents to sleep.

Dusty and Scout sat with Mike for a long time. Finally Mike said, "Hey, I can sit up. I'm feeling better."

"Okay. Do it slowly." Dusty helped Mike lean against a log still within the heat of the fire. Dusty had been feeding it small pieces of wood to keep it going and keep the snow from accumulating.

"Do you want any stew?" asked Dusty.

"I would like to try something. My stomach is growling."

"Let me just check your pupils again." Dusty flashed his light into Mike's eyes. The pupils were still sluggish.

"Am I going to live?"

"Possibly. I'll get you some stew."

Dusty was relieved to see Mike eat some stew and drink a little lemonade. *Maybe he didn't have a concussion after all.* Without warning, Mike began to vomit. Dusty's optimism faded. He grabbed some paper towels and handed them to Mike.

"I feel like crap."

"You better hold off on sleeping for a while. At least until whatever you ate gets digested. I don't want you aspirating in the middle of the night."

Mike said nothing. Dusty wasn't sure he'd understood him.

"So dizzy," Mike murmured, laying back down again.

Dusty got Mike's sleeping bag and covered him with it. He stoked the now small fire. The snow was still falling. He secured the dishes. Scout lay watching him, still lying on Mike's sleeping bag, the wounded man's hand absently on the dog's head.

Dusty sat back down next to Mike. Looking at his friend, he saw his chest rising and falling rhythmically. *That had to be a good sign.* Waiting for a while longer, Dusty made a decision. The snow was coating the sleeping bag in a thin white veneer. If he waited much longer, Mike's bag would get soaked.

Dusty once again carefully lifted Mike up, sleeping bag and all, and carried/drug him back to his own tent. Mike groaned softly as Dusty lay him down.

He went back out to the fire, now red embers. Dusty banked what was left.

"Come on, Boy. Time to hit the sack."

Scout bounded into the tent and Dusty picked up his sleeping bag and carried it over to Mike's tent. As he laid it out on the floor, Mike started snoring. *It was going to be a long night.* He realized he was very tired. Slowly he untied his boots and laid down. He felt stiff and sore. As he lay in bed almost too tired to sleep, his mind kept going over Mike's injury.

What had happened to him? Honestly, it looked like someone had bushwhacked him. Dusty knew right off the bat who it wasn't: the other two people they were with were in camp getting drunk. So then who? His mind raced. Nothing he could think of would cause that kind of injury. He shook his head. *It looked deliberate— an ax or rock, or something. The scalp was split open.*

Dusty didn't know how long he lay awake. Sleep was hard to come by. He knew he'd be carrying his Ruger from now on. The forest felt a little less friendly. He looked over at Scout and the dog lay stretched out on the tent floor without a care in the world. Mike lay in his sleeping bag breathing regularly. Every once in a while he'd turn over and groan.

Finally, Dusty drifted off to sleep. The only sound was the slight swiping as the snow hit the nylon tent.

Chapter Seventeen

Dusty wasn't sure what woke him up. It was dead silent. He looked at Scout. he was curled in a ball, his sides rising and falling. Mike was still sleeping. Finally Dusty realized it was the lack of any sound at all that bothered him. He sat up and looked around. The top of the tent was sagging dangerously. It was only about a foot above his head. Instead of letting the muffled light in from outside, it was dark. He quickly bent down and put on his Sorel boots, glad that he had thrown them in. He grabbed the Gore-Tex-lined gloves out of his saddlebag. Scout watched him as Dusty got dressed. Putting on his Schaefer jacket, he shoved on his hat, threw back the rain fly and exited the tent.

Looking around, Dusty thought it would have been a whole lot easier to have stayed in bed. The tent had at least two feet of snow on it. The whole airstrip was now a white blanket. Looking at the gray sky with bulging clouds, Dusty's heart sank. More was on the way.

Mike called out to Dusty. He was waking up. Hurrying back to the tent, Dusty checked on him. Mike looked groggy. The bandage around his head was soaked with blood in the back. Dusty looked into his eyes. The pupils looked okay, but his eyes were still not focused. They looked fuzzy and bloodshot. He didn't know what that meant, but his friend was not looking very good.

"Hey," Mike croaked out weakly.

"How'd you sleep, Buddy?"

"Kind of a bad headache. Thirsty." Mike weakly put his hand up to the back of his head.

"No, better not touch that. I need to get a new bandage on you." Dusty carefully set his head down. "Why don't you just rest? I'll get you some water and be back with some bandages. How's that?"

"S-sorry, Dust...wish I could help," Mike murmured.

"No problem. You've helped me so much as it is." Dusty said earnestly. "Just rest now and feel better."

Dusty zipped the tent behind him and surveyed the campsite. Both Reggie's and Cliff's tents sagged under the snow. Neither one was awake.

The horses were stamping in the drift corral, anxious to get some feed. Dusty looked at the snow-laden airstrip. This was deeper than he had ever seen the horses paw through. He wasn't sure they could do it. He had grain with him—but it wouldn't last long.

Brushing the snow from the horses' hooves, he buckled the hobbles on and turned them loose. They hopped and bucked out into the airstrip and then stopped, digging to find food. After getting Mike a water bottle, Dusty looked for firewood. He had some from the night before, but everything else was under a white blanket.

Using his hands, he dug around the bottoms of the trees and looked for twigs and anything else he could use to start a fire. Dumping what he could find at the fire ring, he went back out and scavenged. Some big logs were still in the fire from the night before. He dug out the whole ring, brushed off the old wood and laid the new in there. Soon he had a small fire going.

Dusty took the coffee and dumped out the grounds from the night before, then filled it with snow and set it on the fire to melt. One by one, Reggie and Cliff staggered from their tents.

"Coffee will be ready in about 10 minutes." Dusty informed them.

"Crap, we had some kind of snowstorm last night," exclaimed Reggie, as he looked around in awe. "Now what?"

"Yes, we did. Now we have to see if it's going to stop." Dusty grabbed some bacon and eggs out of the pack box cooler.

"And if it doesn't?" asked Cliff, with concern etched across his face.

"Plan B," replied Dusty.

"And what specifically is Plan B?" asked Reggie.

"We make it up as we go," answered Dusty.

"Just lovely," said Reggie, disgustedly.

Dusty looked through the trees at the sky. It was a steel gray. If he wasn't mistaken, those were snow clouds. He really hoped he was mistaken. This was not a great place to be in a storm. The good thing was it had stopped snowing for now. He scooped up snow in a plastic bag and took it with him into Mike's tent.

Cleaning the wound this morning, he got a lot better look at it. It looked almost like a hatchet wound. Crazy. How could that be? Who would want to hatchet Mike in the back of the head? And how would they know to find him here? As Dusty carefully cleaned it, he flushed it with hydrogen peroxide.

"Any idea what happened to you out there?"

"Sorry, nothing. One minute I was looking at the horses, the next minute you were carrying me. And I had a huge headache."

"Don't worry about it." Dusty had always heard not to stress out people with head injuries by asking too many questions. "Mike," he finally said, "This looks like it needs stitches."

"You have some thread?" Mike asked weakly.

"Yeah."

"Go for it." Mike coughed and painfully rolled on his side. "Have you got any hooch?"

"Well, I did, but I think Reggie and Cliff hit it pretty hard last night."

"Anything would be good."

"I'll check. Be right back."

Dusty headed for the pack boxes. The Jack Daniels was gone. He did find a big jar of vanilla extract, and that was about 35 proof. It ought to do the trick. Taking the extract, bandages, first aid kit and purified water, Dusty headed back over to his friend.

"Vanilla?" gasped Mike.

"It's real potent." Dusty insisted. "But you don't need to take anything if you don't want to—I'll just sew it up."

"Ewww—give me the vanilla."

"Just swig it down real quick."

"Sounds like the voice of experience to me," Mike commented, as he plugged his nose and drank half the bottle in one swallow.

"Hold on there; that should be good," Dusty cautioned, grabbing the container of vanilla back.

"Easy for you to say. You're holding the needle."

"I'll be gentle," assured Dusty.

"Oh, please. I've heard that before. Let's just get this over."

Dusty used his straight razor to shave the hair and then he began making little stiches holding Mike's scalp together. When he finished, he looked at his work. "Not bad, if I do say so myself."

"God, I hope so," said Mike. "You really have me at a disadvantage here."

"Not for long. You'll be good as new in no time." Dusty bent down to get out the tent door. "Get some rest. I'm making breakfast and I'll bring you some."

"Great. Thanks." Mike sounded like he was already almost asleep.

Dusty put the cleaning supplies away and washed his hands. The pot was at a rolling boil, so he added in the coffee and moved it aside to sit.

Reggie was studying Dusty as he worked in camp. "So what kind of a job do you do when you're not outfitting?"

The question stunned Dusty. Nobody point blank asked him what he did. It wasn't the usual course of conversation up here. But then, Reggie didn't seem to follow any of the rules.

"Just a little of this, a little of that," Dusty said obtusely, as he flipped the bacon over.

"Hmm," said Reggie, sounding unconvinced.

Cliff studied Dusty with renewed interest. Obviously they'd had some kind of conversation about him.

"Your name is Dustin Rose, right?" Reggie sounded like he was interrogating a witness in a Perry Mason trial.

Dusty slumped a little lower, hoping to become invisible, and continued cooking. "Been called that a time or two."

"Dustin Rose as in a world class lawyer who also happened to have one of the largest personal injury settlements in King County to date. Would that be the same Dustin Rose?" Reggie obviously was missing the courtroom, because he had a huge *aha* look on his face.

"Actually, I think you may be referring to my dad."

"I knew it!" blasted Reggie, whacking Cliff on the back. Cliff remained stoic through the beating, but interest sparked in his eyes.

"I heard Dustin Rose had a son," Reggie continued victoriously. "And I heard his son's a lawyer too."

Dusty couldn't take it anymore. "Guilty as charged."

"So all this time you knew exactly what we were talking about," Reggie stated more rhetorically than anything else.

"I don't actually listen," said Dusty. "But if you don't want people to hear you, then you probably shouldn't talk in front of them." He scraped the eggs and bacon into three separate bowls, "I've got some warm biscuits in the tinfoil by the fire if you want any. Honey and butter is on the pack box."

Dusty grabbed a plate for Mike and hurried to his tent. He felt violated. Strange analogy, he knew, but being who he was in the wilderness was so completely personal and private to him—and now it was out for everyone to discuss. He was sure that he was reincarnated. He held fast to the adage that a man was the measure of who he was and not what he was. Sure, he wanted to do a good job for his clients, damn it. He liked to win! But not here and not now. He was a packer for an outfit, and that was good enough for him.

Dusty shrugged off the bad feelings, put a smile on his face and entered Mike's tent. "Wake up, Sleeping Beauty. Got some food for you."

Mike's head was obviously bothering him. "Here, let me help you sit up so you can eat," said Dusty. He set the food down, grabbed Mike's duffel and set it up behind his head. He carefully helped him into a sitting position, then placed the food in his lap. "I'll be right back with some coffee. Make sure and take small bites. I don't want to have to perform CPR on top of all my other first-aid duties today."

"Yes, sir," said Mike, with mock seriousness. "I never knew my friend was so talented."

"Well, neither did I. Just rising to the occasion, I guess." Dusty disappeared to get the coffee.

Chapter Eighteen

By midmorning Dusty had the dishes washed in snow water and dried. Mike was sleeping, and Reggie and Cliff had gone hunting. The lawyers showed Dusty their already downloaded GPS coordinates, so he wasn't too worried about them returning. If you didn't have a compass, the GPS would work. At least from what he'd read about them. This was not a good day for landmarks as everything was uniformly white. The winter sun had peeked through the slate gray sky and Dusty felt like perhaps all of this snow would go away and they could go on with their business. He knew that was also pretty optimistic, since the only thing you could rely on in Pasayten weather was that it was completely unreliable.

The Seattle attorneys had really laid off on the sarcasm and pushiness after figuring out who Dusty's dad was and that he was one of them. He hated the idea they would treat him any differently because of his job, but whatever. He was just going to stay low. The horses had dug into the snow and found graze, but Dusty wasn't sure how long they were going to be able to do it. He rounded them up and gave them some grain. There was an icy creek that ran just below the log cabin, so the horses were able to water. Dusty busied himself with picking up what firewood he could find and cutting some larger limbs.

The laceration on the back of Mike's head was doing okay, but he wasn't going to be able to stay in the backcountry for long with it. There was too great a chance of infection. Dusty knew that they couldn't go out the way they had come in unless the snow went away. The hills were too slick and dangerous into Hidden Lakes. He wanted to give Reggie and Cliff the opportunity to hunt over here, since it had been so important to them.

In his wood hunting Dusty lucked upon some cottonwoods. He took his ax, which was really sharp, and peeled off as much bark as he could. He took some limbs too. He kept loading it up into the afternoon until he had a pretty good pile of wood. Unlike the other wood, this wasn't for firewood. Mountain man lore was that horses would eat the cottonwood bark—he'd found it to be true. They not only would eat it, but they'd pass up other food for it. The bark was supposed to be sweet. He wanted to be ready in the event of more snow. He also continued to gather firewood with his saw and brought large pieces back to camp and split them. They would be set up for a few days, anyway.

As Dusty just finished splitting a round, he wiped his hand across his forehead. He caught a movement out of the corner of his eye. Mike had his winter coat on and he shuffled slowly out to the fire ring and sat heavily down on a log.

"How's your head?" asked Dusty solicitously.

"It's been better. It feels really, really tight."

"Yeah, I bet it does. Those stitches needed to hold it together and it looked like a lot of swelling." Dusty stopped and sat down on the log across from Mike. "I wanted to talk to you about this. I really think we need to get you an airlift out. The bleeding's stopped, but you need to have your head looked at by a doctor."

Mike bristled. "I'm not going to leave you with this whole deal by yourself."

"Mike," Dusty said, his voice calm. "I totally understand that, but I want you around for a lot more rides than this one. We got plans."

"Yeah, we do." Mike continued stubbornly.

"Well, think about it and see how it goes. If things don't improve by tomorrow, we're going to have to make a move, anyway. At least call Uncle Bob by radio and let him know we're not coming back, at least not in the near future." Dusty stood up and stretched his back. "I've also got a SPOT satellite with me, so just say the word."

"Nice," said Mike. "I don't exactly have insurance for the $25,000 Life Flite either." He looked earnestly at Dusty.

"Seems kind of cheap when you're talking life and death," Dusty insisted.

"It would appear that we got the death thing handled for the time being," Mike insisted.

"Okay, then. We may have to get an air flight, anyway, depending on the weather. So let's just wait and see." Dusty turned to the kitchen area. "How about some lunch?"

"That sounds good to me," said Mike.

Reggie and Cliff were out the better part of the day. When they came back they were dragging a deer with them. Reggie had a big grin on his face.

Dusty walked out to give them a hand, "Nice going, Reggie! A three-point." He looked down at the deer admiringly.

"Isn't he a good-looking buck?" agreed Cliff.

"I'll say," said Dusty.

Reggie actually looked embarrassed over all the praise. "Thanks, you guys. Couldn't have done it without you."

Dusty thought he was going to like this new Reggie. He hoped he kept it up. The three men dragged the deer past the campfire a ways and dressed it out, and strung the meat up high to keep it out of the reach of animals. *With the drop in temperature, it ought to be frozen solid by morning.*

Dinner went quickly with stories of the hunt. The lawyers turned in early and Dusty and Mike sat for a while around the fire.

"So you think we can leave tomorrow?" asked Mike.

"I guess we'll just have to see what happens. I hope so. You can get your head looked at and Reggie can get his meat out."

Mike snorted, "I think either one is going to be okay. I still would like to know what hit me. I hate to think that there are detached meat cleavers or axes waiting for people to walk by in our forests."

"What a thought," agreed Dusty.

Scout curled up by the fire in a ball, careful to keep his fur far enough away to not catch on fire.

"I think I'll call it a day," said Mike. "I need to take both of my heads to bed now—or at least that's what it feels like—the inner head and the outer head."

"That can't be good. You want some more Advil?"

"I thought you'd never ask," Mike joked, and held out his hand. "Just four, please."

Dusty gave him the Advil and banked the fire as Mike walked back to his tent.

The lower light was earie against the snow and the branches of the trees cast shadows. Scout suddenly sat up growling. He quickly changed up to snarling and baring his teeth. Dusty tried to follow his gaze into the forest. He couldn't make out what Scout saw, but the hair on the back of his neck was standing straight up. It had nothing to do with the fuss his dog was making. Someone was out there. He could feel it.

Slowly Dusty walked to his tent, purposely not showing any alarm in his casual gait. Undoing the rain fly, he quickly picked up the Ruger lying next to his bed. Tucking it into his belt, he headed back to the campfire. *Let's have the son of a bitch show himself.* Unless Mike fell over backwards on a meat cleaver, somebody was out in these woods and they meant business. Dusty was going to give it to them. *This one's for Mike.*

Chapter Nineteen

"Whoever is out there, make yourself seen, or you're going to be talking to the business end of my Ruger." Dusty stood facing the area where he'd heard the rustling, his weapon drawn. Scout was done waiting, and with a snarl he launched himself through the snow.

"Call off your damn dog, Dusty! It's me, Pinto. Your uncle sent me down here to check and see how you are doing." The smaller man appeared from behind the trees.

Scout didn't hesitate in his launch at the small man. It caused Dusty a twinge of uncertainty. He'd never known Scout to be wrong before. This was perplexing. Finally, he pointed his gun down. "Scout, come." The dog still growled but reluctantly obeyed Dusty.

He turned to Pinto. "So where's your horse?"

Pinto became embarrassed and even kicked snow with his foot. "When I was coming up Tatoosh Buttes trail out of Hidden Lakes he fell out from under me. I lost him and hiked down here, hoping you could horse me up."

"We don't have any extra stock. Especially now that Reggie has gotten his deer."

"I seen that," Pinto said, gesturing at the meat hanging over camp.

"We'll help you with what we got. Kind of trying to decide what to do next." Dusty said, as he banked the fire. "Really hoping the snow stops."

"It is a worry," Pinto said sympathetically.

"So you got an outfit?" Dusty said, looking around.

"Well, not exactly, but I got my bedroll, so I should be okay."

Dusty wasn't about to share anything with this kid. Camp hospitality was one thing, but there was something pretty crazy about his behavior. He didn't trust him. "All right, then. See you in the morning." Dusty turned and started walking to his tent. Without looking back, "Come on, Scout." The Aussie, keeping an eye on the young wrangler, slowly trotted after Dusty.

Once again, Dusty did not sleep well. He was worried about a lot of things, the weather being near the top, but Mike was right up there. He didn't hear any more noises during the night. Glancing down at Scout, he verified that fact.

It was quiet. Too quiet. Dusty swore he heard the skim of something against the nylon of his tent. He lay completely still. Dread filled the pit of his gut. Finally, he willed himself to pull open the tent fly. He was greeted by a wall of white. *It was still snowing!* Dusty hurriedly pulled on his Sorels, grabbed his jacket and gloves and shoved on his hat as he headed out the door—or rather, began fighting his way through the snow. As he looked around, he could only see the tops of the other tents, it must have snowed about four feet overnight. In all his years in the backcountry, this was the first time this had ever happened to him, and he was at a loss.

Looking over at the log cabin next to them, he saw a curious sight. Smoke was coming out of the chimney. Without wasting a second, Dusty broke through the snow and headed over to the cabin. He stamped his feet on the old log porch and knocked on the door. Expecting a Forest Service person, he was greeted instead by the small red-haired wrangler. "What are you doing in there?" Dusty sputtered.

"Well, sorry, Dusty. But it started snowing really hard and I figured the Forest Service would probably want me in here, rather than freezing to death out in the snow."

"How did you get in?" Dusty was confused. The door he had knocked on looked flawless.

Pinto lowered his voice. "I kind of let myself in through the back door."

Dusty threw up his hands. "Whatever." It doesn't appear to be letting up at all, so we're all going to be moving in here." He strode back through the snow to camp, kicking a trail the best he could. He got Reggie and Cliff up first and told them to move their gear over to the log cabin, and then he went to Mike's tent. The flap was shut and Dusty called through it. "Mike, you awake?" A groan emanated through the camper cloth. Alarmed, Dusty pulled open the tent fly. Mike lay on his bed. His head wound showed red blood through the back, a sign of recent bleeding.

"You have a rough night, Mike?" Dusty asked, pulling himself into his friend's tent.

"I guess. I was okay for a while and then I had a terrible nightmare, like I was in a fight."

"Kind of looks that way, buddy. Your head is bleeding."

"Rats. I must have lost then," Mike said sadly.

"We'll deal with that later. Right now we need to get you into the log cabin. It's snowed about four feet and it's not showing any signs of letting up." As he spoke he was picking up Mike's duffel. "Come on. I'll grab your sleeping bag. Get your boots and coat on." Moving at half speed Mike completed the tasks. Dusty carried his sleeping bag and duffel as Mike leaned on him walking through the snow.

The cabin was large and open, one big room. There were some bunks in the corner—the bottom one had been already claimed by Pinto. Dusty laid Mike's sleeping bag down on the next bottom bunk, and helped Mike to lay down. "I'll get that bandage changed for you when I come back."

"Pinto, can you help me haul the supplies in here? Reggie and Cliff, you guys need to get your gear out of your tents and bring it in here, I don't know how much longer they are going to be standing."

Dusty and Pinto made trip after trip hauling the pack boxes, extra wood, the bark for the horses and grain. When Dusty went out to the corral, eight sets of eyes were trained on him expectantly. There was no way now they were going to be able to forage for food. He broke down a path for them to get down to the stream, but with the rate the snow was falling, it seemed to half fill in before he got back up to get the horses.

Snapping the lead on Muley, the big blue roan Appy followed him down the trail without question. One by one, Dusty led them down to drink. Having accomplished that, he gave them each a scoop of grain and then a small pile of the bark to chew on. *That ought to keep them busy for a while, while I figure out what to do next.* Dusty walked back up to the log cabin. After being outside in the white scape, the warm wood and fire in the Franklin stove felt cheery.

Reggie and Cliff were talking with Pinto about their hunt. If the young wrangler had any bad feelings towards the lawyers, they seemed to have disappeared. He was laughing with them and slapping them on the back. Dusty shook his head. He grabbed the first aid kid and went over to where Mike still lay down. Carefully peeling the bloody wrap off, Dusty used scissors and cut fresh gauze. He carefully wrapped it around his friend's head. "We're going to need to get you out of here, Buddy, insurance or not."

"I was afraid you were going to say that," Mike said, a faint glint in his eye.

"Yup. Riding buddies like you are too hard to come by. I've got an interest in seeing you pull through."

"Thanks, Dusty. I feel the same way." A small tear formed in the corner of Mike's eye and trickled down his cheek.

"Aw, Mike, it ain't near to being over yet. Don't worry about that!" He gave Mike a quick hug.

Chapter Twenty

For some reason, Dusty didn't want to tell anybody that he was calling on his SPOT for an airlift. Some unknown voice was telling him to keep it quiet. He put the satellite in his pocket and slipped on his coat. He walked down to the corral first. The horses were in a tight herd and looked dejectedly at him through the falling snow. Dusty passed them and walked to a clearing with no foliage above. He pushed the button on for Help/Airlift and sat it up as high as possible on a rock. He could only pray the signal would work through the snow. He knew the SPOT would radio their coordinates for an airlift and that was as much as he could hope for. He returned to the cabin.

Inside the cabin the mood was still jovial. Jokes were being traded between Reggie, Cliff and their new pal Pinto. Dusty shook his head and dug in the pack box for his radio to Uncle Bob. As he set it up on the wooden bench, Pinto suddenly stopped laughing. "What's that for?"

Dusty wasn't sure, but he could have sworn he saw anxiety pass over the small wrangler's face. "I need to let Uncle Bob know what's going on down here, that's all."

"Well, I'm sure he's got his hands full too with the snow up there."

"Maybe so, maybe not. The Pasayten is real funny about which areas are hit. It can vary quite a bit, even over a few miles." Dusty punched in the radio button. "Bob Rose, this is Dusty. You read me?" Dusty waited a few minutes and tried it again, "Bob Rose, this is Dusty at the Pasayten Airstrip. You read me?"

Crackling emanated in the background and then a faint voice, "Dusty, this is Bob."

"Uncle Bob, we've had some problems down here. Mike is hurt pretty bad with a head wound. We've got four feet of snow and not much feed. And it's still snowing."

"We got about a foot up here. What do you need?" Bob's voice was barely audible through the squawks and static.

"I called an airlift for Mike, if it makes it. And we need to get everybody out of here, and some horse feed."

"I've been having some problems here. Pinto—"

Before Bob could finish what he was saying, the little wrangler threw himself across the room and slapped the radio out of Dusty's hand. Before the bigger man could react, Pinto pointed a gun in Dusty's face. "Keep your hands where I can see them or you're gonna get some more of what your buddy over there got," he said sternly. His face now resembled the mask of hatred that Dusty had glimpsed before. Pinto's eyes were slits and his mouth a slash of cruel grin.

The rage in Dusty began when the little man slapped the radio out of his hand. But upon hearing this is who had hurt Mike, white hot rage filled him. Dusty heard a roar in his ears. All he knew was he wanted to obliterate the wrangler.

Mike sat up. He had seen the whole thing. He knew Dusty better than anyone. He knew once Dusty lost it, he wasn't going to stop. "Dusty," he said in a very even voice. "Just stay calm."

Dusty looked at Mike, but didn't appear to comprehend what he was saying. He squared off with Pinto and the gun.

Reggie and Cliff had gone to the far end of the cabin and hunkered down the best they could behind a cabinet.

Pinto began to rant. "So you remember Clem Stanton? You remember that man that you kilt in cold blood? Well, that was my daddy, you son of a bitch. You kilt my daddy!" The wrangler's voice took on a shrill quality as he screamed accusingly at Dusty.

"He wasn't nothin' to you, but he was ever'thin' to me and you kilt him. Well, you son of a bitch, you say good-bye now, 'cause I'm sending you straight to hell!" At the same time a perceptible click sounded—he cocked the trigger. Dusty roared like a wild animal, grabbing the wooden table, upending it, and throwing it on top of Pinto. The bullet shot through the wood as Dusty got on top of it and jumped with all of his 225 pounds. After the ringing of the gunshot, the roaring of Dusty, and the crashing of the wooden table, the cabin was silent.

Reggie turned to Cliff. "Jesus, this is more excitement than we paid for!" Both men turned their eyes back to Dusty.

Feeling emotionally and physically exhausted, he cautiously pulled the table off Pinto. The man's neck was bent at an odd angle and the gun hung uselessly at his side. Dusty carefully eased the gun away from the body and set the table back up. All four of the men stared silently at the contorted figure on the floor.

Dusty's neck was tight. He felt a headache begin pounding in his temples, the aftermath of the huge adrenaline outpour. The black, uncontrollable rage, usually kept at bay, had escaped him. Dusty knew he was powerless. Once he lost control, he couldn't stop. Stopping drinking had definitely helped. *Sarah, his ex-wife's face cowered in terror as he shouted and slammed his fist through a door.* Shame burned through him like a hot poker. *That's not me. It's not who I am.* Yet there lay Pinto.

"Dusty." Mike sat up on his bunk. For the first time in minutes, Dusty noticed his friend looking at him, concern carved in his face. His brown eyes boring into Dusty's. "It's okay. You did what you had to do."

Mike knew him better than he knew himself. Dusty willed himself to repress the bile that rose in his throat, "I guess we better roll him up in a mantie and hang it outside. That's the best way I can think of to preserve him."

"Makes sense," said Mike, his voice flat.

"I guess we know what happened to your head," said Dusty.

"Yeah. I'm feeling kind of fortunate now."

Dusty turned to the dudes. "I'm really sorry, you guys. I know you signed up for a hunting trip, not a western shootout."

"No apologies necessary," said Reggie, beaming. "This has been one of the most exciting trips I've had. Beats the heck out of the cruises to Mexico or the Bahamas that my wife always makes me go on. I'd take this any day of the week."

"Ditto here," said Cliff. "It's good to know that the manly men are not a lost breed, Dusty."

Manly men. Jeez, is that what they call it? The image of Pinto under the table flashed through his mind—he quickly repressed it. He knew it would hit him later, but he still had an outfit to take care of. "I think I'll put on a pot of coffee, if anybody's interested," he said, all business. He pulled the pot out of the pack boxes and set it on the stove.

"Count me in," said Reggie. "And me," joined in Cliff. "I'd like a cup too, if you don't think I'm too broken down for it," said Mike.

"No way, Mike. It's the best thing for you. It will be done in a few minutes."

Chapter Twenty-One

The fire in the wood stove flamed and the four men sat in the log cabin drinking their coffee. The snow continued to fall. Dusty felt himself relax, the adrenaline leaving his body. He literally felt like he had a hangover. He never allowed himself to lose control, especially since he no longer drank. *It just goes to show, in the right situation anything can happen.*

Reggie took a drink of coffee and stared curiously at Dusty. "So what was that really about? Why was he so convinced you killed his father?"

Dusty figured this was going to come up, so he was ready for it. Patiently he explained. "Last summer Mike and I went on a pack trip into Corral Lake to visit Uncle Bob and spend some time in the backcountry. A family, the Rosses, had picked the same time to enjoy a family backpacking trip. In a series of events, a couple drug runners, Clem Stanton and Tom Flannigan, had picked that same time to come through the wilderness for a client. Tom was a pedophile. The family was ambushed and their daughter, Sally Ross, was taken hostage. Trying to protect his family, Albert Ross was fatally injured. Mike and I became involved when we found a young boy in the trail, Sally's brother, bruised and exhausted, but able to tell the story of the brutal abduction of his sister.

"We were finally able to locate the young girl with her captors. We freed her and took the men captive. Clem was shot attempting to escape and re-kidnap the girl." Dusty left out the fact that he wasn't the person who shot Clem—he'd just as soon let them think he was. If this attack was leveled at Clem's shooter, let it be him.

Reggie and Cliff listened with rapt attention to the story, their eyes never leaving Dusty. "Wow," Reggie said, shaking his head when it was over. "You guys really do live the Old West up here. Who knew?"

Cliff nodded in agreement. "Who knew?" he echoed.

Reggie asked, "So that's two dead guys in two trips?"

Dusty hadn't thought of it that way, "Yeah, I guess so," he said pensively. "But I've been on plenty of rides where everybody has lived too."

"I'll vouch for that," Mike said.

"Thanks, Mike."

"Just thought I'd help," Mike said, the corner of his eyes crinkling.

Glancing outside again, Dusty set down his cup. The snow was worrying him. "I'm going to go out and check on the horses."

After putting on his winter gear, Dusty attempted to push the cabin door open. It moved very slowly. It had been snowing at a steady rate and it had drifted against the door. It was now approaching five feet, without showing any signs of stopping. The door slammed into the snow bank. Dusty backed into the cabin and looked around for a shovel. He was in luck; there was one next to a broom by the door.

He began to dig a path. It had been tromped down earlier when they moved into the cabin, so it was only a couple of feet high on the trail. As he worked, he sweated. He took his jacket off, careful to lay it right where he could find it on the path. The corral wasn't far from the cabin, but it took a good hour of digging to get to the horses. They were huddled dejectedly together under a tree. Their corral was full of snow and they were shaking.

This wasn't going to work. Dusty looked at them. He was going to have to get them shelter—and soon. If they went into shock and collicked, he'd lose them all. Despite his circumstances, Muley's penetrating eyes looked directly at Dusty. *Do something now!* Walking back to the cabin, he knew what he had to do.

Mike was laying down and Reggie and Cliff were sitting at the old log table. "We are going to do some rearranging in here," announced Dusty, walking in the door. "I'm bringing the horses in." To the lawyers' astonished looks he replied, "If I don't, they're not going to make it." Dusty began moving things out of the way. He had some highline ropes in his pack boxes. Taking them out, he roped off half the cabin, saving the bunk area and the kitchen. It was definitely going to be a little cramped, and they'd have to keep up on the manure, but the horses needed the shelter.

After recovering from their shock, Reggie and Cliff helped Dusty reorganize the room. Once the area was roped, Dusty grabbed lead ropes and headed down to the corral. He snapped the lead line on Muley and Cheyenne first. They followed him without question, right up to the front door of the cabin. Gently, Dusty coaxed first Muley and then Cheyenne through, carefully lowering their heads with his hand as they crossed the threshold so they wouldn't bang their heads on the low doorway.

After that he made trips in until he had all eight horses in the log cabin. It was a tight fit and the horses wouldn't have a lot of room to lay down, but they were warm and dry and that's what mattered. Dusty set about feeding them each some grain and cottonwood bark. Then he found a big pan and set it on the stove. Bringing several small buckets, he filled it with snow. The horses would have water shortly. Dusty wasn't sure how long the airlift was going to take, but he wasn't going to lose any stock over it, of that he was determined.

Having the horses in the cabin wasn't too bad, or at least not as bad as he initially feared. Dusty kept vigilant, shoveling all the manure as it arrived. He would have liked to have some shavings for the urine, but they apparently didn't stock the cabin with everything. Mike was a little surprised when he woke up, but he was happy to see Toby and Duke.

It was difficult to tell day from night as the snow continued to pile up on the windows. This was definitely a record snowstorm, Dusty thought. He couldn't remember hearing of anything like this before, and he knew he had never been in any snowstorm like this. He hoped, one way or the other, the airlift had gotten word. He knew that Uncle Bob would have told them. Bob also needed to get his dudes evacuated. They were set for a week and Dusty knew that had to be about up.

The cabin was supplied with canned goods. Added to the dry goods that Andy had supplied him, Dusty had plenty of food for the four of them. He could last a couple of weeks. He shuddered at the thought of a couple weeks. It was way beyond what he'd like to do. He was going to have to make another dry wood and cottonwood bark run. The horses kept themselves occupied by chewing on the sweet branches and they were getting some nourishment out of it.

Mike was still doing a lot of sleeping, so Dusty had been getting the wood himself. As he put his coat on to go outside, Reggie stopped him. "Hey, you need a hand? I could use some fresh air."

"That sounds like a good idea," chimed in Cliff.

"Another pair of hands would always help out," said Dusty, pulling on his gloves.

The two men joined him and they set out into the pale afternoon. In the gray sky and snow, the woods looked sad to Dusty. It was easier to stay on the path he had dug earlier, so they walked down to the corral. Dusty showed them where to look for firewood on the off side of the trees from the blizzard, and the kind of trees that had the sweet bark on them. They dug around and formed a pile of wood to burn and bark to feed. After a couple of hours they had plenty. They each grabbed an armload of as much wood as they could carry and took it up to the cabin. Several loads later they were hanging their coats up in the cabin. The horses were happily chewing on the bark and Dusty was stoking the fire. The piles they had gotten would last them for a few days.

Dusty put on another pot of coffee and Mike was beginning to wake up. He seemed to sleep for stretches of time that exceeded the time he was awake. Dusty was worried about him, but so far he wasn't burning up in fever, so it appeared the healing process was taking place.

Chapter Twenty-Two

There were four bunks against the far wall. Dusty took a bottom one so he could be ready if Mike needed him. Mike had the other one so it was easier for him to get in and out with his head condition. The cabin was quiet except for Reggie and Cliff snoring. At least they wouldn't have any trouble sleeping.

Dusty was pretty much wide awake. The events of the day had taken a toll on him. It wasn't his usual practice to throw tables on people in anger—let alone kill them. The pit of his stomach clenched in a tight knot. The site of Pinto's broken neck kept popping up in his mind. He'd seen murder scenes in past trials, but being personally involved was another matter. He felt a cold calmness descend over him, *I did what I had to do.* The other issue was: *was it he who was meant for Clem's avenging offspring? Who knew?* Dusty didn't know the procedure for that kind of behavior. *Did they have a list in the family to take care of him?* He supposed when he got out of here and Mike was on his feet again, maybe he ought to have Mike investigate that for him.

It also seemed kind of odd, since they were avenging, that they had the wrong person. Maybe the thought of their father being done in by a beautiful woman like Cassie was just too emasculating to be tolerated. It was much better to be done in by a man. Dusty didn't know the protocol. Then there was the body. He was going to also have them airlift that out. He hoped they had a big helicopter to get all of them out. There would be three of them and Pinto. Dusty would be staying. He needed to get the horses out. There was no way he was going to leave them.

Dusty willed himself to lay still and try to rest. He tried to dream of Cassie. Nothing happened. It seemed like he dreamed about her all the time—except when he consciously tried. She was probably wondering where he was by now. Dusty wondered if she had gotten ahold of Uncle Bob. He figured he was flattering himself. She would probably just keep herself busy with work and riding until she heard from him again. He felt pained inwardly. He knew he hadn't been the most predictable person to date. Maybe she'd just think he'd gone off again on his independence deal. He shook his head. He hoped not. He was really going to have to try to work on his interpersonal relationship skills with her. So far he'd done a really poor job of communicating.

The horses were quiet on the other side of the cabin. They seemed to accept their "barn" and seemed at ease, despite the close proximity to humans. Even the black quarter horse who had been nothing but trouble—starting with the wreck and ending with horse fights, biting and kicking—stood quiet. The cold had probably just shocked it out of all of them.

Dusty lay back down on his bunk. *Everything was going to work out just fine. Hadn't Uncle Bob said they'd only gotten a foot up at Crow Lake? They were bound to send an airlift in at the first opportunity.* He wasn't sure how long it was after that that he drifted off to sleep. He first felt the light colored hair sweep across his cheek and the hot breath. He groaned and threw his arm around—Scout.

The Aussie jumped back and looked expectantly at Dusty. It was pretty clear that it was bathroom time and his dog needed to get out the door. Dusty stiffly pulled himself to his feet and walked over to let Scout out. The flakes had gotten perceptively smaller than before—probably a good sign. Scout ran down the trail and then stopped before he got too far, probably realizing that grass was out of the question. Dusty noticed another six inches of fresh snow. He was glad the cabin was here, or he wasn't sure what they would have done.

Scout finished his business and bounded back to Dusty. As he shut the door behind him, he noticed that Reggie had gotten up and was sitting at the table. "Having trouble sleeping?" Dusty asked.

"A little bit," replied Reggie.

"Sorry about your trip," said Dusty apologetically, figuring that's why he was sitting up.

"You have nothing to be sorry about," said Reggie emphatically. "I was just thinking about going back. I'd really rather stay here."

"You're kidding," said Dusty, mystified.

"I know. I have it all, right? Senior partner in one of Seattle's biggest law firms. I inherited money and position, so that naturally leads to more money and position." Reggie corrected himself, "As long as you work. But it really struck me hard when I figured out who your dad was. He's one of us." The lawyer paused for a minute. "And you're not," he said in a voice that was so quiet Dusty had to strain to hear it.

"No, I guess not," he admitted.

"You do what you want to do. You have control of your life and your law practice." Reggie ran his hand through his hair, "You got out. How?"

Dusty felt he was getting entirely too much credit. "Actually, it wasn't something I really planned. I just couldn't…"

"Couldn't sell out to the system, right?" Reggie cut in. "Bigger job, bigger house, bigger cars, bigger trips, more money and bigger cases. At some point you forget exactly who you are and where it all began." He dropped his head in his hands and almost whispered, "And you forget how to get out."

Dusty felt a lot of empathy for Reggie. He understood what had happened to him. Dusty thought back to an ex-girlfriend whom he met in law school. It was going to be perfect. Her father was going to get him a job in one of the most prestigious law firms in Seattle. It was old money. She was in a sorority and beautiful; he was in a fraternity. But he had to call it off. It was probably one of the most difficult things he had ever done. He thought he was in love with her, that he could be that guy for her. She was ready to marry him. The only problem was when it came down to it, he couldn't do it.

He could thank Uncle Bob all those years ago for giving him an insight as to what kind of man he was. Dusty had experienced true happiness in the woods with the horses. Nothing could compare to it. It was an intoxicating high to him. Probably the most important thing was it exceeded the value of money. He could see Reggie's pain and he understood it completely.

Dusty sat quietly at the table. "You must have been looking for a different life or you would have never seen it," he said.

"You're right, of course. I guess I've been looking for a way out for a long time." He seemed to age as he talked. "I'm with a woman I fell out of love with years ago. I work at a job that I despise. And my social life is a great big void—fueled by my socialite wife."

"Well, I guess that's a start then, Reggie," said Dusty. "Nobody's a victim here. Probably least of all you. You're a smart man. If you want off the merry-go-round, get off."

Reggie looked at him as if really seeing him for the first time. "You're right. You know, I can do anything I want. I just need to make up a plan."

"That's right," encouraged Dusty. "We all only get so many years. Make them worth your while."

A huge grin split across Reggie's face. "I can't believe this, coming from one of the greatest trial attorney's—son."

Dusty looked embarrassed, "Yeah, well, I guess I have always been kind of a disappointment to my dad, but—"

"No, Dusty, you're every bit the man he is. I see it clearly now. And the fact that you're doing what you love, despite your father's wishes, is a huge endorsement to me on how to live a life." He put his hands down on the table, his eyes wide in earnest. "I'm going to do it. All I needed to know is that it could be done."

The smaller man got up and slapped Dusty on the back, "Thank you. This is huge. I'm going to come back next year." Then he bent down and whispered in Dusty's ear, "And we'll see if Cliff the yes-guy is with me or not." He winked and headed off to his bunk.

Dusty felt a tickle of happiness inside his chest. He wasn't sure what had just happened, but he felt it was probably a really good thing. He smiled into the darkness.

Chapter Twenty-Three

Dusty got up and put the pot of coffee on to boil. Eight pairs of equine eyes stared at him from across the room. He still wasn't used to it. Despite his efforts to keep the manure removed, the urine was another issue. The cabin was pretty much smelling like a urinal at this point. Dusty wished he could find some straw or something, even pine boughs, but with all the snow, no such luck.

He walked over to the door and shoved it open with his shoulder to take a look at the weather. The flakes had stopped falling and Dusty swore he actually saw a glimmer of sun. It was probably about time to check with Uncle Bob on the progress of the airlift and whether the craft would be big enough to evacuate the dudes too.

Dusty picked up the radio. "Uncle Bob, this is Dusty. Come in." The static crackled and there was no reply. He tried it two more times and then set down the headset. Mike got out of bed shakily and walked over to the table and sat down. Reggie got up, followed by Cliff. They each poured themselves a cup of coffee.

Picking up the cottonwood branches, Dusty tossed some in to the horses to eat. "If it thaws some more, we can put these animals back outside," he remarked. Just then one of the horses let loose with about five gallons or urine. As if on cue, the other horses, one by one, joined in on the bathroom break.

"Probably the sooner the better," Mike said dryly.

The radio cracked with static, "Dusty, are you there?"

High Hunt

He ran over and picked up the headset. "Yes, Uncle Bob, I'm here."

"Well, thank God for that. I wondered what happened when we got cut off yesterday. I didn't know if it was the weather or what the heck happened."

"A little bit of everything," replied Dusty.

"Oh," said Bob, still confused. "We got a 'copter coming today, if the weather conditions line up. I'm not sure about the landing, though. If there's as much snow as it sounds like, they're probably going to have to drop a line down and pick you guys up that way."

"We need a carrier. Mike is in no shape to be picked up by just a line and harness, so request something they can carry him out with a head wound."

"Will do," said Bob.

"One more thing."

"Shoot," the outfitter waited.

"We had a casualty. We're going to need some kind of carrier that he can ride up in." The radio crackled again.

"Waaaht? Not again." Bob was clearly stymied. "Please don't give me any details on this channel; it's open, as far as I know. Fill me in later. I'll let them know," he finished.

"Thanks, Uncle Bob. They are only going to be airlifting four men. Scout and I are staying here and taking the horses out." Dusty took a drink of coffee.

"Are you sure about that, Dusty? It's going to be pretty dangerous finding the trail and breaking it with all that snow for all those horses."

"They're my horses," he said with finality.

"Thanks, Dusty." Bob knew not to argue. Horsemen take care of their horses—end of story.

"I'll call you when we get out. Over," said Dusty.

"Over and out, Son." Bob regarded Dusty as his son and often used it as a term of endearment to the man he loved as his own.

Dusty caught it, and there was a catch in his throat as he clicked off the radio. He knew, despite what his uncle had said, Bob was proud of him. Dusty had made the right decision in his and his uncle's eyes.

Three pairs of eyes had been watching the exchange at the table.

"So we're getting out today?" questioned Cliff.

"It sounds like it, as long as the weather holds up."

"Hallelujah!" said Cliff, then quickly looked to Reggie to see if he agreed.

Reggie seemed different since their exchange last night. He just smiled, but there was a light of determination in his eyes that Dusty hadn't seen before.

"For now," responded Reggie. "But I'm coming back."

"Oh...yeah. Sure. Great." Cliff seemed a little uncertain what to say.

Mike's dark brown eyes focused on Dusty. "You're taking out the horses all by yourself?"

"Yes," Dusty said firmly.

"Can I help you?" Mike inquired, looking directly in his eyes.

Dusty hated to say it, but Mike had forced him. "I can't let you do that, Mike. I could lose you on the trip. I won't do it." He saw the pain flash through Mike's eyes.

"Okay," Mike said softly, and looked away. "Take good care of Toby and Duke for me."

"Will do," Dusty said brusquely. Then he stood up. "Who wants breakfast?" And went over to the pack boxes and began rummaging around.

Reggie walked up. "I'll give you hand."

"Great," said Dusty.

Cliff looked confused. Offering help to other people was completely out of his skillset, so he was quiet as he watched Reggie break the eggs into the skillet while Dusty fried the bacon.

Mike watched with a slight smile tugging at the corners of his mouth. This wasn't the first man he'd seen changed by the wilderness experience, and he felt certain it wouldn't be the last.

Chapter Twenty-Four

The weather held and they heard the sound of rotor blades hovering above the strip in early afternoon. Dusty and Reggie weren't sure what kind of room the chopper would need, so they had spent the better part of the day digging out a big area in the airstrip. It wasn't for the aircraft to land, but rather, a marker to pick up passengers.

The helicopter was bigger than the small Lifeflite 'copters Dusty had seen in the past, so Uncle Bob must have gotten through to them. They hovered above the cleared patch of snow and dropped down a medic first. He unsnapped himself from the harness and walked up to Dusty and shook his hand. "I heard there was a head injury here."

"Yes," said Dusty, returning the shake. "He's laying down in the cabin."

The man looked very healthy, suntanned and athletic. "Let's take the litter. Can you give me a hand?"

The helicopter had lowered a litter to the ground. Dusty grabbed the other end and Reggie grabbed the middle and carried it to the log cabin. The snow was stable at 5 feet. The sun was out, but the melting hadn't started yet. Walking to and from the airfield had helped to tramp down a path, so carrying the litter was not difficult.

They threw open the door and brought it in, setting the carrier on the floor with a thump. The helicopter's rotors were loud as it hovered. It sounded like it was inside the cabin. Mike tried to sit up, but the effort cost him.

"Just relax, Buddy. Help has arrived," Dusty said soothingly.

"I'm not really into flying, Boss," Mike attempted humor.

The medic assured him. "You'll be there before you know it. And helicopters are a lot better than planes when you want to get somewhere." He winked at Dusty.

Squatting down to Mike's bunk, he pulled a small penlight out of his pocket. "Let me check those pupils." Mike obliged, opening his eyes and looking into the light, first on one side and then on the other. "Hmmm," said the younger man. He put his light away and put his hands on either side of Mike's neck, feeling his lymph nodes for swelling.

"Oww," offered Mike.

"Looks like you've got a bit of swelling going on in your neck. You're probably getting out of here just in time. Could I get you to sit up for me?" The medic sat back. "Slowly." He helped Mike into the sitting position so he could check the bandage. The bleeding had stopped, but a little bit of greenish yellow ooze was around the cut. "Nice job on the stitches."

"Thanks," said Dusty. "It was my first time."

"Only the best for me," Mike quipped.

"Looks like your wound is trying to heal. We'll get some antibiotics in that and get it really clean at the hospital when we land."

"Hospital?" said Mike tentatively. "Are you sure? I try to stay away from those."

"You'll be in and out of there as quickly as possible," the paramedic said calmly. "I'll see to it."

"It's doesn't get any better than that, Mike," Dusty said, encouraged.

"Okay, Boss," Mike said finally.

"I'll check up on you as soon as I take care of your horses."

"Thanks, Dusty. That means everything to me."

"Let's get loaded," said the paramedic. "We don't want the 'copter to run out of fuel. Everybody else ready?"

Reggie and Cliff stood by, their duffels in hand. "Yes, we are," said Reggie. He slung his bag over his shoulder and picked up the litter again. Surprisingly, Cliff did the same thing, and it was even lighter on the way back to the airfield.

Dusty stood on the ground as Mike's form got smaller and smaller and finally was enveloped into a hatch on the underside of the helicopter. The lines came down with an empty harness on it and the medic called, "Next."

Cliff looked at Reggie hesitantly and Reggie said, "Go ahead, Cliff."

He was harnessed in and airborne in a couple minutes. They watched him disappear into the bottom of the craft.

As the harness descended again, Reggie turned to Dusty, "I can't thank you enough for the whole trip. This was so much more than a hunting trip to me. It was a wake-up call on how I want to live my life. Sometimes you just have the truth standing right in front of you before you realize what the answer is."

"Thanks, Reggie," Dusty said modestly. "It works both ways. Talking to a guy like you makes me appreciate my choices in life. Sometimes I take it for granted. You remind me that this kind of lifestyle has been born into us, and in order to be happy on this planet we have to live it."

"Well said." Reggie shook Dusty's hand firmly.

Dusty returned the shake and pulled Reggie into a hug and slapped him on the back. "Take care on the wild streets of Seattle, Buddy."

The medic began to slip the harness on the lawyer. "Look me up when you're in the city. We'll have lunch."

"It's a deal," yelled Dusty, as he watched Reggie and his duffel go higher and higher and finally disappear into the aircraft.

The next drop contained the empty litter. Dusty and the medic loaded up Pinto. This time when it rose it turned a couple times, the dead weight throwing it off. *Maybe it was Pinto doing his last thing to say 'In your face. This ain't over.'*

Dusty and the young man stood as the harness came down for the last time. "I can't thank you enough for all your help," said Dusty.

"It's my job." The young man said, and they shook hands. He snapped himself into the harness, pulled on the line and began to raise off the ground. "Hopefully I won't see you again any time soon!"

"Amen to that," said Dusty.

He and Scout stood for a long time out in the airfield. The hatch closed and the helicopter took off, flying vertically above the trees. It soon became a small dot and disappeared altogether.

"Well, let's head in, Boy. We've got a big day tomorrow." Dusty walked back to the cabin, Scout trotting over the chunks of frozen snow.

The cabin seemed lonely now that everyone had left. Dusty turned on the radio and tried calling Uncle Bob. "Bob, this is Dusty. Do you read me?" Static crackled over the line and then remained silent. He waited for a couple minutes and tried it again. "Uncle Bob, this is Dusty. Can you read me?"

Just as he was going to give up, a voice sounded through the static. "Bob Rose here, Dusty, is that you?"

"Yes."

"How are things at the airport?"

"The helicopter came and everyone loaded up. They brought a litter for Mike, and it was a good thing too. The medic felt there was some infection starting, so we got him just in time"

"That's good news," replied Bob through static. "How about Reggie and Cliff; how did they do?"

"They did well. Reggie is a good guy," said Dusty.

"Good," said Bob. If he was surprised, he didn't show it. But Dusty knew, being in the business as long as he was, nothing surprised him about people anymore.

"I'm going to pack up their meat and go out with the horses tomorrow. I'm going to have to head out Robinson Creek."

"That's the only way that makes sense," agreed Bob.

"Hear anything on the weather?"

"This is supposed to hold for a few days, I'm taking out the

Boeing Boys tomorrow. Like I said, we didn't get hit with nearly as much snow as you did. You take care and call me as soon as you get out."

"Reggie got a deer. We'll need to get that on ice too. I'll let you know my progress."

"Oh, one thing. That Robinson Creek trail takes a lot of turns. It basically follows the creek out, so don't be surprised if you can't get ahold of me. You should have no problem at the trailhead, though."

"Okay. I'll keep that in mind," said Dusty.

"Take care. Keep the wind at your back, Son."

"Back at you, Uncle Bob," Dusty smiled, disconnecting the radio.

The horses stared at him from across the cabin. A couple nickered encouragingly. He grabbed scoops of grain and fed them and then loaded them up with some more cottonwood bark, saving a little bit for the morning. "Muley, you make a better horse than a roommate." The smell of urine was strong now in the cabin. When one horse would relieve themselves, the rest would join in. That was a lot of urine on one little log floor. Dusty felt bad about it. Maybe he'd try to ride some lime in later and try to mitigate the smell before the Forest Service used it again.

With the horses occupied, he dug in his pack boxes and looked for something for dinner. It was going to be a long trail tomorrow.

Chapter Twenty-Five

The log bed was uncomfortable. Dusty kept switching sides to get comfortable. Waking up, he swore he heard something, but looking at Scout and then over at the horses, nothing seemed to be amiss.

It was hard to get the death of Pinto off his mind. It actually was the first time he had killed anybody and it wasn't entirely on purpose. As he thought about it, he had to admit he squashed him like a bug. Geez! The thought made him sick. But if that little guy went to all those lengths to avenge his father's death and he thought Dusty was the killer, what would he have done to Cassie? He shook his head. He wasn't going to think about it.

Laying still, he was almost asleep. Suddenly he heard the deep-throated howl of a wolf. No mistaking that. Scout sat up, his ears perked straight forward. The horses crowded closer together and their hooves shuffled on the wood floor. The wolves sounded like they were right outside of the cabin—thank goodness they had gotten Pinto transported. But what about the deer?

Dusty waited. Growling and snarling sounded from the direction of the meat pole. *Reggie may not have anything to show for his hunt pretty soon. He may have to come back and get another one.* The wolves were aggressive. They could smell the horses in the cabin and circled around the outside, jaws snapping in angry growls. So far they hadn't been able to get the meat. It was tied twelve feet off the ground in anticipation of predatory animals.

Dusty hoped it held. His Ruger was loaded and right next to him.

Why does this stuff always happen in the middle of the night? And why does it always happen after everybody else is gone? Maybe they'd been watching the place. Who knows? But it wasn't going to be easy for them, he could guarantee that. Dusty cocked his gun.

He laid his head down again to sleep. He was grateful the Forest Service had covered the windows with wire mesh. At least the wolves couldn't get in that way. He could hear growling and then thudding outside. He got up and peeked out the window. A small pack of four or five skinny wolves were slinking around the trees. One of them sniffed in the air and howled with an ungodly urgency. He heard slamming against the cabin door, then clawing on the timbers. From his side, the thick logs rattled. *Thank God it was made in the old days, when things were made to last.* Then another huge thud resounded against the door, Dusty saw the nails in the hinges give a little. *I forgot about the hinges.* Shining his light on them, the rust was apparent. His stomach dropped, *How many more times was it going to take before it broke?* The horses quivered nervously together, their flight mode in full gear with nowhere to run.

An earsplitting mournful howl resounded off the cabin walls and the door was silent. Dusty crept over to the window and looked out again. The wolves were leaping in the air trying to get ahold of Reggie's deer. One would jump, fall short and then another would take his place.

Just when it looked like the meat might actually be safe, a very large wolf stepped forward. Dusty was thinking that he must be the pack's alpha male. The giant wolf sized up the meat and the height, took one mighty lunge and sunk his teeth into the flesh. The rope groaned under the weight and snapped. A feeding frenzy of snarling and slashing of teeth ensued. Within a couple minutes all that was left of the deer were pieces of bloody bone laying on the ground. One last circle around the cabin and the pack disappeared into the woods as quickly as they'd come.

Dusty breathed a sigh of relief. He wasn't going to become wolf food tonight after all. The horses visibly relaxed as well. They stood quietly, the fidgeting over.

The gray light of dawn came quickly. Dusty felt like he had just laid his head down to finally sleep when Scout was nuzzling him. Dusty cautiously opened his eyes. The horses stared at him from across the room. It really was the oddest feeling, he thought—literally being stared awake. He got up, put the coffee pot on, threw the horses some grain and the rest of the bark and put the pan on to boil some water for the horses. He probably didn't need to, but might as well start out the day right.

While the horses ate, he began to throw his things together for the ride out. Normally, pushing it, he could ride out with just one night on the trail, but with the trail conditions unknown, he knew he better be prepared for more. His grain was running low, but he'd take what he had and hope for some kind of graze along the way. He packed his tent, sleeping bag, supplies, heavy coat, boots, gloves, long johns and anything else he could think of to ward off the cold. He also threw the SPOT satellite in. He'd already had to use it once on this trip, but if those wolves came back, he'd rather be safe than sorry. He also took care to pack all the rounds of ammunition that he brought with him.

Dusty threw the pack boxes on Cheyenne and Duke. He knew his and Mike's packhorses the best. They were both reliable. He still had misgivings about the black quarter horse. That gelding had single-handedly caused the wreck on the way in. He couldn't afford another one on the way out. The snow was deep and the trail was going to be tough. It was going to take every bit of his energy to break through and get back as it was.

Saddling up Muley, Dusty double checked his latigos. It didn't seem that long ago that somebody had tried to mess him up by cutting them. They were all hard and fast, the new leather he'd purchased in good condition. After carefully checking the pack saddles, Dusty put breakaways on the packhorses. These breakaways were actually going to break if there was an issue, unlike the trip over here. Tying horses hard and fast could be lethal. Dusty knew of a packer up in Stehekin that had been subject to that folly. He had gotten killed when his packhorse fell off a steep embankment, taking him with it.

Dusty cleaned up the cabin as best he could and, one at a time, he led the horses out, taking care to hold their heads down as they passed under the door. He didn't need any injuries at this point. Once outside the cabin, the snow trail remained pretty much the same. The side walls were still close to five feet high. In the night that had passed since the snow fell, a slight glazing of frost covered the snow, making a hard shell on top. Dusty had a plan.

As he headed out of camp, he led out with Muley. His horse would use his chest and literally push against the snow, breaking it up like an ice breaker. The horses behind would follow with considerably less effort. Dusty had studied the maps before he left and he knew that Robinson Creek trail ran right by the cabin. After careful searching, Dusty found a slash in a tree. The trail signs were still buried in snow, so he was going to have to do it the old-fashioned way.

The landscape was beautiful. A virgin, untouched blanket of snow covering the forest floor. As the trail wove through trees, from time to time it broke up and was easier to push through. But as soon as Dusty got in the open, Muley had to push it with his chest again. This worked well for an hour or two, but then Muley started losing steam. He was a tough horse and had a lot of heart, but carrying Dusty and pushing the heavy drift was a lot to ask out of any horse. He needed a break. So Dusty put Cheyenne in front, climbed on him bareback, using the halter and lead rope for a bridle, and pulled Muley behind. The rest of the string followed him. At first the big white horse didn't want to lead, but after some persuasion, he began pushing the trail through the snow.

Dusty wasn't sure how far they'd gone. It was much slower going than if he was just riding down the trail. The horses hadn't had as much food as they normally would and they were more easily fatigued. He had switched out Muley and rode Toby for a while, alternating on pushing the snow and breaking trail. He'd put both Cheyenne and Duke in front and driven them from the back. The stock was getting tired. The smell of damp snow and horse sweat was pungent, mixing with the crisp fir trees and cold air. Dusty figured he wasn't going to be able to push them much farther, so he started looking for a place to camp. Thinking about the wolf pack that wasn't so far away made him extra particular about where he wanted to stop.

Finally, he came to a large thick group of fir trees, so close together it appeared almost dark to look through them. The snow was really light underneath them and Dusty could actually see grass sprouting up through the snow. He pulled Toby over and looked at Scout. "We're home." Scout wagged his tail. He was tired and wet too, so it looked like anyplace they were stopping was great with him.

Dusty put a bell on Muley and hobbled the horses. The fact that there wasn't much grass made it all the more important to hobble the horses. They may be inclined to search so far and wide to find grass that it would make it difficult to find them. This time he wasn't going to wait for the black quarter horse to pull his trick of leading the herd away. Dusty tied a third hobble to the back foot, using the lead rope, and tying a back foot to the front hobbles. That made the black horse's progress much slower.

Later, looking at his maps and the mountains, as best he could tell, he was about a third of the way out. Not bad for extreme conditions. He felt that it had gone pretty well, all things considered. He should be at Robinson Creek Trailhead within two days, at the most.

As he lay in bed that night, he thought one of the first things he would do when he got home was go visit a certain lady. He fell asleep smiling.

Chapter Twenty-Six

Dusty opened his eyes. It was dead quiet. His stomach lurched. *That can't be good.* He pulled his boots on, grabbed his gun and threw open the tent fly. Scout scrambled out in front of him, alerted by his haste. The horses stared at him questioningly as he burst from the tent. He instantly felt foolish. "Good morning, guys." Then, walking over to them, he said, "How about some breakfast?" He would let them graze for an hour or so, watching them paw at the deep snow and nibble in the lighter areas under the trees. Then he packed his gear.

As he finished lashing the packs onto Cheyenne, Dusty looked at the sky. Snowfall looked possible. The smell was strong in the air. Dusty felt his heart sink. He had to get out of here before any more snow. It was getting to be a matter of life and death. The horses only had so much feed they could forage, and he had some grain in the bottom of the bag—that was it. He was amazed it had even stretched this far.

The trail was slick with ice and slush, sometimes weaving high above the creek. The footing was bad. More than one horse fell to its knees and then clambered back up again. Once the sorrel even fell all the way off the trail—its breakaway broke and he came very close to falling in Robinson Creek. It would have meant certain death for the horse. The water was bursting over the banks and white with frost and ice. If he didn't drown falling in the water, being sucked under one of the many logs and snags in the creek would kill him.

Dusty and the eight horses had slipped, slid and pushed their way through the snow for a few hours when they came upon a huge creek flowing into Robinson Creek. There was so much water, it looked like a river. Dusty had ridden this a couple of times before. He should know its name. He was sure this was not the way it usually looked; it was swollen with melted snowfall and ice chunks.

He studied the approach for a few minutes. There really didn't seem to be a good way to cross. It looked like he was going to get soaked. He was going to have to carry Scout. As good a swimmer his dog was, he was no match for the turbulence of this creek. He grabbed his dog and lay him across the saddle in front of him. Holding tight to the lead rope of the horses behind him, he spurred Muley across. The mighty Appaloosa bowed his neck and bent into the creek—just as he would any wall of snow. The water frothed and splashed, creeping up Dusty's pant legs over his boots. Scout was riveted in place, his eyes glued to the turbulent water thrashing wildly below him.

It looked like the crossing was going to be successful, right up until the black quarter horse panicked. He was last in line. The black squealed, braced himself and reared up. He pushed the other packhorses back with his weight. Muley was stepping carefully when he suddenly went down in a hole. At the same time he was regaining his balance, the string pulled back. It knocked him off his feet. Dusty plunged into the ice cold water with Scout. He could feel Muley next to him, frantically kicking to get to his feet. The water closed over Dusty's head and it felt like a block of ice. His head was pounding with the cold of the creek. It sounded like a freight train in his ears.

It was pure pandemonium. Horses thrashing in the creek. Scout frantically dog paddled to the far side of the creek, barely avoiding ice and being sucked under debris. Dusty surfaced. It was difficult to swim with his winter boots and coat on. It wasn't that deep, but it was swift and hard to keep his feet under him. A fallen log was on his right and the current was strongly pulling him towards it. He dug in deeply in a crawl stroke to stay back from it, but it was closing in on him. Just as it seemed there was no way out, he felt warm fur and a saddle next to him. It was Muley thrashing through the creek, having regained his footing. He was closing the distance to the shore. Dusty threw a frozen hand out and grabbed the stirrup as it passed by. Muley dragged them both to safety.

Dusty lay on the snow in shock for a few minutes. When he opened his eyes, he saw a pile of Aussie fur next to him, with the sides breathing in and out quickly. *Scout made it!* Dusty sagged with relief. He lay on the frozen bank, drained. Dusty thought he'd lay there for just a few minutes. He was so very tired. He just needed to gather his strength—and he'd get up and find the other horses.

Dreams finally came to him. He felt warm and safe. Cassie was with him. Her arms felt good around him. He could finally rest.

Cassie rolled her wheelbarrow to her horses, Prince and Murphy. They stood by the pen, stamping and pushing each other, their eyes never leaving her. The horses encouraged her by nickering in between running back and forth along the fence line.

"Take it easy, you guys. I can only go so fast."

Sammy, her Australian shepherd, hearing Cassie's voice, took charge and began barking at the horses.

"It's okay, Girl. They're just hungry."

Cassie smiled. *That was the beauty of dogs—their size never got in the way of what they wanted to do. They were always as big as they needed to be.* She tossed the flakes of hay over the fence into the feeders. *It was a pretty good way to live. Don't let things you have no way of changing get in the way of your goals.*

She brushed off the pieces of hay that clung to her plaid shirt and watched her horses eat. The satisfied munching and smell of horses always calmed her. The vine maple in the pasture had burst into striking color under the green fir trees. The madrona and dogwood were dropping yellow leaves. She loved the colors of fall. The sky was quickly switching from gray to black and the air had a bite to it. She rubbed her arms to warm up. The horses continued eating, their thick winter coats impervious to the cold air.

"Come on, Sammy. Let's go have some dinner." She turned and walked to her house, her dog trotting behind her.

Sammy stretched out in front of the wood stove, and Cassie sat down on the couch with a mug of steaming tea in her hand. She had a pile of files with her, as always. She flipped one open and began to read.

The sudden ring of her landline next to her made her jump. It didn't ring very often, and she had to admit, night calls always put her a little on edge after her experience a few months ago with the crazy guy from the Buck Creek work party.

Roy had seemed a little off when she'd met him at the trailhead, but she had no idea how bad it was going to get with his constant phone calls and finally breaking into her home.

Cassie involuntarily touched the gun she always carried. She had resolved a long time ago that she wasn't going to let it change how she lived. She picked up the phone. "Hello."

"Cassie," said the caller in a weak voice. She instantly recognized Mike and she stiffened.

"Hi, Mike. Are you okay?"

"Yeah, I'm at the hospital in Wenatchee. They were going to send me to Harborview, but they're just watching me for now."

"What happened to you?"

"Well, I did get a little cut on my head. I had to be airlifted out. While they were at it, they took the two lawyer dudes with me."

"Go on?" She felt ice in her veins.

"I'm going to be fine. It's Dusty I'm calling about."

Cassie felt her stomach clench and she stopped breathing, "Is he okay?"

"He was fine, last I saw him."

She felt like she was in a trance as Mike told her about the hunting trip. His voice hesitated and faltered. He gathered himself to speak.

"So where's Dusty now?" she asked, willing her voice to be calm.

"He's taking the stock out. We couldn't just leave them there. There's a lot of snow." Mike's voice broke. "I should be there."

"Hey," she said in a soft voice. "You're fine. Dusty would want you to get help. He's a tough guy." Even as she spoke the words, she couldn't repress the dread forming inside her. "Thanks for the call, Mike. You better get some rest."

"I'm pretty tired."

Hanging up the phone, Cassie stared at Sammy. Her dog, sensing her owner's mood, looked back at her, alert. *Size never gets in the way of what you need to do.* Tossing her files in a stack, Cassie stood up to begin packing.

Chapter Twenty-Seven

Cassie parked her truck at Robinson Creek Trailhead. She needed to chain up to make it up the grade. Her rig was the only one at the trailhead. The snow was pristine and untouched except for her tracks. After talking to Mike last night, she had called Uncle Bob early this morning and left a message. Once he called her back, Bob Rose had stressed more than once, "Do not go. Dusty is fine. He can take care of himself." She had assured Bob she would not go, then hung up the phone, packed her gear, grabbed her horses and headed for the Pasayten Wilderness. As she passed through Wenatchee, she was able to talk to Mike again at the Regional Medical Center. They still hadn't transferred him to Harborview in Seattle, so that was a good sign, since it was the closet trauma unit.

"So you're going."

"Felt like I needed to. He might need help."

"He might. That is a lot of stock to push through that much snow," Mike agreed.

"You sound better this morning."

"I got a little bit of sleep. They always wake you up in these places, though. I'd really like to get out."

"Take it easy. With a head injury, if they have you in here, they're not going to let you leave until it's stable."

"Maybe," Mike said, unconvinced. He filled her in more on the hunting trip. The situation with Pinto was unreal. It sounded like some avenger for his father, but he had made a mistake on who shot him. She guessed no one bothered to tell Pinto who really killed his dad. Knowing Dusty, it wasn't going to come from him.

Her trip last summer in the Pasayten still haunted her. She preferred not to think about it. When that crusty old man pulled the young girl off the horse with Dusty and Mike helpless to do anything, she had had no choice. The old man had made his plans pretty clear he was going to rape and kill the girl. Cassie felt her stomach churn and repressed it. She didn't have time to relive that now. She had things to do.

Mike told her Dusty had taken all the horses out through the snow and ice. *Figures—the most dangerous thing he could do.* But she also knew it was no question that he would save the horses. It was how he was put together. *So was she.*

The drive to Robinson Creek Trailhead was long with switchbacks. She took the corners very carefully. It hadn't been so long ago that they only allowed stock trucks up there, because of the turns. She got to the trailhead about 11:00. Visiting with Mike had taken a little time. But she knew Dusty would want to know how he was doing. It wasn't the earliest start time, but she wanted to go right away.

Cassie locked her truck. Swinging into the saddle, she grabbed Murphy's lead rope, and small light flakes of snow began falling. She checked her gun and her rifle and reined her horse to the trailhead. "Let's do it, Boy." The big horse lunged up the snow and ice, occasionally slipping to his knees. He rebounded quickly to his feet. Murphy dug in behind her and seemed to have better footing than Prince—but maybe he saw the mistakes the lead horse made and he didn't want to repeat them. The horses were dripping with sweat in the first mile. The snow and ice made the trip much more difficult.

Cassie did not bring Sammy with her this time. She talked to Terri and it just seemed too risky. Normally there was no question, but with the icy freezing conditions, the creek crossings and fallen logs, Cassie didn't want to do it. The farther down the trail Cassie went, the deeper the snow became. Prince was sweating, but he settled into his work and was still making decent time. Cassie figured at their present rate they should make it about halfway into the Pasayten Airstrip by tonight. She hoped, anyway. The sooner she got there, the sooner she could help Dusty with the horses. One side of Murphy's pack contained horse feed. She figured with eight head, he was probably going to need it to give them enough energy to get out.

The hours crept by slowly and she ate a sandwich while she rode. The trail was boring. It followed a creek bed for miles, winding around the corners with large side walls, and every once in a while an interesting rock erosion. The slickness and boiling creek below kept her attention on her horses' footing, but the scenery didn't change much.

The small flakes became larger, and Cassie hoped they would find a place to stop pretty soon. The sky was turning grayer and she knew it would get dark quickly. She needed to find a camp.

She rode up a rise and the creek dropped far below her. The creek bed opened up into a wide valley. The trail descended some switchbacks and on the left was a large flat area with trees bordering the creek. Judging by the white expanse, it looked like an old horse camp. As she got closer and looked up, sure enough, she saw some nails still left in the trees. She remembered reading about the early trapper Billy Robinson for whom the drainage was named. There were supposed to be some ruins of his old cabins in the area too, but with all the snow she hadn't seen them. Cassie unsaddled her horses quickly in the fading light. She lay her gear on the mantie tarps and quickly highlined her horses. She gave them each pelleted feed; the graze was covered under a couple feet of snow. She put her tent up and threw her personal gear in it. She was using her flashlight by the time she finished. The only sounds were the creek rushing next to her and the horses stirring on their leads.

She heated a cup of tea with her PocketRocket stove and chewed on an energy bar. The snow had stopped—for now, anyway—and the sky was bluish black. No stars and still overcast. It looked like snow. She crawled into her sleeping bag and lay down, more exhausted than she realized. As she was drifting off to sleep, she swore she heard a faint howling. A wolf? Reflexively she reached down for her .38 where it lay comfortingly right next to her.

Chapter Twenty-Eight

The sky was dark and chilling. The clouds looked heavy and swollen. Dropping temperatures signaled a fresh snow was about to arrive. The horses had already pushed through three feet on the way up. Cassie hated the thought of any more snow. It would only make it that much harder. She shrugged it off as she covered her pack with the mantie. There was no time for negative thoughts. She would do what she needed to do to find Dusty—of that she was certain.

Prince stood saddled and she grabbed her bridle. Breaking down her camp and loading up Murphy had kept her warm. As she stood still to bridle, she shivered. The cold settled over her like a blanket. She held Prince's bit in her gloved hands and blew on it. He wouldn't want his tongue frozen any more than she would. As she looked around her, the snow scape looked gray and gloomy, a direct reflection of the sky. The sun made all the difference, and she noticed it most up here in the wilderness. The lakes were deep blue and the trees were emerald green in reflection of the light. But in its absence, a foreboding swept across the landscape; the lakes and rivers became gray and the trees a drab olive green.

Her horse shifted position bumping into her. She came out of her thoughts. Carefully she placed the now warm bit in Prince's mouth. She picked up Murphy's lead rope and swung into the saddle. She tightened her Sorel boot against her horse's side.

"Let's find Dusty," she said resolutely. Her horses slipped and slid through the deep snow back to the slashes in the trees which marked the now buried trail.

She could hear it before she saw it—a huge creek boiling down the mountain side and intersecting Robinson Creek. She looked in awe at the frost-covered logs and ice shooting down the river. The center current was moving and strong as the shores of the creek stood white and frozen. As she stared in dismay, something on the bank caught her eye. It was a pile of clothing laying on the snow by the creek. Not very far away stood a few horses, one with a riding saddle and two with pack saddles. *Muley! Cheyenne! Duke!* Icy fingers crawled up Cassie's spine. *Dusty!*

Riding closer, she saw Scout, lying next to Dusty. The dog wagged his tail at her as she approached.

"Hey, Scout, what happened?"

The Aussie wagged his tail harder, standing up.

Cassie jumped off Prince and ran across the snow to the inert form. She put her hand under his nose. She could detect faint breath. He was alive, but barely. She had to move fast. She ran over to her packhorse and quickly untied her pannier. Reaching in, she grabbed her tent and sleeping bag. Without wasting time pitching the tent, she just laid it out on the shore away from the creek. She quickly shook out her sleeping bag. Laying it next to Dusty, she rolled him onto the bag and dragged him over to the laid out nylon tent. It was no easy task. Cassie congratulated herself on being in shape with all her farm chores. She had to admit, the slick surface and slick sleeping bag helped.

Once on top of her tent, she stripped off his wet clothing, beginning with his boots. He was blue around the mouth. The rest of his skin was pale white. Once he was naked, she wrapped her sleeping bag around him and zipped it up. Then she stripped herself. She slipped inside the sleeping bag and covered his body with hers, willing the coldness to be soaked from his skin. She began rubbing his arms and legs to bring back the circulation. He moaned faintly and she kept going, encouraged.

She could feel one warm spot on Dusty, where Scout had lain, she knew. *His dog had kept him alive.* The cold assaulted her body and her heat descended into his. Exhausted from the long ride and her efforts to revive him, she dozed off, her head on his rising and falling chest.

Chapter Twenty-Nine

Cassie wasn't sure how long she had been sleeping, but she knew she needed to get their camp set up and the horses settled. Dusty's breathing had become stronger now. As she started to get up, a hand weakly held her.

"Ca—Cassie, are you sa-saving me again?" he said softly.

"Trying. You need to get some rest right now. Let me set up camp and I'll be back." Cassie noted his chest felt warmer as she lay her hand against it while she got up. Her clothes were right where she left them, so she got them on quickly in the frigid air. Dusty's eyes were closed and he seemed to go back to sleep.

Cassie found a copse of trees not far away. All the horses were still close by, *thank God!* Cassie gathered them up, unloading her pack boxes and the feed in the trees. Then she highlined the horses and gave them each some grain. "I know it's not what you want, but it's all we've got tonight." She stroked Prince's silky coat. Scout followed her as she set up camp.

Putting the tent up was an issue. Dusty was in her sleeping bag and laying on it, so without moving him she wasn't going to be able use it. She rooted around in his gear and found a tent and sleeping bag. It was a simple dome tent, so she had it up in a few minutes. Now the hard part, getting the 6'2" man dragged through the snow and inside it. The light was just about gone by the time she was done setting up the tent. She picked up a corner of the tent he was laying on and began to drag him to her camp. Luckily there were no big logs in the way and she was able to move him. With a mighty heave, she got his body across the threshold and into the tent.

She put on a pot to boil some soup. The best thing was to get warm liquids inside him. Anything that could bring his body temperature up was a good thing. As she worked she tried not to think about what would have happened if she had not come. She shook her head. *I'm not even going to go there.*

Cassie brought a steaming cup of broth into the tent. Scout lay next to Dusty and looked at her, wagging his tail. "Dusty." He lay still. "Dusty, are you awake?" Nothing. She sighed. She was going to have to get back in again and see if she could warm him up. She grabbed her fleece sleeping bag liner. She always used it in the mountains because of the low temperatures. She'd wrap herself in the liner and then crawl in the sleeping bag. For the second time that night she stripped down and got into the sleeping bag. This time he at least had some body heat, which was better than before. It was so warm that it actually reflected the heat from the bag. She could feel it escape the bag around her head. That's what she needed now. She couldn't get in it like she normally did, but she wrapped it around the both of them the best she could and waited for the warmth to descend on them.

Dusty slowly began to regain consciousness. He felt like he was finally dreaming of Cassie. He dreamed she was naked in his arms. This was the best dream so far. Maybe he didn't want to wake up. But he had to take care of the horses. *Where in the heck had they gone?* He swore he could smell Cassie, the scent of her perfume— or was it her shampoo? He pushed his head into her hair again and inhaled deeply. No, it was her shampoo. He was sure of it.

Cassie pushed him back and looked at him. *Why did she do that?* He wanted to ask, but the words came out in a groan.

"Dusty. Dusty, are you awake?"

Dusty groaned again. *This was the weirdest dream. It seemed he couldn't talk.*

Cassie began rubbing his back. *He could get used to that. He hoped she'd keep doing it.* "Dusty. Come on, Babe, talk to me," she pleaded.

"Caaassie?" he murmured thickly.

"You're okay! You're going to make it!" Overjoyed Cassie hugged him.

Dusty did his best to hug her back. "Is this a dream?" he managed weakly.

"You fell in the river. I found you by the shore passed out. You got hypothermia. The creek must have been crazy cold." Cassie continued to hold him.

"Damn black gelding did it again," Dusty croaked.

"Again?" she asked.

Dusty suddenly had a lot to say. His words were barely a whisper. "He caused a wreck in the string on the way down to the airport. I knew he was just going to be no good. And sure enough, he did it again in the creek. Upset all the horses, threw Muley off, and he stepped in a hole. Scout and I went down." Dusty spoke almost in a continuous sentence. Finishing, he closed his eyes. He was exhausted.

"Scout?" he tried to sit up.

Cassie understood. "Scout's right here, Dusty. He's fine."

Upon hearing his name, Scout moved closer to Dusty.

"Good," Dusty said thickly and shot his hand out to awkwardly pet him. Scout inched closer and lowered his head under Dusty's hand.

Shortly after talking, the man's breathing became heavy and soon he was sound asleep. Cassie tossed out the soup and zipped the tent door. She snuggled close to Dusty and fell asleep.

The high-pitched call eerily split the night a short distance away. Cassie didn't know how long she'd been asleep, but it felt like she'd just shut her eyes. A couple more howls chorused in and the result sounded loud and forewarning. Scout was staring at the side of the tent, cowering and shaking.

"They were at the airport," whispered Dusty. "Must have tracked us."

"Great," said Cassie. "Any ideas?"

"They ate all of Reggie's deer and that held them off for a while, but they're probably hungry again."

"What about the horses? Should I go out there?"

"Not by yourself. Let's listen to them and see if anything happens."

No sooner had Dusty said that, then there was a shrill squeal from the horses and the thud of a kick connecting with something.

"Okay." Dusty sat up slowly, "Where are my clothes?" he asked.

"I'm not really sure," said Cassie embarrassedly. "I was in a hurry to get them off you."

"Oh, really?" Dusty looked at her speculatively with a half grin on his face.

"You're kidding, right?" said Cassie. "We have wolves about ready to attack our stock and you want to do that?"

Dusty sighed. "Maybe later then." He looked around. "I just need to find whatever I can to put on."

Cassie threw her clothes on and pulled on her boots. Grabbing her gun and flashlight she said, "I'll be right back."

"Well, wait a sec..." Dusty started, but saw the tent flap close behind her.

Cassie flashed the light on the horses and saw two wolves circling them. "Get away from there," she shouted with a bravado she didn't feel. Cassie hoped it wasn't apparent. This was the very last instance in which to show fear. The wolves didn't give ground. They just stared at her. She raised her rifle. It was tough to shoot because the horses were panicked and kept moving around. One wolf, who must have been the alpha, finally left the horses and advanced towards her. She took aim, careful to wait until he was away from the horses. She fired and caught him in midair, just as he began to charge. With a loud yelp, the wolf hit the ground. The other one whined a little and backed off.

Where there were two, there were probably three. She stood uncertain what to do next. If she went back into the tent, they may go after the horses. If she stood still, they may begin to circle her. Obviously, she couldn't stand there all night.

"Nice shot," a voice sounded behind her. Dusty was standing in boots and a jacket—no pants on.

"What are you doing?" Cassie was appalled. "You're going to get hypothermia again!"

Dusty looked embarrassed. "I wanted to help. I just couldn't find anything but the coat and boots."

"Come on. Let's get back in the tent. I'll find your stuff." Cassie looked down, hiding the grin on her face. If the situation hadn't been so dire, it would have been pretty comical. Dusty standing there in his boots and jacket. *Some help. Maybe it was moral support.* She tried to calm the laughter that was threatening to spill over as they walked back to the tent.

Dusty went in ahead of her, took off his jacket and crawled back into the sleeping bag.

"I'll check by the river and be right back." Cassie shown her light on the ground, following the skid marks of dragging Dusty from the swollen creek. It sounded like an ocean as she got closer. Near the bank were some dark pieces of material that she recognized to be his clothing. *I can't believe he had his boots on!* Bending down to gather them up, she felt prickles in the back of her head. She was being watched.

Chapter Thirty

"How much ammunition do you have?" Cassie asked, as she checked her saddle bags.

Dusty yawned, still tired from the ordeal, "I've got what's on my ammo belt. I'm not sure how much survived the swim, but they'll dry off."

Cassie found her extra cartridges and put them in her pocket. "I'm going out to check your saddle bags. I left them out with the tack."

"Wait," said Dusty, sitting up. "I'll give you a hand."

"I'm fine," said Cassie firmly. "Just rest."

Once again, as Dusty looked for his boots, he watched the tent door close. A hand reached underneath and zipped it shut.

Geez, that woman could be impossible. He picked up his pants and shirt, still soaked. Dusty hesitated. It was almost better not to wear them than to freeze again. He needed to get his duffel bag and see if anything was dry in it. Pondering his situation, a shot rang out. He heard the horses squealing and moving around. Scout shook harder and scooted closer, trying to dig under the sleeping bag.

"It's okay, Boy," Dusty stroked his back soothingly. His dog had never cared for gunfire and that compounded with his innate fear of the wolves. "I've got to go."

"Damn it," he muttered, grabbing his boots, coat and gun, and rushed back outside, pausing only to rezip the tent with Scout inside.

It was dark with a half moon; the light reflected on the creek. The snow added contrast to the dimly lit forms.

"Got him," said Cassie. He looked over and saw the tall woman standing over a dark carcass, rifle in hand.

"Good job. Two for two," Dusty congratulated her.

"Oh, there's a lot more than that out there. From what I could see, there are at least three more."

Dusty felt his stomach lurch. Bad news. The stronger the numbers, the more aggressive the wolves became. It was becoming clear he wasn't going to get much sleep tonight. "Let's move the horses closer and build a fire. Maybe a couple of them."

"Okay," said Cassie. "I've read that campfires don't really deter wolves. They'll even run through them at times, but it's worth a try."

Dusty wasn't really familiar with wolf attacks; in fact, he'd never heard of them in the Pasayten Wilderness. He knew that as a protected species they would "breed like hamsters" with no natural predators. It was becoming obvious that was just what they were doing, pouring out of Yellowstone and into all the adjoining states. *Here we go again*, he shook his head. *Our forefathers got rid of them for a reason.* He really hoped he wasn't going to find out what that reason was tonight.

"What would you suggest?" he asked, looking directly at Cassie.

She faltered, "I—I didn't really have any other ideas. I just wanted us to be ready if they charged again."

"Well, at least they'll be closer and we won't have to look for the wolves in the dark." Dusty shown his light on the trees and began snapping off some dead branches near the bottom. "I'll start the fire if you want to move the stock."

Cassie was already walking to the highline and unsnapping horses' leads. "Will do."

Between the two of them they got all ten head of stock moved and a huge fire roaring within a short amount of time. The horses were jittery and wouldn't stand still. Dusty didn't blame them. The wolves were the biggest threat they would probably encounter in their lives. Even Muley, the fearless, stood shaking with his eyes ringed with white. Dusty couldn't help himself. He walked over and stroked the horse's muscular neck. "It's okay, Boy. We're going to get you out of here." The only sign that his horse heard him was the flicker of his ear toward Dusty's voice.

Dusty walked back to the fire. "Have you happened to see my duffel bag? I'd really like to see if I have any dry clothes. I know I had one dry pair of pants."

Cassie had been so focused on moving the horses and the fire, she hadn't really looked at Dusty. He was standing in his underwear, with his coat and boots on. An image of long ago, a King County courtroom and the impeccably dressed attorney, and now this man. Putting her hand to her mouth, she stifled a laugh.

"What's so funny?" Dusty looked at her puzzled.

"Oh, nothing," she said quickly. "You just look so different than when I met you in court."

"Oh, yeah? Well, so do you." He looked at the woman with the cowboy hat, scarf, lined Carthartt jacket, and Sorel boots squatting by the fire warming her hands. Her gun and gloves lay next to her in the snow. This was a far cry from the do-gooder young woman attorney that came into court to defend "the little guy" mill owner. He thought ruefully. *I'd basically had her for lunch.* Dusty hadn't felt good about it at the time, and he felt worse about it now. The wilderness had a way of doing that to a person. Right and wrong became so much clearer out here. It wasn't diluted by all the other things in the city.

Shame burned through him as he reflected on that day in court. "By the way," he said softly, looking at her, "I'm sorry how that went down that day. I never felt good about it."

She looked at him, her eyebrows raised and surprise etched across her face. Before she could reply, he continued, "So do you know where my duffel is? I'm getting cold."

Snapping back to the moment, she gestured toward the canvas mantie a short distance away. "I dragged all your stuff up and put it under the mantie. Your duffel floated for a ways, but maybe something in there is dry."

"Hope so." Dusty turned to go look under the mantie. Suddenly a chorus of yelping began. The horses snorted and jumped in place next to them, whinnying in panic. Cassie flashed her light over to where the noise was coming from. Two giant wolves were dragging the carcass of the dead wolf away, while two others yelped next to them.

Dusty wrapped his hand around the cold steel of his gun. As he watched he felt an icy empty feeling in the pit of his stomach.

Chapter Thirty-One

Dusty found a pair of dry jeans in his duffel on top. Grabbing them and a pair of wool socks, he went back to the tent. The air was full of yelping and snarling as the wolves tore into the body of their pack mate.

The only way Dusty could tell that Scout was still in the tent was that a part of the sleeping bag was shaking. "It's okay, Boy." Dusty reassured him while he pulled on his pants and socks. Scout was so undone that Dusty's voice did little to reassure him. The dog had always been this way and Dusty wasn't really sure what had happened to trigger his huge fear of gunfire. He had gotten Scout at 8 weeks old, and nothing traumatic had happened. Sometimes it just must be an innate reaction, Dusty guessed. He gave his dog one more reassuring pat, then zipped the tent flap down and walked back out to the fire.

Cassie sat on a log she'd dusted off and dragged over. The firelight danced on her face and she sat with her rifle in her lap, slung to one side. In the flickering light Dusty could see fatigue in her eyes and the lines of her face.

"Hey, you can go lie down for a while. We can take turns watching over the stock," he offered. "No sense in us both falling asleep in front of the fire."

"You're the one that fell in the creek and got hypothermia. You need the sleep," she insisted.

"Cassie," he said firmly. "I've done nothing but sleep. It's your turn. You'll be a lot better off with some sleep. Not only have you been doing everything since you got here, but that was a long ride in before that." He stood next to her offering his hand. "What time did you start out this morning, anyway?"

"I had one camp on the way in. I took off this morning at first light." An involuntary yawn emitted from her, as if thinking about it made her tired. She finally accepted his hand and rose.

Dusty pulled her into his arms. He didn't know if that was for him or her. Both maybe. He buried his face in her hair, inhaling the scent of her shampoo and wood smoke. He felt wobbly and intoxicated. He didn't want to let go of her. She returned his embrace and they stood that way for a long time.

He whispered in her ear. "It's going to be all right." She hugged him tighter.

Finally, he forced himself to let go of her. "You better get some sleep."

"Okay," she said reluctantly. "I'll come out in a little bit." She walked slowly to the tent.

He watched her go. "No rush. I'll be right here." He settled down on the log and stared into the fire.

Dusty wasn't sure how long he'd dozed off, but he felt rather than saw the presence. He slowly opened his eyes, taking care not to move. The fire in front of him had grown cold. The horses were shifting on their highlines nervously. At first he saw nothing. Then at the edge of their camp in the trees he saw a lone wolf watching him. Even from the distance, its breath was coming out in streams of cold air. The steely gray dawn provided a dim light against the white snow. The pale edge of the moon was beginning to fade. Dusty slowly moved his hand and wrapped it around his Vaquero.

He wasn't sure if there were any more wolves immediately behind that one, but he doubted it. This looked like a scout. The wolf was close enough to the horses, Dusty knew they'd be panicking more if there were multiple wolves. So far, anyway. Keeping an eye on the lone wolf, he needed to get the fire going again. He was cold and that was dangerous. Dusty's body had already taken one huge shock of hypothermia—he was afraid the next one would kill him. He slowly got to his feet and grabbed what was left of the twigs and small branches he'd managed to collect the night before. Flicking his lighter on, the twigs would catch, turn bright red and turn to white ash. He was going to need a fire starter. It was too cold and damp. There were some in his pack boxes.

Turning his full attention back to the wolf, it was gone. Dusty's stomach contracted. Where? Wolves had been eliminated from the Pacific Northwest years ago, so their behavior was unknown to him. Dusty realized now there was a lot more he needed to know if he was going to coexist with them in the wilderness.

The pack boxes were under the manties by the horses. Cassie had thrown the saddles and boxes together last night and covered them with one of the canvas tarps. The cold metal was reassuring as it fit in his hand and he stiffly rose. He reasoned to himself if the wolf had wanted to attack him, it could have easily done it while he slept. The horses would have alarmed him, but would it have been in time? *No point in giving that any more thought.* He slowly crunched through the frozen snow to the manties, the cold morning air burning in his lungs.

It seemed like much farther, but the boxes and horses were only about 20 feet from the fire. As he approached, Muley nickered to him encouragingly, followed by a chorus from the rest of the herd. They were hungry and probably thirsty too. "Just hang on, you guys. We'll get you some food and water in a little bit." He spoke in a low voice. He didn't want to alert any more wolves. He pulled the tarp off and dug in the pack box. Luckily, he got in the right one on the first try. *How often did that happen? Usually it was the last one.* He felt lighter. Maybe things were looking up.

He turned and started back to the fire ring. He had only gone a couple steps when the hair stood up on the back of his neck. The horses exploded in screams and flying hooves. He pulled his gun and turned. Muley was in a standoff with the big gray wolf. Dusty could see it clearly from where he stood. Its lips were parted in a feral snarl. The yellow eyes were slits. Saliva dripped from the huge jaws, exposing long curved white teeth.

Muley was in attack mode. His arrogant roman nose poised for combat. There was fear in his eyes, but Dusty saw something else—an unflappable will to survive. His horse stood ready for battle. Dusty simultaneously aimed and pulled back the hammer. The click resounded in the cold morning air. The wolf turned his large head and his pale yellow eyes focused on Dusty. Seeming to forget the beast in front of him, the wolf hesitated and then slowly walked around Muley toward Dusty.

Despite the frigid air, Dusty felt perspiration drip down his armpits as the powerful animal approached him. He willed himself to clear his mind and be ready for the fight. Survival was the only thing in his thoughts.

Everything became a blur. The wolf, slow at first, suddenly charged Dusty. As it leapt, a vicious roar split the morning air—but it wasn't from the wolf. Dusty saw a flash of blue merle as Scout launched for the wolf's throat. The wolf let out a huge snarl, but Scout had latched onto the side. The larger animal faltered and went down mid-leap, swiping at the smaller dog.

They became a ball of claws, snarling and fur. Dusty had to take a shot to save Scout, but they kept rolling and turning. He didn't want to kill his dog. Dusty's stomach was filled with dread. The wolf had jaws like a steel trap. He could snap Scout's head in one bite. The dog was tenacious, screaming in pain when a claw got him and then quickly growling in anger. He wasn't going to last much longer.

Getting as close as he could, Dusty took aim and fired at the wolf's head. The roar was deafening in the morning air and seemed to reverberate off all the snowcapped peaks around them. The beast screamed an ear-splitting yelp of pain and then the writhing mass of fur and claws was still.

Chapter Thirty-Two

"What happened?" Yelled Cassie, running from the tent carrying her rifle.

Dusty stood over the pile of fur. The wolf had tried to bite Scout's neck, but his teeth had slipped to the side and a gash was bleeding in the fur. Gently Dusty put his hands underneath his dog and lifted him away from the wolf. Scout made a little yelping sound; his brown eyes calmly looked up into Dusty's eyes with complete trust.

Looking at Scout, Dusty felt a catch in his throat. His dog had thrown himself to the wolf to save him, with no regard for his own safety. Holding his Scout close, he could feel a tear course down his cheek. "I'll get you fixed up, Boy," he said roughly.

"I'll go get the kit," Cassie said. "Just hold him." She ran over to her saddle bags. The first aid kit was exactly where she put it. That was one thing she always kept tabs on.

Scout had a couple minor scratches. The main wound was on his upper shoulder. She cleaned it out with hydrogen peroxide. Cassie kept it in her kit for the horses. It bubbled as she poured it on the wound, but it didn't sting.

"Is it going to need stitches?" asked Dusty. He'd already done one stitching job on this trip. He was ready to do another.

"I'm not sure," Cassie said pensively. "I don't think it's as bad as it looks."

Once all the blood was cleared away, she could see the

laceration had sliced through the fur, but just grazed the muscle. She carefully placed butterfly bandaids over the wound and then laid sterile gauze over that. Scout looked at them gratefully, licking their hands.

Dusty held him inside his coat. "That's okay, Boy," he said reassuringly. "You're going to be fine."

"It looks pretty good, considering what we have to work with," Cassie said, stepping back and looking at the finished product. "I think he's going to be okay, Dusty."

"Thank God." Dusty held him close. "He saved me. The wolf was in mid-air when Scout attacked."

"He's a great dog," Cassie said, with tears in her eyes.

The initial shock of the attack was wearing off and the cold was setting in. "Why don't you just hold him for a while," she repeated. "I'll go get some more firewood."

"Okay. Stick close to camp. There's probably more of them out there," Dusty cautioned.

Cassie took a tighter grip on her rifle. "I will." She walked to the nearby trees to find dead branches.

Once she got the fire going, Cassie found some larger logs under the snow, dragged them over and laid them on their side by the fire to dry out. She lit the propane stove, filled the coffee pot with water from the creek and put it on the flame to boil. "Coffee is on its way," she announced.

"Great," said Dusty gratefully. Sitting by the fire with Scout in his lap, Dusty felt drained. It had been a long week and he wasn't as young as he used to be, or maybe he was never young enough for everything that had happened lately. Scout shifted in his lap. They had given him half a tablet of bute. It was actually horse aspirin and not recommended for dogs, but it was all they had and Dusty didn't want to risk Advil, which could cause damage to the dog's organs. So in moderation, bute was the best choice they had for pain and stiffness for Scout.

Cassie had divided up the rest of the grain and the horses hungrily ate it. Sitting by the fire, she said, "I wish we had more feed."

"Yeah, but ten horses is a lot. I'm glad we packed what we did," Dusty agreed. "We need to get out of here." It was still early morning. The darkness had faded and the sky was a steely gray. No more snow had fallen this morning, although it was hard to tell if it wouldn't.

"Do you think the wolves are coming back?" Cassie asked.

"I wish I knew more about them," Dusty said apologetically. "It's a new thing for me."

"They've been quiet for a while," Cassie offered.

"They had just eaten their buddy last night. If I was going to hazard a guess, that's probably going to hold them off for a little bit." Dusty looked at the carcass still laying where he shot it. "They haven't come for this one yet."

"That's probably because your dog put the fear of the Almighty into them," Cassie teased.

Dusty looked appraisingly at his dog, now bandaged and curled up at his feet. Sensing the man's gaze, Scout looked up at Dusty and wagged his tail weakly. "Maybe so."

"We should be able to get close to getting out if we really push it," said Cassie. "I had to make a camp on the way in because I was breaking through a lot of snow. But now there is a path and it hasn't snowed much since then."

"Our horses are going to get a lot weaker in one more night if we can't feed them, so we'd better try to get out," Dusty agreed. Scout stood up and shook, apparently checking out the new bandage, and took a couple of tentative steps in the snow.

"Are you going to be able to walk out okay, Boy?" He looked at his dog closely. Scout wagged his tail and walked some more. The stiffness seemed to drop off with each step.

"Looks like he's doing okay" said Cassie, watching him.

Dusty felt a big weight lift off his chest. "Yes, he does."

He stopped suddenly and wrapped Cassie in a big bear hug. She whooped and almost fell over. "What was that for?" she asked, laughing.

"I forgot to say thank you." He pulled her close and talked into her hair.

"Thank you?" she said uncertainly.

"Well, let's see. Where should I start? For coming down this God-forsaken trail alone in a blizzard to find me." He paused like he was counting and then continued., "Oh, yeah. For peeling my clothes off me and throwing me in a sleeping bag so I didn't die of hypothermia."

Cassie laid her head again his chest. "Well, it was the least I could do."

"Really?" Dusty said speculatively, "Well, if that's the case, what would be the most you could do?"

She looked up at him, her eyes dancing in mischief. "Well, let's pack up and get out of here and then maybe we can find out what that would be."

"I'm packing now," he said, letting her out of his arms and heading for the tent.

He left Cassie behind him smiling. She walked up to the stock to begin saddling and getting the packs ready.

They worked efficiently as a team and they were ready to go in about an hour. Dusty's duffel was still a little wet, but his horses were okay after their dip in the stream. All of the stock was dancing on the lead lines and in a hurry to move. Hunger was a driving factor. Dusty hoped that Cassie's trail had held and they wouldn't have to break trail through the snow all the way out. It would really tire the stock out and he was worried what another night with no food out in the freezing cold would do to them. They needed to get out tonight.

Cassie led out on Prince, pulling her packhorse Murphy behind her. The snow had a frozen crust on it and it crunched under her horses' hooves. Dusty followed, pulling seven horses behind him. It wasn't the first time he had pulled a big string. Working for Uncle Bob sometimes he would have to do a "turn and burn." In the outfit business that meant riding in, dropping a load, and then back to the trailhead in one ride, the only stops being picking up or dropping gear. The difference this time was he wasn't dropping anything off and he was breaking through snow.

The horses lunged and slipped as they walked down the trail. Cassie's horse jumped ahead from time to time. He was a walking horse, so normally he would be traveling at around four miles an hour. In this snow and ice that wasn't going to happen. They were lucky to make two miles. *The good thing is we know we can get out, because Cassie already got in.* Dusty felt his chest tighten with pride at this woman. Not only was she able to hold her own in a tough profession, but she was perfectly capable in the wilderness. You didn't find that with men very often, let alone women. He was very lucky to have met her.

As Dusty smiled he watched her competently pull her packhorse and negotiate snow drifts and hidden logs on the trail. He wasn't sure how it started, but he began to feel dread settle in the pit of his stomach. This time he knew it didn't have anything to do with his surroundings and everything to do with himself. Was he actually going to be able to go out with this woman? Commitment did something to him. He couldn't explain it. He felt an unreasonable fear. Sometimes he wondered if he wouldn't be better off just to fantasize relationships and never pursue a real one. He sighed and continued down the trail.

Chapter Thirty-Three

They had to cross the creek a couple more times. Each time they did, Dusty would dismount, scoop up Scout, then remount laying him across the saddle in front of him. His dog didn't fight. The point was to keep infection out of the wound, and that's what Dusty was going to do.

The weather held and no more snow fell as they rode into the afternoon. Scout kept close to Muley's heels. No more wolves had appeared. Dusty kept his gun locked and loaded, just in case. The snow began to melt in the afternoon and became more pliable under the horses' hooves. Giant snowballs formed and shot out from their feet as they slipped more, and then less as the day wore on.

Dusty was tired. His bones ached and he felt a dull throbbing in his temples. The past week was taking its toll on him. The stock behind him was doing okay. He had taken care not to place the black by the sorrel again, hopefully avoiding another rodeo. Funny, it seemed like so long ago, but it was only a few days. The mountains had their own time. You didn't need a watch. It was daylight and then it got dark. You did your chores in the order they came—feeding the horses, feeding yourself, cleaning up, going to bed, starting all over again, the huge mural of snowcapped mountains and crystal clear icy streams watching over you.

Lost in thought, Dusty almost ran into the back of Cassie's packhorse as she came to a sudden stop. "Listen."

Dusty listened carefully. He could hear what sounded like

horses, their feet hitting an occasional rock and the sound ricocheting off the mountains around them. There again was the jingle of hardware. It sounded like it was coming closer.

Cassie gave Prince a kick and he lunged ahead on the snowy trail. As they rounded the corner, in front of them stood Uncle Bob and Wrong Way. Their horses were drenched in sweat, steam pouring off them.

"I knew it," exclaimed Bob, his suntanned face splitting into a grin. "I knew you would find Dusty before we did."

Cassie blushed. "I guess you talked to Mike."

"I gave him a call to see how he was doing. I heard he took a nasty blow to the back of the head." Bob sat easily in his saddle and rested his gloved hands on the saddle horn. "He told me you were planning a little trip up here." His deep blue eyes held a glint of humor as he spoke.

"It seemed like the thing to do thing," Cassie replied.

"Yeah," agreed Bob. "I knew you'd do it."

Shifting in his saddle, he looked directly at Cassie, his deep blue eyes serious, "It's not something that every woman would think of or be willing to do, and I thank you from the bottom of my heart for finding my nephew."

"I'm glad I came," Cassie reddened.

"She saved me." Said Dusty from behind her, "My horse fell down in the creek and I was passed out with hypothermia." He sat up in his saddle. "If she hadn't come along when she did, I wouldn't be here now." He looked pointedly at her. "She said she found me asleep on the bank by the creek. And if that hadn't killed me, probably the wolves that came later would have."

"Wolves," exclaimed Uncle Bob. "Really?"

"Yeah," affirmed Dusty. "Have you seen any?"

"Nope," said Uncle Bob with finality. "And I hope I don't. I can't stand those furry murderers!"

"Do we have much farther?" asked Cassie. Prince was starting to cool off and with little food and all the exertion she didn't want him to tie up. "We should get going."

"Just about two miles," answered Bob. "We got it packed down pretty well, so it shouldn't be a problem getting out."

"Great," said Dusty. "Hey, Wrong Way." He addressed the hand who had been silently watching. "Would you mind giving me a hand with some of this stock? Much as I hate to admit it, I'm tired."

"No problem, Dusty. Glad to see you're okay." Wrong Way rode over to Dusty, nodding at Cassie as he passed her and picked up the lead rope. As the wrangler turned, the stock stumbled for a minute, confused about who they were following. Wrong Way expertly tugged on the lead and they straightened out. Cheyenne fell in behind him, the rest of the stock following.

Bob's sharp eyes picked up the bandage as he looked down at Scout.

Following his gaze, Dusty replied, "wolves."

Bob shook his head sadly. "It was only a matter of time. Thanks to them, we're going to have to change the way we do things now in the outfit."

"He's getting along pretty well, I think. Infection has been the biggest worry," said Dusty. "How's Mike doing?"

"He's chomping at the bit to get up here and look for you. He felt just awful leaving you to take out the stock alone."

Dusty chuckled. "I bet he did. But in the shape he was in, I don't think he could have helped much."

"That's a true story there. He was still in the hospital when I talked to him," agreed Bob.

"Ahemm," Cassie cleared her throat and looked pointedly at the men. She tried again, "You think we ought to get going? It would probably be a good idea not to have to spend another night with the wolves."

"Oh, sorry, Cassie," said Bob. "I'm up here so much, I guess I forget sometimes we need to leave. Please, lead the way." He gestured gallantly.

Dusty fell in behind Cassie and Bob followed, Wrong Way in the rear pulling the stock. Scout trotted along beside Muley. Bob was true to his word and the recent action of the horses' hooves through the snow had packed it down for easier travelling.

Continuing on the line of conversation with Bob, Dusty asked, "How did the rest of them do after the airlift?"

"Well, that's a funny deal," said Bob thoughtfully. "The guy Reggie? The one that you didn't seem to really hit it off with? He called me."

"Really?"

"Yes. He was actually excited. He told me he had a great time and he wanted to come back next year."

"Is that so?" said Dusty, smiling.

"What's even curiouser was he offered to help out if I needed it. Said he wanted to pick up the trade of packing."

"He wouldn't be the first wilderness convert we've had, would he, Uncle Bob?"

"I guess not. Maybe that big Seattle lawyering isn't all it's cracked up to be," said Bob philosophically.

"Ya think?" said Dusty. The smell of fir, horse sweat and snow filled his nostrils. He was with the animals and the people he loved. Seattle and the practice of law seemed far away, and he'd like to keep it that way.

Chapter Thirty-Four

Cassie rounded the last bend in the trail and saw Bob's big stock trailer parked next to her rig. Without breaking stride, Prince walked right over to the trailer and stopped. About six inches of snow and ice was on her windshield. *Considering what it could have been, that's not bad at all.*

She dismounted and dropped the pack off Murphy. Her fingers were stiff from the cold and her back ached. *Funny how you never notice that when you're riding.* Clicking her truck key, she was glad to see the battery hadn't died. It had sat in the snow and ice for a while. Sitting in the cab, warming the engine, she looked over at Dusty. He pulled the saddles off and put it in the truck. Muley stood with his head down and steam was pouring off him. Dusty came up with the blanket. He stopped for a minute and affectionately rubbed the big horse behind his ears. Muley bent down and rubbed his big head into Dusty's chest. Cassie felt warm in the pit of her stomach, *Another side to Dusty Rose. He wasn't afraid to show affection for his animals. He obviously loved his dog and his horses.* A shadow crossed her brow. *Was it only limited to animals? She hoped not.*

Heat finally began to fill the cab and she held her hands over the vents to warm them.

It was impressive that one man could bring eight head of horses through outlaws, frozen rivers, snow and wolves, but he was just that kind of guy.

Dusty's head still felt fuzzy from the past few days. He unsaddled his horse. Grabbing a blanket, he threw it over Muley's back. Despite everything he'd been through, the big roan still managed to give him a haughty stare, raising his head high above Dusty. *Nothing broke that horse's spirit.*

As he worked he was keenly aware of Cassie putting her gear away. Once again she'd done it. She'd saved him. He knew that hypothermia would have done him in if she hadn't come along when she did. *How can I repay her for that?* He chuckled ruefully. *With my track record the best thing I could do is get far away from her.* That was usually an easy thing for him to do with women. He looked over at her sitting in her truck. But not this time. He felt a warring of emotions inside of him, the push and pull. So easy for him to go with women physically, but mentally he felt a familiar wall of protection. *For God's sake, she just saved my life.* He grabbed Muley's lead. The smell of horse wafted over him and he felt steady. Wrong Way walked up to take the horse. "I'm going to say good-bye to Cassie," Dusty said, handing the wrangler the lead rope.

"She's some lady," the older wrangler said.

"That she is," Dusty agreed.

As he walked up to the truck, Cassie opened the door and got out. "Another great trip," he said with a wry smile.

She smiled up at him, her light blue eyes questioning.

That was all it took. He amazed himself at how she affected him. Dusty closed the distance in one step and pulled her into his arms. Holding her against his chest he said, "Cassie, I don't know how to thank you for what you've done. But I'm going to keep trying to figure out a way."

"You don't have to thank me. Anybody could have done it." She lay her head against his chest.

"Yeah, but they didn't—you did." Once again, he didn't want to let go of her. Didn't want to walk away. Oblivious to Bob and Wrong Way, he leaned down and kissed her. He needed to be close to her. Heat shot through him; he could feel it down to his feet.

"Whoa," he said, recovering. "That probably wasn't a good idea." He felt even more light-headed, almost losing his balance, and he leaned against her truck.

Cassie's lips turned up at the corners. It was the smile that he'd been thinking about for days on his ride.

"I'd better get going. I need to go get my truck and I'm going to stop in and see how Mike's doing on my way back."

Glancing over at the stock truck, Bob and Wrong Way were sitting in the cab with the motor running. Scout was lying next to it watching Dusty, his bandages still in place.

"I need to get Scout to the vet too." He let go of Cassie and felt a cold draft sweep between them. Dusty involuntarily shuddered.

"I'll call you later." He couldn't take his eyes off her face.

"Sounds good," she murmured, opening the door of her truck.

"You head out and we'll follow." Dusty tore himself away from her and walked back to the truck. Scooping Scout up, he got into the cab.

"Looks like you had quite a ride," said Bob, putting the truck into gear.

Watching Cassie's truck and trailer pull out in front of them, Dusty felt part of himself tear away. "Yes, I did."

Chapter Thirty-Five

Dusty walked into his office in Eagleclaw. It had only been two weeks since he'd left, but it seemed like so much longer. The bell jingled as Dusty walked in. Mrs. Phillips sat at her desk.

"Good morning, Mr. Dustin Rose. Welcome back."

"Thank you, Mrs. Phillips. I hope you had a nice vacation." He hung up his coat.

"Very relaxing. Coffee will be right in," she replied briskly.

"Sounds great." Dusty sat down at his chair and looked at the stack of mail on his desk. He winced. This was the worst part, coming back to a pile of mail. Next to the mail lay a huge stack of files with documents paper clipped to them.

Mrs. Phillips bustled in with a steaming cup of coffee in her hand. "You got so many pleadings while you were gone, I thought it would be most expedient to pull the files and put the paperwork with it."

"Good idea," said Dusty. *What would I do without her?*

Mrs. Phillips beamed. "Thank you." Setting the coffee down, she announced, "I'll leave you to your work. It looks like you have a lot to catch up on."

"Indeed," agreed Dusty.

The older woman turned and as she walked out, she carefully closed the door behind her.

Dusty stared dejectedly at the large pile of paperwork in front of him. This was the last thing he wanted to do. If it were up to him, he'd still be up in the mountains helping Uncle Bob. But it wasn't up to him—at least not yet.

Dusty grabbed the letter opener and began with the mail. Most of it was expected correspondence on cases he had ongoing. Nothing shocking. A few new cases with clients he already represented in other matters. Dusty was about halfway through when the jingle sounded on the office front door. He heard muffled voices.

His office door opened and Mike walked through it. He was wearing a ball cap with gauze showing underneath it in the back.

"Well, hello," said Dusty. "I didn't think I'd be seeing you for a while."

"Nor I you, but you white people always underestimate us Greeks."

"Wow, I'm now a race representative," exclaimed Dusty with mock gratitude. "Really, how did you get out of the hospital?"

"I passed the release test," Mike said. "I didn't want to stay in there a minute longer."

"How did you get home?"

"Terri came and got me," Mike said quickly.

"Oh," said Dusty understandingly. "That explains everything."

"Really?" said Mike.

"No, not really at all. Have a seat and tell me what happened to you."

"That's why I came by," said Mike. "I thought you might want to go to lunch. I wanted to find out if there's any truth to the rumor going around that Cassie saved you—again." Mike's dark eyes sparkled and he looked like he was really enjoying himself.

"Sad, but true," Dusty said contritely. "Let's go. I might as well fill you in on the details." He grabbed his coat off the hook and they headed out the door.

Mrs. Phillips looked up as Dusty walked by. "Going to lunch."

"Have a nice early lunch, Mr. Dustin Rose."

Mike smiled at her as they walked by. Once out the door, "Uh-oh, busted for leaving early," he joked.

"Yup, she got me," agreed Dusty. Laughing, they headed down the sidewalk to Maude's Mountain Café, a few doors down from his office on Main Street.

The late morning crowd was still in the restaurant as they walked in, mostly older men in plaid shirts and work jeans, mulling their days over a steaming cup of coffee. Mike and Dusty took their regular seats at the end of the bar.

Maude bustled over, coffee pot in hand. "Well, aren't you two a sight for sore eyes!" she exclaimed. "Coffee?"

Mike and Dusty turned over their cups almost simultaneously. Without hesitation, she filled them both. "How was your pack trip?"

Dusty said, "Eventful."

"By the looks of it, I'll say," agreed the red-haired waitress, eyeing Mike's bandage.

"Just a flesh wound," Mike assured her, catching her eye.

"Well, that's good."

"Anything new around here?" asked Dusty conversationally.

"You know, the same ol', same ol'." She flipped out her menu. "Speaking of which, would you like the special?"

"Why change now?" said Dusty.

"Ditto for me," agreed Mike.

Scooping up the menus, she said, "Coming right up," and she was gone in a flash of pink.

Dusty stirred his coffee. "Good to be back."

"It sure is," said Mike. "Now tell me about your trip out of the Pasayten. And is it true that Cassie had to rescue you again?" He looked at his friend with mock concern. "If this keeps happening, you may not be able to let her go."

"Yeah, I know. That's what I'm afraid of," joked Dusty. The old twinge of doubt rose up inside of him. With a supreme effort he did manage to suppress it. "Okay. Well, the airlift picked you guys up and then I had to take all the stock out…"

Chapter Thirty-Six

Dusty did a Reader's Digest version of the events of his departure from Robinson Creek. When he came to the part of crossing the creek and falling asleep, Mike's face looked tortured.

"I knew it. I should have been there."

"It would have been nice if you would have been there, but there was no way in heck you could have. It certainly was out of your control," added Dusty.

Then he finished up with Cassie coming just in time and their fight with the wolves.

"How is Scout now?" asked Mike.

"He's doing much better," answered Dusty, with relief on his face. "I took him into the vet this morning. He did walk all the way out. Other than just the exposure and stress from the walk out, he's fine."

"The wound?" questioned Mike.

"My vet was amazed. No infection."

"That was a good move on Cassie's part with the hydrogen peroxide."

"Yup," agreed Dusty.

"So what now?" asked Mike.

"What now what?" asked Dusty, confused.

"Well, Cassie. I mean, is she the one?"

Dusty just about choked on his sandwich. "The one?"

"You know what I mean," encouraged Mike.

"Oh, for crying out loud, Mike. Enough about me. I've been meaning to ask you about Terri. Is she *the one*?"

"Oh, nice try to divert the conversation away from the point."

"Okay." Dusty wiped his mouth with a napkin and grabbed the check. "I think it's time to head back to work."

"Okay, Boss," Mike said compliantly.

They walked out of the café waving to people they knew and walked outside. The sky was gray and unrepentant. It looked like it was going to rain any minute.

"I hate the rain," said Dusty randomly.

"It's a little tough to ride in," agreed Mike.

Dusty paused at his office door, "Thanks for stopping by for lunch. I'm glad your head is doing better."

"Yeah, it is, and no problem." Mike walked away and called over his shoulder. "Talk to you later."

Dusty entered his office again, the bell jingling behind him.

Mrs. Phillips looked up from her desk, "Did you have a nice early lunch, Mr. Dustin Rose?"

"Yes, thank you, Mrs. Phillips." He felt annoyance and an invisible band around his head tightened. Most of the time he really appreciated Mrs. Phillips for her attention to detail, but on days like today, leaving at 11:00 for lunch instead of 12, it grated on him.

Back in his office, Dusty sat at his desk and renewed his attack on the mail.

A short while later the phone buzzed and Dusty picked it up. Mrs. Phillips' voice came over the intercom, "A Mr. Reginald Flynn is on the line."

"Thank you, Mrs. Phillips." Dusty punched the button down. "Dusty."

"Hey, how are you doing?" Dusty marveled at the difference in Reggie's voice. It had changed from imperialistic and demanding to warm and friendly. He wondered how long this "mountain conversion" would last. He hoped forever, because he liked the new Reggie a lot.

"Pretty good," said Dusty. "I made it out in one piece with the stock."

"I was so glad to hear it. I just wanted to follow up."

"Thank you. There were a couple areas of touch-and-go with hypothermia and a few wolves but, you know, the usual fairy tale. A beautiful princess saved me and we rode into the sunset together."

Reggie laughed a deep amused sound. "Well, you can't beat that."

No, you really can't, thought Dusty.

"How is Mike doing? Last time I saw him he was leaving on a stretcher."

"I'd say pretty well. I just had lunch with him."

"Great!" Replied Reggie. "Look, I just wanted to give you a call and thank you again for a great trip. Maybe everything didn't fall in line exactly on the hunt, but you've got to believe me when I tell you it changed my life. I feel like I can finally do the things I've always wanted to do. And for that I am forever in your debt."

Dusty was overwhelmed by Reggie's gratitude.

"Wow. You're welcome," he said.

"Dusty, if you ever need anything at all, don't hesitate to contact me. I mean it, okay?"

"Okay. Thanks."

"I'm going to get back up to Bob's hopefully next summer. In the meantime I think I need to check into buying a mountain horse. Maybe when the time comes you can give me a few tips."

"Happy to," replied Dusty.

"Wonderful," boomed Reggie. Stay in touch."

Dusty could hear a click on the end of the line.

Thoughtfully, he hung up the phone and sat looking at it for a few minutes. Then he resumed opening letters. He wasn't sure how much time had gone by when there was a knock at his office door.

"Come in," he said, absent-mindedly.

Mrs. Phillips stepped in and quickly shut the door behind her. Dusty looked up from his paperwork. She hesitated and then spoke, "There's a, um, gentleman out in the waiting room who wishes to speak to you. I told him you received clients by appointment only. He insisted he is not a client and has urgent business."

The tone of her voice and her demeanor sent an alarm through Dusty. He set the mail down. "Well, send him in then."

Chapter Thirty-Seven

Dusty could smell the man before he could see him. The rank smell of dirty socks preceded the shuffling steps. The man was stoop-shouldered and seemed to drag his right foot. Dusty held back from extending his hand and, glancing at the tobacco-stained yellowish brown fingers on his visitor, he was glad he did.

"Have a seat." He gestured at one of the two chairs which sat in front of his desk. Mrs. Phillips gave him one last look of concern, which Dusty knew her well enough to mean, *If you need any help, let me know.* She silently closed the door behind her.

Dusty watched the gray-haired man position himself in front of the leather chair. Setting his cane to one side, he lowered himself down awkwardly into the chair. His jean jacket was stained and there were also dark spots on his pants. Dusty felt his shoulders tense. He got a bad feeling about this meeting.

Once settled in his chair, the scraggly looking man leveled piercing gray eyes at Dusty and said, "I'm here about my brother Clem and my nephew Pinto." He spat the words out. And then looked at Dusty expectantly.

Taking mental stock of the handgun in his desk drawer, Dusty looked directly back at him in a steely blue stare. "What can I do for you?"

The older man shifted a large wad of chew in his mouth from one side to the other. Dusty noticed the yellow stains for the first time in the man's beard and his stomach churned. Baring yellowish brown teeth, the man announced, "You done murdered them both." He sat back in his chair, leaning on his cane and waited for that to sink in.

In his practice of law Dusty had had a lot of nut cases, but this may have hit the top of the list. Apparently he was supposed to know what this man wanted. Whatever it was, it was sure to have a price tag attached to it.

After waiting what he deemed an appropriate amount of time for impact, the old man said, with a wry curve of his lip, "You gotta pay me fer it."

"Mr…" Dusty tried to remember if he'd been given a name for the man in front of him.

"Name's Buster Stanton. My brother was Clem. You most probably would remember him," he added angrily.

Now it fit into place. The man before him didn't look any saner than his brother or nephew had, so he was going to take it really easy with this guy.

"Mr. Stanton," Dusty said evenly, "Your brother was shot, but it was in the midst of an attempted rape at gunpoint. And—"

"Bullshit!" the old man roared.

The office door opened slightly and Mrs. Phillips peeked in. "Is everything okay in here, Mr. Dustin Rose?"

"For the moment, Mrs. Phillips. Thank you," Dusty answered carefully.

The door softly clicked shut, but Dusty knew the watchful eyes and ears of Mrs. Phillips were close by.

"What would you like me to do?" Dusty tried again. His keenest hope was to have this man leave his office.

"My family, you kil't 'em. Now you gotta pay me!" This time the old man screeched and slammed his cane on the floor.

The situation was untenable. The guy was crazy. Dusty silently studied him.

"Well? You gonna pay me or not?" snarled the unkempt pile of dirty clothes.

"Mr. Stanton," Dusty said evenly. "You need to remove yourself from my office."

"I knew it!" He yelled, slamming his cane down in a series of thumps on the floor to emphasize his words. "You're just a God damned piece of shit! Well, let me tell you, you uppity white trash, you're gonna pay!" The man was frothing at the mouth, little flecks of foam at the corners.

Dusty was flummoxed. Things were escalating and he wasn't sure how to eject this man from his office. As he pondered the situation, the bell jingled and almost simultaneously the door to his office opened. Two uniformed officers walked in. Dusty recognized them from Maude's Café.

"Everything okay in here?" A young blond-haired, blue-eyed police office questioned Dusty.

"As a matter of fact, Mr. Stanton was just leaving. Maybe you could help him out?" suggested Dusty.

The blond-haired man's partner stepped over to the old man in the chair. "Can I help you, sir?"

The elder man trembled in rage, oblivious to the officers, "Yer gonna pay me!" he screamed at Dusty. Then he finally recognized the dark-haired policeman. "This man's a murderer. He kil't my brother and my nephew."

The officers got on either side of the man and took an elbow. "Come on, sir. It's time to leave now," the blond policeman said calmly.

The man jumped to his feet with unexpected agility and spat his wad of tobacco hitting Dusty's files and shirt—just missing his face with the stinking wad.

"Okay. That will be enough of that." The blond-haired officer firmly propelled the old man toward the door.

"We're taking him down to the station for assault, Dusty. Would you like to come down and file some paperwork?"

Dusty sat momentarily surprised and immobilized by the onslaught of tobacco juice. He looked down at his sodden paperwork and felt his stomach clench in revulsion. "Yes. Please just get him out of here. I'll be down in a little while."

His voice was almost drowned out by the now ranting man.

"You son of a bitch. You'll pay! You're nothin' but murderin' white trash." The man shuffled out under the power of the police officers and finally the door closed behind the men.

Dusty stared down at the chair and saw the gnarled wooden cane still resting on the side of his conference chair. As he stared at it, Mrs. Phillips rushed in and began spraying air freshener. Glancing down at Dusty's desk, she said, "Oh, my." She hurried into the back room and in minutes rushed back with a warm bucket of water and soap. Blotting at the files and desk, she murmured, "Tsk, tsk, tsk. People are getting crazier all the time." Stepping back she regarded her employer sympathetically. "Mr. Dustin Rose, you should go home, shower and change that shirt. I will have no trouble running the office in your absence."

For the first time Dusty looked down at his shirt. The yellowish brown stains appeared on his chest. He stood up and pealed his shirt off quickly. "Thanks for pointing it out."

"No problem at all, Mr. Dustin Rose." She rung out her rag in the bucket and tackled the blotches on the desk and the files. "I hope we won't be seeing him again."

"I'm not so sure about that," Dusty said thoughtfully, and then added, "Thanks so much for calling the police. That was good thinking. The situation got out of hand a little quicker than I'd anticipated."

"No problem, Mrs. Dustin Rose. That's my job," she said smiling. Her cheeks flushed and her eyes sparkled at his compliment.

"I'll be back shortly." Shirtless, Dusty pulled on his leather jacket and walked out the door. The sky was gray and cold, way too cold to be shirtless. He zipped up his coat and walked to his car. *This is the second time in as many weeks a woman has saved me.* He felt a rush of heat in his face. *Things have just not been going the way they're supposed to lately. Mike's been having such a great time with the latest Cassie rescue. I sure hope he doesn't get wind of this one.*

He tried to shrug it off and got in his pickup. *It's not over yet, in more ways than one.*

Chapter Thirty-Eight

Pulling into his driveway, the gray sky had patches of white and the winter sun was occasionally peeking through. Dusty hated the winter. Sure, he could still ride in Western Washington, as long as he didn't mind getting rained on. Muley and Cheyenne stood in their pasture watching his arrival attentively. Scout ran off the front porch as he pulled into the clearing by his log cabin. As Dusty stepped out of his truck, his Australian shepherd emitted a few high-pitched barks in welcome.

"Hey, Boy." Dusty reached down and patted him on the head, careful to avoid the bandage. The dog was healing fast. Dusty walked in the back door and set his briefcase down on the kitchen table. He walked into the living room and hesitated. The old hewn logs, the river rock fireplace and the fir trees always calmed him. He didn't feel like going back to the office—maybe he wouldn't. *The files probably won't be completely dry until tomorrow, and I could swing by the police station in the morning.* He teetered in indecision. *One thing for sure, I'm taking a shower.* He turned and ran up the stairs to his bedroom, taking them two at a time.

The whole situation with Buster Stanton required more than a clean shirt. Dusty took a shower as much to erase the mental image as the physical of the old man. Spitting on a person in Washington state was 4th degree assault. The maximum penalty was five years and/or a $5,000 fine. The odds of him actually getting jail time were slight, Dusty calculated, although criminal law was not his forte. He could only hope. If the way the guy smelled in his office was any indication, he could only assume the police would want him out of their jail as soon as possible.

Dusty poured himself a cup of coffee. Putting on his coat, he went out to the porch to think. It was cool out, but he always preferred to be outside. Muley and Cheyenne nickered to him encouragingly, reminding him they were ready to eat.

"You're a little early today, boys, but nice try," he replied, smiling at them. As he sat his coffee cup down, a furry head worked its way under his arm for the most opportune spot to be petted.

Dusty accommodated his dog, looking at him fondly. "We've had quite the ride lately, haven't we, Boy?" Scout opened his mouth in a big dog grin, wagging his tail so hard it looked like he might split in half.

As he took another drink of coffee, his landline went off in the house. Dusty debated whether to ignore it. *The way things have been going lately, I'd better see what it is.* Still holding onto his cup of coffee, he went back in the house.

"Hey, Boss."

"What's up, Mike? And how did you know I'd be here?" Dusty held the phone in one hand and pulled off his coat.

"Process of elimination."

"Okay. So Mrs. Phillips probably already filled you in on our visitor this afternoon."

"Yes, she did. That's why I'm calling."

"Can't be a good sign," Dusty sighed.

"Well, I guess that depends who you are," Mike answered calmly.

"Okay. Well, how about if you're me?"

Mike seemed to think it over. "Maybe not so good."

"Okay, Mike. Enough. What did you find out?"

"I guess the main thing is that Buster Stanton is who he says he is, meaning he is Pinto's uncle and Clem's brother."

Dusty felt the wind go out of him. His mind drifted back to the pack trip to the Pasayten when the young family was assaulted and the little girl was kidnapped. Had it not been for Cassie's quick thinking, there might have been a very different outcome to the story. As it was, due to the attack by Clem and his rapist, pedophile buddy Tom, Sally and her brother Scott lost their father. He was pushed off an embankment by the derelicts when he tried to rescue his daughter. Their father died from head injuries.

"And now what?" Dusty asked to himself as much as Mike.

Mike said honestly, "That part I don't know yet."

"Well, he came into the office yelling at me I've got to pay him. It never really was clear whether he meant money or my life."

"It might be good to find out," Mike suggested.

Dusty felt heat crawl up his back., "How many of those people are there, anyway?" He shifted positions angrily and looked out into the fir trees surrounding his cabin. "Are they going to just keep pouring out of Canada like roaches, or what?"

"Hard saying." Then Mike said encouragingly, "Don't worry. We'll get this sorted out, Boss. As of right now, it's just another nutcase. I'll try to find out as much as I can about the family and who's who." He paused for a minute. "I thought the most important thing at the moment was to let you know he is legitimately who he says he is."

"Well, I guess knowledge is power. Thanks, Mike." Then as an afterthought he added, "Find out who the family members are and what the charges are. Felons usually don't think of it all on their own; it tends to run in families."

"Will do, Boss."

Just as he was about to hang up, Dusty quickly added, "Oh, and Mike, I did it. Anyone asks, I shot Clem."

Mike didn't need any explanation. "Right."

Dusty hung up the phone and grabbed his jacket. *If nothing else, he'd protect Cassie by taking the blame for Clem's shooting. The family was nutty enough. Who knows what kind of revenge they might try to get.*

Getting down to the police department and filing charges had taken on a new importance to him now. As he walked out to his truck, the feeling of security he got from the close proximity of the fir trees changed a couple of degrees. The darkened depths and pine needle strewn forest floors looked dark and foreboding. Dusty looked at Scout, Muley and Cheyenne. All three of the animals had their eyes riveted on him. If there was anybody else around, they would let him know. At least that was the hope, even though it was maybe getting close to feeding time.

Shrugging off the thought, Dusty jumped in his truck and drove quickly down the driveway.

Chapter Thirty-Nine

It hadn't taken as long as he thought at the police station. They were going to hold the old man, at least overnight. But he might bail out sooner if he got an attorney. *They probably really hope he gets an attorney.* Dusty wasn't sure, but it seemed the Eagleclaw Police Station had already taken on a new scent—for the worse.

Dusty had swung by his office and grabbed his files, now dry, thanks to Mrs. Phillips. He figured he'd work on them at home. It was as good as anyplace and sometimes he was actually able to get more done there.

Pulling back into the driveway, Dusty still felt a gnawing sense of unease. He hated it when this stuff followed him home. The log cabin sat silently, like it had for years, in the grassy clearing. The trees shadowed around it and the white-rimmed windows looked like dark vacant teeth.

Scout ran up to meet him and he walked in the back porch and flipped on the light. Walking into the kitchen, he dropped his files on the red checkered tablecloth. He flipped on the lights in the living room, just for good measure. Everything was the way he left it, so he went out to feed.

Grabbing a couple of flakes from the barn, Muley and Cheyenne whinnied and ran up and down the fence line. As he threw the flakes of hay in each trough, they tore into them eagerly. Scout and he watched for a minute and then went back in the house. With everything that had happened, Dusty hadn't had time to talk to Cassie. He grabbed his cell phone and hit the number.

She picked it up after a couple of rings. "Hi, Dusty."

Dusty smiled into the phone—so convenient that people knew who you were before you said anything. "Hey."

"How's Scout?" she asked.

Dusty was impressed that she'd think of his dog first. "He's doing pretty well. Really well, as a matter of fact. We'll probably have the bandage off in a couple of days." He hesitated before he added, "Thanks to you."

"He's a great dog," Cassie sounded embarrassed. "I didn't do very much."

"You're right, not much," he agreed. "Only saved me and my dog's life."

"Oh, Dusty, please. I don't want to talk about this anymore. I did what anyone else would have done in the same situation." She cleared her throat. "The outdoors sometimes takes no prisoners, and you gotta do what you gotta do."

"Okay, yeah. Well, I really appreciate it." Then he lowered his voice and surprised himself at the seductiveness of it. "I'd like to make it up to you."

"Oh." Cassie paused for a second and asked breathlessly. "When?"

The sound of her voice drove him crazy. He wanted to hang up the phone and head straight over to her house. A feeling of panic and lust overcame him. He looked at the files on his table. "What are you doing now?"

"Waiting for you," she answered simply.

"Give me five." He hurriedly clicked off his phone. He looked around for a minute, trying to figure out what he needed. Realizing he couldn't think, he grabbed his coat and his keys and headed to his truck, only stopping to lock the door behind him.

The drive took him less than 10 minutes, but when he thought about it later, he couldn't remember any of it. As he pulled into Cassie's driveway, Sammy barked at his truck. He turned it off and slammed the door. Walking up the stairs, he saw Cassie standing in the doorway. His heart quickened and he practically ran up the steps.

He pulled her into his arms before she even closed the door and they kissed. It was a crazy kiss. He wanted her and kissed her in a way he had never kissed a woman before. She returned it and moaned in the back of her throat. He tore her clothes off and carried her up to her room. His need for her obliterated any other thoughts and she met him equally. At one point he thought his head was going to explode and he saw stars. Was it the evening sky? Or was it heaven?

Laying on her bed with his arms around her, he felt such a peace. The silkiness of her hair was under his chin. The rhythm of her breathing calmed him. He closed his eyes and felt exhausted. It occurred to him he'd never talked to her at all, but then, in a way, he guessed he had. He closed his eyes and slipped into darkness.

When Dusty woke, light filled the room. Cassie lay next to him on her side spooning in the conformation of his body. He pulled her close. She opened her eyes sleepily and smiled at him. "Hypothermia over?" she murmured.

He feigned thinking it over. "I am feeling a little cold still."

She pulled him close to her and kissed him. Kissing her back, he felt warmer than he could remember.

Feeling relaxed, Dusty turned to look at the clock. "What time is it, anyway?" He had a hard time focusing. "Is this the right time?"

"Whaat?" Cassie asked groggily. She looked at the clock, and then attempted to refocus. "Oh, shit."

"Boy, that's right," agreed Dusty. It was almost 10 o'clock. He was late. Mrs. Phillips expected him in the office by 9. He hadn't fed the horses or anything else. "I've got to get out of here."

"Me too," agreed Cassie.

They both jumped out of each side of the bed and grabbed their clothes. Cassie, unable to find hers, pulled on a robe. Dusty had more success and began pulling on everything lying on the floor at the foot of the bed.

He buttoned a few buttons on his shirt. "I'll call you later on."

"Tonight is the Eagleclaw Trailriders meeting. Are you going?"

Dusty hesitated. He hadn't remembered it. "Sure. I'll pick you up at 6, if you want to go."

"Sure," Cassie kissed him. "Wouldn't miss it."

Dusty kissed her back. "See you then, Babe."

Running out of the house to his truck, he realized he hadn't thought once about being boxed in by a relationship. *Maybe I'm starting to get better, or maybe Cassie is just the most amazing woman I've ever met.*

As he drove home he wondered why everyone was waving at him. He didn't realize he was smiling so brightly, they couldn't help themselves.

Chapter Forty

Despite feeding the horses, showering and driving into the office like a madman, Dusty still didn't make it in until a little bit after 11. Mrs. Phillips looked at him with concern, "Are you feeling okay, Mr. Dustin Rose?"

"Yes. I just had a few things I needed to take care of before coming into work," he mumbled, trying to get down the hall to his office as soon as possible.

"I couldn't get ahold of you for your 10 o'clock client, so they are going to call back to reschedule."

"Darn it, I forgot about it," Dusty slapped his head. *Figures he would have a morning appointment today of all days.*

"Mike has tried to call you a couple more times."

"Okay, I'll call him back." Dusty started down the short hall to his office.

Mrs. Phillips called after him, "A man named Raleigh Higganbotham called. He said he was representing Mr. Stanton."

Dusty froze in his tracks. He hesitated a moment and then walked back to her desk. "Do you have that number?"

"Yes," the elderly lady replied. "It's right here." She tore the *While You Were Out* slip off and handed it to him.

Interesting choice of lawyers. Raleigh Higganbotham was known for wrongful death cases. He'd had several multimillion-dollar settlements over the years. He was known as one of the big guns in the business. Dusty tossed the files down on his desk. *How in the heck would that old guy know to pick that lawyer?*

Dusty called Mike. "So what do you know about an attorney by the name of Raleigh Higganbotham?"

"I've heard of him. He seems to do pretty well for his clients." Mike sounded puzzled, "Why?"

"That's Buster Stanton's new attorney."

The line was silent. Just when Dusty was wondering if they had been cut off, Mike spoke again. "You're kidding?"

"Nope. That bad, huh?" Dusty felt the bottom of his stomach drop and he knew it showed in his voice.

"Well, you know him too. What do you think?" Mike urged.

"I think that this case is serious and it just got a whole lot more difficult."

"What can I do?" asked Mike.

"I need whatever information you can dig up. I know you verified that Buster is the real deal, but I need to know everything I can about the family. What are their legal records? Past arrests, lawsuits, et cetera. Whatever plays into this nut job's reliability. We know that Clem ran drugs and hung out with pedophiles. That has a way of not just stopping with one person in a family." Dusty suddenly remember the stench in his office. "And by the way that guys smells, I can't believe there aren't other issues too."

"Got it, Boss."

"Get back to me as soon as you find out." Dusty sat in his office chair and ran his fingers through his hair.

"Will do."

"Thanks." Dusty set the phone down. He stared at it and tried to decide when he would call back the attorney. He wasn't sure what the call was about, but when he did talk to Raleigh, he wanted to have as much information as possible. It was always easier to actually know, than to have to act like you do. Dusty figured he'd give Mike at least a couple of hours.

He sat at his desk and stared into space looking for answers. The buzzer on his desk rang and Dusty jumped.

"Do you have everything you need for your 2 o'clock deposition?" inquired Mrs. Phillips.

Stunned, Dusty quickly collected himself. "No, I think I'll be fine—just need the file."

"That's on the corner of your desk. It's the Renfro file."

"Oh, course. There it is. Thank you, Mrs. Phillips."

Dusty glanced quickly at the clock. 11:30. *Great. If he worked through lunch he might be able to pull it off and not look like a complete idiot.*

This case, thank God, was just an easy automobile accident. His client had crossed the intersection and gotten T-boned. The insurance attorney was deposing his client. Dusty willed himself to calm down. No big deal.

Dusty hated not being organized. Stopping briefly by Cassie's turned into an all-night deal, and from there his entire schedule went out the window. He felt a warmth in the pit of his stomach when he thought about her. *He was really looking forward to seeing her tonight. Going to the Eagleclaw Backcountry Horsemen meeting with a woman was going to be a little bit different for him, maybe because it would the first time ever, but what the heck. Why not?*

He wasn't sure how long he went through his files preparing for the deposition. It seemed to take a long time, because when he wasn't thinking about Cassie, he was thinking about Buster Stanton.

His buzzer on his desk rang and once again he jumped. "The court reporter is here for your 2 o'clock deposition." Dusty quickly glanced up at the clock, 1:30 already.

"Thank you, Mrs. Phillips. Please send her in."

As he stood up to open the door, the auburn haired small woman appeared in his doorway. She pulled a small suitcase on wheels and carried a briefcase.

"Hi, Dusty." He did a double take at the woman.

"Terri, what a surprise." *I should be getting used to surprises.* "Please go ahead and set up over there." He gestured to the conference table in the back of his office by a window.

"How have you been doing?" he asked politely.

"Fine." She bent down setting up her equipment and then looked up at him, "The better question is, how are you? I heard you've had a rough couple of weeks."

Dusty laughed wryly. "It was quite a ride, for sure."

As Terri turned on her computer and set it up, she asked, "Any idea how long this is going to go? I was hoping to go to the meeting tonight."

"I can't think it would go that long. It's not my client, but not that much happened to the guy."

"Great," said Terri. "Don't worry, I wouldn't hold you to it. I know you never know."

Mrs. Phillips buzzed in again. "Dallas Renfro is here."

"Send him in, please." Dusty stood up and shook hands with his client and directed him over to the conference table. The man was in his early 40s and wore a suit and tie. He looked nervous.

"Do we need to talk about anything before I do this?" he asked Dusty.

"No, Dallas. I think it's pretty cut and dried. Just be honest and up front with any questions he asks you. Don't add anymore than you need to and just answer the questions."

"Okay." Dallas didn't look convinced.

"Water? Coffee?" asked Dusty.

"Water would be great." Dusty walked out to get it and came back in with opposing counsel. "Everyone's here now, so we're ready to go."

The insurance attorney carried out the deposition a little longer than Dusty thought he needed to, but by 4 o'clock he was winding down. He wanted to talk to Mike about the results of his investigation into the Stanton family. He really wanted to call Raleigh back today.

Dusty waited politely for Terri to pack up her equipment before he called Mike. Interesting—while she talked a lot with the horses, she talked less here. Maybe Mike was starting to rub off on her.

"Thanks a lot for coming, Terri. Maybe I'll see you tonight."

"My pleasure, Dusty. I hope so." She smiled and left.

Dusty leaped to his desk and grabbed the phone. Mike answered on the second ring. "What did you find out?"

"I can be there in 10 minutes."

"Great. See you then." Dusty hung the phone up and stared at it. *If Mike wanted to come in, it must be serious.*

Chapter Forty-One

Dusty heard the office door jingle in exactly 10 minutes. Mike said hello to Mrs. Phillips and knocked on his door. "Come on in."

Mike flopped down in one of his conference chairs. "What a day."

"Yeah, I know what you mean," agreed Dusty. "What's the story?"

Mike began. "Buster Stanton is basically the patriarch for the Stanton clan. He and Clem were brothers, but he was the stable one. Pinto was his nephew and, unfortunately, had a lot of his dad in him. He had a rap sheet a mile long, like his uncle. So if he hadn't gotten accidentally killed on the pack trip, he had plenty of other people that wanted to see it happen."

Mike paused and took a sip of water. "From what I can tell, Buster was not satisfied with the outcome of Clem's wrongful death action. Losing his nephew pushed him into action. He wants to bring a civil suit, since he views the criminal suit as a failure."

Dusty looked at Mike thoughtfully. "Kind of an OJ Simpson thing."

"Yup," agreed Mike.

Without hesitating, Dusty grabbed the phone and dialed in the Seattle attorney's phone number. After a minute he said, "Raleigh Higganbotham, please. My name is Dustin Rose."

Mike raised his eyebrows.

Dusty covered the phone, "It's always better to start with the upper hand."

Before he could say anything else, the attorney answered on the other end.

"Dusty, good of you to call me. Thought I was just going to have to send you a letter."

"No problem, Raleigh." So much for the formal address, thought Dusty."

"I wanted to just give you a heads-up. I am now representing Buster Stanton. I wasn't sure whether you were going to be getting a lawyer." He cleared his throat. "I certainly would if I were you, but I wanted to find out who I'm mailing the notice of appearance to."

"And what are the claims?"

"Two claims of wrongful death," Raleigh answered with no hesitation.

Dusty felt his stomach tighten and the heaviness hit his shoulders. Thinking about the term was a lot different than having someone actually say it. That was no laughing matter, and if, by an insane twist, Buster prevailed, Dusty could be looking at a sizeable amount of money. His stomach twisted at the threat to his dream of retirement and full-time riding and packing.

"I'll get back to you later, Raleigh—either I or my counsel."

"Fabulous," boomed Raleigh. "And sorry about the call. Hate to ruin your day with this."

Dusty couldn't tell whether he was joking or sincere. He pretty much doubted there was any sincerity in what the lawyer said. After all, Dusty needed to go down in order for him to win. Dusty hung the phone up.

He and Mike stared at each other for a few minutes and finally Dusty said, "I think it's probably time to give Reggie a call."

"The mountain convert," remembered Mike.

"None other. Let's just see how sincere he was when he told me if I ever needed anything, just call."

"Seems like it might be a good time to check," agreed Mike.

Dusty doubted he'd get ahold of anyone at Reggie's Seattle firm at 4:45 p.m., but it was worth a shot. The receptionist answered on the first ring. "Reggie Flynn, please. Dusty Rose." His call was directed to Reggie's office and it immediately went to voicemail. No surprise. The traffic was bad these days in Seattle. Everybody either left way early or late to avoid the worst of it.

"Reggie, this is Dusty Rose. I need to talk to you about a personal matter. Please call me at your earliest convenience." He left his cell phone number and hung up.

"Not tonight, I guess?" asked Mike.

"Nope." He scooped the files off his desk and put them into the drawers. "You going to the meeting tonight?"

"Yup," said Mike.

"I'm picking up Cassie and I'll see you there," Dusty said casually.

"Oh?" Mike looked surprised.

Dusty figured Mike wasn't going to be the first one surprised tonight. He wished he didn't have to go at all. He felt bone tired. But as he knew from experience, nothing that a quick shower wouldn't cure.

"That's great. I'm happy for you, Boss," said Mike, as they walked out the door together.

"Thanks. What about you? Are you going with anyone?"

Mike winked at him. "Going solo. See you tonight."

Dusty shook his head. As long as he had known Mike, he never quite understood him. That probably wasn't the most important thing, anyway. He put his truck into gear and drove home. He felt apprehension in the pit of his stomach. It had nothing to do with Cassie and everything to do with Raleigh Higginbotham announcing he was filing a wrongful death lawsuit against Dusty. That was a big deal. And it was problematic. The main issue was he didn't kill Clem Stanton, accidentally or otherwise. He did accidentally kill Pinto, but that was in self-defense.

Dusty had no problem protecting Cassie from these lunatics by letting them think he killed Clem. But letting people think something and going on trial for it are two different things. He couldn't get on a witness stand and perjure himself—he'd lose his license to practice law. Once they got into the case they were going to find out the truth, anyway. It was going to take them awhile. He was going to have to talk to Cassie about this. It could very well be they were going to both need a lawyer.

He sighed as he turned into his driveway. No point in putting the cart before the horse, though; he had to receive service of suit first. *And besides, did Raleigh really think he was going to bring that smelly little man to court?* Stranger things have probably happened, but Dusty couldn't think of them.

Chapter Forty-Two

Cassie was sitting on the front porch next to her dog when Dusty pulled up. He felt a lot better after his shower. She looked beautiful as she got up to meet him. He jumped out and ran around to open the door for her.

"Wow, I'm impressed," she laughed.

Dusty was going to reach for the door, but changed his mind and instead pulled her into his arms. He couldn't help himself. She always had that effect on him. He kissed her. Her hair smelled like that shampoo he loved. "Are you sure you want to go?" he whispered in her ear.

"Yes," she said breathlessly. "They're having a vet talk tonight and I really wanted to hear him."

"Okay," he said, not wanting to let go of her. "Maybe later on?"

"That's a possibility."

Dusty released her and closed the door after she got in. Cassie sat next to him in the truck.

"There's a seatbelt in the middle." He leaned over to pull the end up and help her fasten it.

She laughed, "Wow, what did I ever do without you?"

"Good question."

When they arrived at the grange hall everybody was inside. Now that it was winter, the old-timers who usually hung outside the front door had moved inside where it was warmer.

As they walked in the door, there was a dull roar as everybody talked and laughed. Coffee was available. Dusty saw Mike off in the corner talking to the old-timers.

Shelley came up. "Hey, you guys. How are you doing? I heard what happened to you up in the Pasayten. I'm so glad you both made it out okay."

"Thanks, Shelley," said Cassie.

"Thanks a lot," echoed Dusty.

"I think I'll go get some coffee," said Cassie. "Can I get you any?"

"Sure," said Dusty. "I'll just go over and say hi to the guys for a minute."

Mike was talking to Val and Eddie. Russ and Walt were in a big conversation. Everybody stopped when Dusty walked up and they all pummeled him with questions about his harrowing pack trip in the Pasayten.

"Is it true you almost died up there?" asked Val incredulously.

"Yes, it sure is."

"Hey," Eddie chimed in. "I heard that you just about died of hypothermia and had to get in a sleeping bag naked to survive."

"Something like that," Dusty said quietly, feeling his cheeks burn. He didn't want Cassie to hear them.

"Wow. Some guys get all the luck," Russ chimed in.

"I wonder if Mary would do that if I was dyin'?"

"I don't know, Val. That's a good question," Russ said, and they all dissolved into loud guffaws.

"Nice seeing you guys," said Dusty. "Talk to you later."

As he turned, he saw Cassie not too far away with two cups of coffee in her hands.

"Sure, Dusty," said Eddie knowingly. "You don't want to keep the little lady waitin'." Laughter rippled through the men once again.

Dusty headed back over to Cassie. He was about halfway there when a tall, striking brunette intercepted him. She had dazzling blue eyes. "Hi, Dusty," she said softly. "Do you have a minute?"

He could feel Cassie's eyes on him questioningly when he

stopped to talk to the woman. Dusty turned his attention to the woman. She was tall, like Cassie. She had an expensively tailored leather jacket and jade earrings. They accentuated her eyes.

"I've been wanting to ask you," she looked at him, her blue eyes wide. "I have a, um, a slight problem." She hesitated, "It's, um, a little embarrassing. Could I talk to you someplace more private for a minute?" Her eyes appeared glossy and a tear slid out of the corner.

Dusty was intrigued and surprised. Forgetting himself for a minute, *What could possibly be wrong?* He studied her. She had been at meetings in the past. He knew he had seen her from a distance. *She was hard to miss.* The word was she had come from old family money. Her clothes and the way she carried herself would certainly back that up.

Seeing that Dusty hadn't moved, Cindy began crying softly, genuinely distressed. Dusty instinctively put his arm out to comfort her. She immediately clung to him. The heat flowed from his cheeks down his back. *This was not what he intended.*

"Ma'am," he stumbled.

"Cindy," she purred.

"Cindy," he corrected. "I'm not sure what I can do for you or what your problem is, but I need to get going."

"Oh, Dusty," she sobbed, leaning into him. "It's been so awful. My ex-boyfriend broke into my house, and he...he...struck me. He won't get out." Catching a quick side glance at Dusty, she still didn't seem to have his full attention, so she poured it on more. "I just don't know what to do."

Dusty stood awkwardly with the model-like woman clinging to him, now sobbing so hard her shoulders were heaving. He was shocked. Nothing like this had ever happened to him before. *Why now of all times?* All he could think of was to get this woman away from him. Looking around helplessly, he tried to think of what to do. "You need to get ahold of yourself, ma'am." He tried to set her back. "Maybe you should go home."

That set her off worse, "Oh, no, not there," she sobbed.

"Do you have a friend you can go to?" He looked around again frantically, "Did you come with anyone."

"I came alone," she replied mournfully. "You're the only one I could think of that could help." She showed no inclination to let go of him.

"I'm really sorry, but I have to go. I have a—a date that I came here with." He finally managed to get a little distance from the woman. "Call my office and make an appointment. I can see what I can do to help you then."

"A date?" The dark haired woman said, her tears stopped. "Where?"

Dusty looked where only minutes before Cassie had been standing. Nobody was there.

"Let's call this meeting to order," called a man from the front of the room. Frantically Dusty looked around the room. He saw Cassie nowhere. He finally located Mike just sitting down in the back.

"Mike, could you come here a minute?" Mike's face looked purposefully blank.

"Sure. What's up, Boss?"

"Have you seen Cassie? I came here with her and I can't find her."

Mike's face looked strained. "Um, I think she left."

"Left? What? How?" Dusty was genuinely confused. "She came with me."

Mike squirmed and looked like he'd rather be anywhere else. "I know. But she came up to Terri when I was talking to her. She asked to talk to Terri for a minute. Then Terri told me she was giving Cassie a ride home."

"Seriously?" Dusty's stomach hit bottom. "Okay. Thanks." He turned and walked out of the grange hall into the night.

As he drove home, he passed a tavern along the way. There were several cars in front and the lights inside looked warm and inviting. He hadn't felt like he really wanted a drink in a very long time, but he could almost smell it right now. He pulled into the parking lot and just sat in his car. The loss of Cassie was like a knife in the heart. The pain was palpable. *I am so incredibly stupid.* The scene played over and over. *What could I have done?* He laid his head against the steering wheel and shut his eyes.

A rap on the window startled him. Looking up, he saw a flashlight in his face. Dusty rolled down the window.

"Hey, Buddy, do you need a lift home? Maybe leave your car here?" A man in his 30s in a jean jacket and plaid shirt stood before him. He had a cigarette in one hand.

He thinks I'm drunk. "No, thanks. I was just a little tired." He answered sheepishly.

"Well, you don't sound wasted. Just take care. We don't want any accidents from drinking and driving from our place." By way of explanation, the man continued. "I was just on my smoke break and saw you out here. Wanted to make sure you were okay." The man smiled at him with crooked teeth and took a drag off his cigarette.

"No, problem. Thanks for checking." Dusty rolled the window up and put his truck in gear. *Nothing like making a bad evening worse.* He turned out of the parking lot and headed home.

Chapter Forty-Three

Standing with the coffee cups in her hands, Cassie hadn't noticed anything. She said hi to a few friends and noticed Dusty was over talking to the old-timers. Not coming to a lot of meetings, Cassie wasn't familiar with the women members of the Eagleclaw Backcountry Horsemen. She could not remember seeing the attractive brunette that hurried up to Dusty.

As the woman lay a proprietary hand on Dusty, Cassie felt her back tighten. *Who is she?* She watched how that woman looked at Dusty. *Oh, please. If that's not obvious.* Watching Dusty's handsome suntanned face break into a beautiful white-toothed grin, Cassie's stomach wrenched. *That woman is trying to pick him up.*

Dusty smiled and leaned down to speak with the woman. Then he looked confused. The woman, apparently not close enough, started crying and then plastered herself onto him. Cassie felt rooted to the spot. It was as if she was disembodied and watching from above. *He was enjoying himself.* As Dusty's hand rubbed the woman's back consolingly and the woman planted her face into Dusty's shirt, Cassie felt heat burn into her cheeks and down her back. Shades of the arrogant asshole at the King County Courthouse flashed through her mind. *I should have known. God, I am so stupid!* Making her mind up, she set the two cups of coffee down and sought Terri out.

She found Terri and Mike talking. "Could I talk to you for a minute?"

"Sure," said her auburn-haired friend. Walking a little distance away, she asked, "What can I do for you?"

"Can you give me a ride home?" Cassie asked calmly.

Terri appeared confused. "Sure. What happened? I thought you came here with Dusty."

"Um, I did, but something came up and I've got to get home."

"Okay. Let me just tell Mike real quick and we can go."

"I'll meet you outside." Without waiting for a reply, Cassie hurried out the door. The sooner she left the meeting and the embarrassing scene behind her, the better. *To think she had stupidly ridden all the way into the Pasayten Wilderness in a snow storm to rescue that sorry excuse for a human being! It was more than she could swallow. And he actually talked me into seeing him again! Like being shut down and made a fool of once wasn't enough.* As Cassie walked to Terri's car, she felt tears burn in her eyes. *Oh, no. Having him humiliate her at the meeting wasn't bad enough. Now she was going to cry.*

It took all the strength she could muster not to cry. When Terri got into the car and started it up, Cassie sat silently.

Terri made it as far as the street before she couldn't stand it, "What happened, Cassie? Really."

Her voice flat, Cassie responded, "I got an email about a file and it couldn't wait."

"Oh, yeah, right." Terri said sarcastically. "And Dusty refused to take you home?"

"He, um, had his hands full."

"You mean with Cindy?"

"So you saw that…that whole scene?" Cassie was barely able to contain herself. Even saying it was bringing back the mental picture.

"Cindy throwing herself at Dusty and him not knowing what to do with her? I might have noticed something along those lines."

"Well, okay, then," Cassie said with finality and threw herself back against the seat.

"So I asked Mike who she is," Terri said, and then let it hang.

Cassie waited for a while and then responded. "And?"

"She has a thing for unavailable men. According to Mike, anyway," Terri added. "He thought about asking her out at one point, but since he's single, he didn't breathe air, as far as she was concerned."

"That's pretty twisted."

"It is," agreed Terri.

"But Dusty liked it. I saw him," Cassie said forcefully.

"Honestly? I saw him too, Cassie. And what I saw was Cindy closing in on him and doing her best to get what she wanted. He looked embarrassed and confused to me."

"Why didn't she ever do it before? Surely this wasn't her first BCH meeting if people knew who she was."

"All I can figure is she saw him come in with you. He looked pretty crazy about you, Cassie. It was all over his face. Cindy must have thought it was now or never."

And she'd left. "Oh, crap, Terri. I'm so stupid." Cassie felt tears stinging her eyes again. "I'm just not cut out for the dating scene. I'm no good at it."

"It's okay, Cassie. Just a little misunderstanding. It's not the end of the world," Terri said soothingly. "Do you want to go back?"

"No," barked Cassie. The thought of returning was more than she could fathom. "Let's just leave it. I want to go back to the ranch." The security of her home played out in her mind. She'd feel much better there.

"Okay. Don't get upset. I'll take you home." Terri clicked on the country radio station and they continued to Cassie's house.

The two woman drove the rest of the way without talking, listening to the radio. *Why does every song have to be about cheating men and broken hearts?* Cassie sighed and looked out the window.

Chapter Forty-Four

Dusty felt awful as he walked into his office, and he was sure it showed.

"Good morning, Mr. Dustin Rose," Mrs. Phillips greeted heartily.

"Morning," he ground out.

His elderly secretary raised an eyebrow at him, then shrugged as a duck shook water off her back, and continued on. "I'll bring coffee into you in a minute."

"Thanks," was his muffled response as he walked into his office and shut the door.

Sitting in his office Dusty was relieved. It was difficult to even come in. He had an overwhelming desire to ride. He knew he couldn't get up to the high mountains now, but there were other places to go. There's something about being on the back of a horse in the woods that straightened everything out. His mind flipped back to the previous pack trip, and then his thoughts turned to Cassie and his dark mood once again descended upon him.

He snatched up the files on his desk and was just beginning to read as Mrs. Phillips walked in with a steaming cup of coffee.

"Thank you," he muttered, not looking up at her, hoping to appear immersed in his files.

"Mike called and would like you to return his call."

"Great," he replied. *That's the last person I feel like talking to right now. Between Buster Stanton and my dream date last night,*

I'm ready to get out of here. "I'll get back to him." *Yeah, right. Maybe in a month or two.*

"All right, then. Please let me know if you need anything."

With one eye, Dusty watched her back as she shut the door. She knew him so well—sometimes it was unsettling.

As he picked up the first letter, the header caught his eye, Raleigh Higganbotham. *Boy, that guy doesn't waste any time. Must have sent it by messenger.* He was going to have to do something about this case. The notice of appearance now made it official. Buster Stanton had filed a lawsuit against him. The truth was all going to come out about Cassie shooting Clem. It always did in these things. Dusty was surprised that he hadn't found out yet. Raleigh had Dusty down for the wrongful death of both Clem Stanton and his nephew, Edward Stanton, a/k/a Pinto Stanton. Dusty stared at the paperwork.

He picked up the phone. When the receptionist answered, he said, "Dustin Rose, for Reginald Flynn."

"Dusty," a warm voice greeted him seconds later. "Great to hear from you."

"Good to hear from you, Reggie, but I wish it was under other circumstances," Dusty began.

Reggie instantly sounded concerned. "What can I do?"

Dusty outlined the situation for him.

"Sounds like you need a lawyer," Reggie surmised.

"My thoughts exactly."

"Shoot. I wish it could be me. But of course, it can't."

"Nope," agreed Dusty.

"Both Cliff and I witnessed the, um, accident with Pinto, so we're out."

"I was hoping you might know somebody who works in these kind of cases."

"Let me think about it and get back to you. I want to get you the best," added Reggie.

"I appreciate that and, unfortunately, I need it."

"We'll have to figure out what to do about the first incident with Clem too, since it isn't applicable. Buster's going to find out when they do the records release. Funny why he wouldn't know already from Tom."

"He's in prison."

"True, but they do get word out," Reggie said.

"Just a matter of time," agreed Dusty.

"I'll get back to you with a name. Don't worry too much about this. It's all going to work out. These cases can take a couple years to get to court. As you know."

"Yeah," agreed Dusty. *Easy for you to say.* "Thanks a lot. I really appreciate it."

"Oh, you'll get me back, Dusty. Remember, I want to learn how to pack."

"It's a deal," Dusty said, and hung up the phone.

The morning dragged on and just before noon he grabbed his coat and headed out the door.

Undaunted, Mrs. Phillips called out, "Have a good lunch, Mr. Dustin Rose."

"Thank you," he muttered. "You too."

The sky was gray and the wind blew as he walked to Maude's Mountain Café. Dusty gathered his coat closer to him. Ever since the hypothermia he avoided getting cold. The image of Cassie naked in the sleeping bag with him coursed through his mind, and what was left of his mood sank.

As he walked into the door of the café, the warm wind hit him in the face. Since it wasn't quite 12 yet, the early coffee crowd was still there. Old-timers in plaid shirts with suspenders, old jeans and Romeo shoes. They nodded to Dusty as he went to his regular spot in the back of the bar.

Maude bustled up to him, "Hi, Dusty. Coffee?"

"Hi. Sure." Dusty used as few words as possible and held out his cup.

"Waiting for anybody today?" she asked.

"Nope," he answered quickly.

"Okay. Food will be up in a couple minutes." Reading his

mood, the savvy bright-red-haired waitress worked with people enough to know, sometimes it's best to get away as soon as possible.

Dusty drank his coffee and stared straight ahead morosely.

He was so engrossed in his pain, he didn't even hear her come up. A small hand patted his arm, "Hey, Dusty. You mind if I sit down?"

He turned and looked at her. "Help yourself, Shelley."

She hopped up on the bar stool, her bracelets jangling. Her little booted feet swung in the air. Maude ran up and Shelley said, "I'll just take a coffee."

Dusty did his best to smile at her. Apparently he didn't do a very good job.

Shelley smiled at him sympathetically. "I figured you might need a friend today, so I came up here on purpose." She took a sip of hot coffee. "I also wanted to tell you everything is going to be all right." Then she added emphatically, "I just know it, Dusty."

He didn't say anything and looked down at his coffee.

"You may wonder why I know that," she continued. "Well, I've been a woman for a long time, and I know how we think. Cassie is crazy about you."

"Is that right?" Dusty finally said. "She's got a funny way of showing it."

"It was just a little misunderstanding. You two have been single a while. You need to get on the same wavelength is all."

"Is this seat taken?" A deeper voice sounded behind Dusty. He turned and Mike was settling into the seat next to him.

"Wonderful," observed Dusty. "Is this the revival committee, or what?"

Mike smiled at him sadly. "Last time I checked, we were friends. And this is what friends do."

Dusty felt shame burn through him. Mike was right. "I'm sorry, Mike. I guess I wasn't thinking right." Then he added, "Thanks for coming, you guys."

"Our pleasure," concluded Shelley for both of them.

Talking to the two of them over lunch, Dusty actually was able to drag himself out of the hole he'd dug for himself. He actually felt a little better. He still wanted to go riding and weighed the options of going back to the office. As he went outside, he noticed the wind had calmed down. It still wasn't the brightest of days, but it wasn't raining. And on the West Side of the mountains, that would be considered a good day.

Making up his mind, he passed the office and went to his car. Dialing Mrs. Phillips, she answered on the first ring.

"Something's come up and I'll be out of the office until tomorrow. If I have appointments, please reschedule them. If I have calls, I'll get them back tomorrow."

Mrs. Phillips listened patiently. "Very well, Mr. Dustin Rose." Then she added, "Have a good ride."

"Thank you," he said. As he walked to his truck, his step was lighter.

Chapter Forty-Five

Dusty pulled Muley out of the trailer at the old mill site. Scout stood by. Dusty felt a lot better being out in the woods and the smell of horse balanced him. There were only a couple other trailers in the parking lot. During the week it was usually light in traffic, and the large fee they charged to ride on their property kept a lot of people away too. But he didn't care. When he couldn't go up to the mountains, the foothills was as good as it got. He swung into the saddle and headed up the hill, Scout trotting behind Muley's heels.

For years the Weyerhaeuser property had been open to the public to ride. The Pierce County Backcountry Horsemen had even made signs for the trails, and had work parties to keep the trails clear. They had the annual work party and chili feed every spring. It seemed like it never failed to rain that day either, but it didn't dampen the fun. Dusty enjoyed going to them.

Muley kept up a good pace on the hillside. He was in shape and raring to go, so the elevation barely seemed to affect him. As Dusty rode his thoughts were free. *I've got to figure out what to do about this civil case. Once they investigate me and figure out that I only could be linked to one death, are they going to then go after Cassie? Will we be codefendants in the same case? It's going to be all about money, so if they think they can get more with one case, that's the way they'll go.*

He crested the top of the hill. He could see the whole valley with Highway 410 on the bottom. The cars looked small from up there, like little ants. Across the road he could see the old red painted buildings from the Weyerhaeuser sawmill. It seems like only yesterday it was in operation. He remembered taking his son up there on a Boy Scout outing a number of years ago.

Dusty reined Muley around and headed up a particularly steep grade known as "Knee Knocker." The big heavy-muscled horse dug in and stepped up the hill with no hesitation. As the ground flew by and the smell of fir trees and horse sweat hit his nostrils, a familiar calmness settled over him. He knew it was going to be all right.

By the time Dusty got to his trailer, it was dusk. He pulled Muley's tack off and threw a light blanket over his horse. He didn't usually cover his horse. He wanted him tough for the high country. But with the cold mountain air and a sweaty horse, he made an exception.

Driving home, Dusty heard the beep of his phone. *I hate that thing.* He got so many calls at work, he just didn't want to deal with them in his spare time. *Only a few people do have my cell phone number, though*, he hesitated and picked up the phone. Three messages shown on it. Dusty threw it down again. He'd check it when he got home. Scout looked at him questioningly. "It's okay, Boy." Dusty patted his head. The Aussie stretched out on the seat next to him.

As the dark trees flew by, his mind unwittingly returned to Cassie. *Maybe Shelley was right. Maybe it was just a misunderstanding.* Everybody seemed to think so. He smiled, *Maybe she wasn't any better at dating than I am.*

Dusty pulled into his driveway. His yard light shone brightly illuminating the back yard and parking area. He walked into his house through the back door and turned on some lights inside and the porch light. Cheyenne nickered in greeting and hunger from the front pasture. "Hang on, I'm getting there." His big packhorse responded by tucking his head, galloping and bucking up and down the fence line. Scout joined in, running on the other side and barking. Dusty chuckled and walked Muley over.

Once inside the cabin, he put on a pot of coffee. He made a small fire in the fireplace. It was a damp and cool night. Scout immediately lay in front of it and stretched out appreciatively, closing his eyes. The wood stove was his only source of heat besides the big stone fireplace in the living room, so it took a few minutes to get the room warm. His dog apparently didn't need to wait.

Grabbing a steaming cup of coffee, Dusty sat down in his recliner in front of the fireplace. He picked up his cell phone and listened to the messages. The first one was Mrs. Phillips, "Mr. Dustin Rose, you received a call from Mr. Reginald Flynn. He seemed very eager to talk to you, but I did not give him your cell number without your permission." *Good girl, he thought.* He could always depend on Mrs. Phillips. *I don't know Reggie that well, so I don't want any private numbers exchanged at this point.*

Next call. "Hey Boss, I couldn't bring it up in front of Shelley, but I have some more information concerning Buster Stanton." Mike cleared his throat. "I also talked to Terri today. Thought you might want to hear about that. Give me a call."

Dusty stared at the phone thoughtfully. *Maybe that's good.* Seemed kind of stupid to have to always hear things through other people, kind of high schoolish. But maybe that's just where he and Cassie were. He knew alcohol hadn't exactly matured him. He'd heard that you quit maturing when you started drinking. But the good news was once you quit, you catch up a lot quicker. *I've probably got a ways to go yet on that.*

He clicked on the last message. A deep whisky voice came across the phone; he recognized it instantly. "Say, Dusty. This here's Buster Stanton. I went and got me a big Seattle lawyer today. I'm going to sue the shit out of you." He laughed a low gravelly voice. There was a pause and he sounded like he took a drink. "I was doing some thinking about it. This is going to cost us both a bunch of money. Why should we give it all to those God-damn low-life lawyers?" Then he laughed again at his own joke. "How's about we make our own little deal?"

Dusty's mouth dropped open. *How did that slime ball get his cell phone number?*

The message continued, "Oh, don't worry about me having your cell phone number. Money talks." A raucous laugh. "You remember that." The message ended and Dusty was left to stare into the phone slack-jawed. Recovering, he tossed it down like it was hot. He went upstairs to his bedroom and took his Ruger out of the drawer by his bed. Walking downstairs he felt somewhat better. The curtainless windows of his living room now seemed to yawn open. In the past he had never wanted curtains. He didn't want anything to stop the light from entering. With the log interior, it was almost a part of the forest to him. At least growing up and coming over to his then grandpa's house, that's what it had seemed like. Never once had he thought about the openness of his house—until now.

The fact that Buster had his cell phone number made him feel violated. If he had the phone number, what else? Carrying his gun with him, Dusty walked in the kitchen and poured himself another cup of coffee. Scout still lay before the now warm parlor stove. Dusty grabbed a couple more pieces of wood and loaded it in the stove. Dusty sat down at the kitchen table and picked up his landline. He felt more comfortable using that at the moment.

Mike picked up on the first ring. "Hey, Dusty."

"So what's the news on Buster?"

"I checked into his criminal background further. He's a pretty scary guy."

"Do tell." said Dusty, taking a sip of his coffee.

"Oh?" said Mike, picking up the sarcasm in his friend's voice.

"I got a little phone call from him tonight."

Intrigued, Mike asked, "What did he have to say?"

"He wants to talk to me; make some kind of deal without the lawyers." Dusty watched Scout groan and roll over. "Kind of interesting, since I just got served today by his lawyer."

Mike laughed. "That's always a hit when your client hires you and then starts ignoring you on the very first day."

"Stellar, right?" Dusty lowered his voice in a more serious tone, "Mike, how did he get my cell phone number?"

"There's ways, Dusty. And unfortunately, it's just not that hard. The people search sites on the internet, Intelius. All you have to do is buy the information."

Dusty's stomach sank. His beautiful secluded log cabin suddenly felt isolated and alone. "I suppose that includes my address?"

Mike's voice was sympathetic. "Unfortunately."

"Well, I'm not calling him, but I suppose he'll just keep calling, anyway."

"That's how it seems to go with these kind of people."

"Can you stop by the office tomorrow? I'd like to go over your information."

"No problem, Boss. I'll be there first thing in the morning."

"Great." Dusty hung up the phone and decided to check his house and make sure he locked the door. Scout was softly snoring by the woodstove, so it didn't appear anyone was around who didn't belong there.

Later, unable to sleep, Dusty flipped through the channels on his very seldom used television. It occurred to him he forgot to ask Mike what Terri had to say.

Chapter Forty-Six

Dusty actually felt decent as he came through the door of his office. Mrs. Phillips greeted him and he knew she didn't miss his elevated mood, in contrast from the day before.

"How was your ride, Mr. Dustin Rose?"

"Just what the doctor ordered," he said jovially.

"Good," she said.

"Thank you for not giving out my cell phone number to Raleigh Higganbotham. I actually don't ever want it given out, for what good that does."

"Of course not." She frowned, cocked her head and looked at him quizzically.

"Buster was able to get it. He left a message right after yours."

"Really?" she gasped. "What a world we live in."

"Money talks. I wonder what Raleigh would think of that? His client calling me on my private cell phone. Maybe I'll call him and find out." He went into his office and closed the door, leaving Mrs. Phillips shaking her head.

Dusty picked up the notice of appearance he'd received yesterday. He dialed Raleigh's number. The receptionist put him right though.

"Dusty Rose, what can I do for you?" he boomed magnanimously. Then he hesitated, "You don't have a lawyer yet, do you?"

"No, Raleigh, you're fine. I wouldn't be calling you if I did."

High Hunt

"Oh, good." The Seattle attorney's voice relaxed.

Dusty decided not to beat around the bush. "Your client called me on my private cell phone last night."

"What?" said Raleigh, incredulous.

"I thought you'd want to know."

"I do. And thank you. It would seem that Mr. Stanton and I need to have a little discussion about what the word *represent* means."

"Apparently he thought it was cheaper to move forward without you."

"Indeed," said Raleigh. Then abruptly, "I'd better have this conversation with my client, not you. Then I can see if I still have a client." And as an afterthought, he added, "Thank you, Dusty. And I'm sorry about your private phone. I'll talk to him about that."

"Thanks, Raleigh. You'll be the first to know when I find a lawyer."

"Perfect." Dusty heard the dead line in the background.

He turned back to the ever present pile of paperwork on his desk. The little bit he'd done yesterday was already buried by the new mail. It never ended. Even the snowstorm in the Pasayten was looking pretty good right now. Thoughts of the snowstorm turned his thoughts back to Cassie. He sighed, turning a page on a report. He knew that he would never think of hypothermia in the same way since that pack trip.

Dusty wasn't sure how long he'd been working, but the office door jingled and he could hear Mrs. Phillips in the front office. Pausing, Dusty could hear footsteps. His office door opened and Mike walked in carrying a large folder in his hands.

"Here's the complete criminal record on Buster Stanton," he said, handing it over to Dusty.

Dusty immediately pulled the paperwork out and began pouring over it.

Mike added, "When I think of their family, for some reason, the term *nest* comes to mind."

Skimming through the paperwork, there was crime after crime

with the family members. It started with their parents' parents and made its way through the kids and cousins. *It wasn't usually that lucrative to do the kind of crimes this family did. Clem must have come up with some cash somewhere along the line.* Dusty considered the report. *I wonder what the payout had been on his last job? I know he didn't have to share any with Tom Flannigan, his sidekick. Tom went immediately into the state pen. Tom had so many felonies, it was a no-brainer to take a plea, rather than risk life imprisonment.*

"I hope his lawyer can talk some sense into him," said Dusty, finally.

"Yeah," agreed Mike. "By the way, have you gotten one yet?"

"Not yet. Reggie's working on it for me. It's going to be a mess, no matter how you look at it."

"For sure." Mike sat back in his chair.

"Does she know?"

"Not yet. Or I guess, as far as I know," corrected Mike. "I haven't said a thing to Terri, just in case."

"Wise move." The conversation drifting toward Cassie again caused him an unexpected pain in his stomach. He finally couldn't help himself. "So what did Terri have to say? You never told me." Dusty picked up his coffee cup and straightened the papers on his desk. He didn't want to appear that it mattered as much as it did.

Mike's face broke into a faint grin. He knew Dusty too well. "Terri and Cassie had a little conversation after they left the grange hall. Cassie thought the worst and Terri told her what she'd seen." Mike yawned and took his time finishing.

Dusty couldn't help himself from staring at Mike, willing him to finish. Finally, he couldn't take it anymore. "And?" he said pointedly.

"According to Terri, by the end of the ride Cassie realized she had made a big mistake."

"Why didn't she come back?" asked Dusty, dismayed.

"Really?" Mike looked at Dusty. "After walking out of there on the big first date, is she really going to go back?"

"I…guess not," Dusty said slowly.

"Yeah," Mike said with emphasis. "Terri even said she thought Cassie was crying when she ran into her house."

Dusty was speechless. *Cassie crying? I would have never thought that.*

Mike stood up. "Well, Boss, I better head out. If there's anything else you need, let me know."

"Okay," Dusty answered, dazed. "I will."

Dusty stared at the door for a while after Mike left. What should I do? *This is so awkward. I've got to tell her about the lawsuit, though. She's going to need a really good attorney, or it's possible she could lose everything she has in the outcome.*

He reached for the phone. As he listened to it ring, suddenly a huge commotion broke out in the front office. He could hear Mrs. Phillips shouting and he dropped it back into the receiver.

Chapter Forty-Seven

"I want my lawyer!" Came an anguished cry. "I need to see him now!"

"Young lady, you need to just settle down. Mr. Dustin Rose takes appointments, not drop-ins."

Dusty stepped in the front office. The statuesque woman stood dabbing at her eyes. Her cheeks were turning dark with running mascara.

"Dusty," she cried, ignoring the now-standing Mrs. Phillips. She dashed over to him and threw herself into his arms.

He felt helpless as Cindy hung unto him and sobbed uncontrollably. "You need to just calm down. It's going to be okay," he soothed, in a combination of patting her on the back and trying to put some space between them.

The tall dark-haired beauty would have none of it and she clutched tighter. Finally, in a hiccupping voice, "He...he went nuts. Somebody told him about the...the Backcountry Horsemen meeting and....and...about us." She bent her head, crying softly. Dusty felt like he was on a sinking ship. *Eagleclaw is not that big of a community. I'm doomed.*

"Mrs. Phillips, can you please get her some Kleenex? You need to calm down, Cindy." Dusty firmly, but gently, removed her arms from around him. He turned and resignedly walked toward his office. "Come on back and let's get the process going."

Dusty had the paperwork finished and Cindy had finally

regained her composure as she signed the restraining order. "You need to remove yourself from your joint residence, immediately. This restrains him from being within a thousand feet of you. He can't do that if you're living together."

"I...I don't have anywhere to go." She looked at him demurely under her streaked mascara eyelids. "Unless maybe I could come and stay with you?" She smiled at him hopefully. "It would only be for a little while."

Oh, no, here we go." I'm sorry, but that would be impossible." The finality with which he said *impossible* shocked even him. Cindy sat back in her chair, surprise etched across her face.

Before she could try anything else, Dusty stood up and stacked his files. "I've got another appointment, so if you don't mind, I'll walk you out." Before Cindy could speak, Dusty was out the door pulling his coat from the coat rack.

"I'll be back this afternoon, Mrs. Phillips," he said, holding the door open for Cindy.

"Have a good lunch, Mr. Dustin Rose."

The sky was full of gray swollen clouds and it looked like rain any minute. Dusty and Cindy walked the few steps out of his office. She stopped at her car, "Dusty," she said, grabbing his arm. "I'm so thankful for everything you've done for me..."

Dusty wasn't sure what caused him to look up at that precise moment, but he did. And to his horror, he saw Cassie a few feet away from them, her face a mask of revulsion.

"I've got to go," he said hastily to Cindy, turning out from under her grasp. Before she could say a word, he was walking toward Cassie at a fast clip.

Catching up to her, he said, "Hey, I wanted to talk to you."

"You son of a..." Not finishing the sentence, she threw a small bunch of flowers at him and ran to her truck. Dusty saw the flowers hit the sidewalk. He felt his chest clench painfully.

This was getting to be more and more of a bad dream. Heat rose up his spine to the back of his neck. *I know I'm not very good at dating, but this is ridiculous. She has to at least talk to me.* He watched as she jumped into her vehicle and sped off. Then he ran to his own truck parked behind his office. He roared through Main Street of Eagleclaw in hot pursuit of Cassie. *If people were watching the scene, let them.* He pushed his foot harder on the gas.

Cassie gripped the wheel of her truck. Terri had called her again after talking to Mike. The only thing she wanted to do was apologize for the misunderstanding. *That arrogant ass. She had been right from the moment she saw him in the trial in downtown King County. He's just a womanizer.* Cassie was so angry. The betrayal cut through her like a knife. *I was right the first time. What is wrong with me?* She was too wound up to go back to the office. She turned down the road to go home.

As she neared her ranch, she noticed in the rearview mirror a pickup truck. He was driving like a bat out of hell. *What the heck?* Turning into her driveway, she got a side view of the rig—Dusty Rose. The anger was white hot as it poured through her, *Wasn't one woman enough for this cad?*

Sammy barked in greeting as she got out of the truck. She stopped barking and looked quizzically at the pickup coming to a screech behind Cassie's. Dusty bailed out and walked towards her. "I want to talk to you," he began, forcefully.

Cassie stood imperiously with her arms folded across her chest. Her light blue eyes glinted. Dusty faltered for a minute, "I—"

"There's nothing to say. I saw everything I needed to see."

"No, you didn't." Indignation welled up inside of him. "You saw me saying good-bye to a client. That's all you saw."

"Oh, Dusty," she said disparagingly, "You really expect me to believe that? I think it's pretty obvious to me and the rest of Eagleclaw," she added with emphasis.

He closed the distance between them in a couple of steps. Standing inches away from her, he said, "I'm not interested in any other woman. You have to know that." Dusty shocked himself with the force of his own words. "Cassie, I've never met anyone like you in my life. If I can't be with you, then I'm done."

Confusion passed over her face. Whatever Cassie had been about to say never came out. Dusty took her hesitation as a good sign. He pulled her into his arms and kissed her deeply. When she kissed him back, he picked her up and carried her into the house.

Dusty lay on his back, Cassie was on his chest breathing evenly. He thought about the last few days. *Talk about highs and lows.* If he'd gotten any work done lately, he'd surely forgotten what it was. *I need to get back to the office and talk to Reggie. We're going to need two lawyers now, at least co-counsel for the case.* Dusty put his hands behind his head and stared at the ceiling thoughtfully. It was better to be ready ahead of time, rather than just be served. Cassie was going to be involved, that was a given. He gently moved Cassie, set her carefully on the bed and then got up.

When he came out of the bathroom, Cassie was sitting up. She had her bathrobe on. Dusty was buttoning the sleeves of his shirt. She looked at him quizzically.

"I need to talk to you about something." He sat down on the bed next to her. "I got a notice of appearance from a Buster Stanton." He paused. "Does the name ring a bell?"

She frowned. "No, not off the top of my head."

"Well, it will. His son was Clem Stanton, formerly of the Pasayten."

"Notice for appearing in what?"

"A civil action in the wrongful death of Clem and his son, Pinto."

"Oh, no, Dusty," she said, understanding spreading across her face.

"Apparently they think I'm responsible for both deaths. I haven't done anything to try to straighten them out one way or the other." He touched her face. "But they're going to figure it out."

"I'm sure they will," she agreed quietly.

"I put in a call to Reggie. He's supposed to get us lined up with some good attorneys. I better go back to the office and see what he's found."

"Yeah, I guess so."

He leaned over and kissed her. "I'll call you later. Maybe we could go get something to eat," he suggested. Then added. "That is, if we can get along."

Cassie smiled crookedly at him. It was the smile he'd thought about all through the Pasayten. "Well, that just depends if you can keep your hands off all the other women long enough to go out to eat."

Dusty hesitated. "That's kind of asking a lot, isn't it?" Then he turned and ran down the stairs, narrowly avoiding the pillow being launched out of the bedroom. He called over his shoulder. "I'll call you later," and he was out the door.

Driving back through town Dusty made it a point not to have eye contact with any of the curious onlookers. It was a small town, and not every day did two trucks race through the middle of it. Carefully going the speed limit, he parked his car behind the office and went in.

Mrs. Phillips asked cautiously, "Is everything okay, Mr. Dustin Rose?"

He frowned a little at her like he didn't know what she was talking about and said, "Couldn't be better." He stopped at her desk, "Did I receive any calls while I was out?"

"Reginald Flynn called."

"Perfect. Thank you, Mrs. Phillips."

Chapter Forty-Eight

"Any luck finding anybody?" Dusty asked as soon as Reggie picked up.

"As a matter of fact, yes. It just took me a while because he's really busy and he's been out of town. His name is Bill Grisham. I thought you guys would get along really well. He rides horses. He comes from a big cattle ranching family in Wyoming."

"I like this guy already."

"Yeah." Reggie warmed to his topic. "He calls them the way he sees them and doesn't take any garbage." He chuckled. "He's not real popular because of it." Reggie paused. "That, and he wins a lot."

"Not too busy for my case, I hope?"

"I talked to him. He can get you in, so no worries," Reggie assured him.

"What about Cassie?" Dusty asked. "We need someone for her too."

"I talked to him about that. He's got another lawyer he works with that could probably do it. His partner is actually a long-time attorney. They have got offices in Spokane, Moses Lake and Seattle. His name is Garth Danner. Bill talked to Garth, and they felt it was kind of a humanitarian thing with two lawyers being sued." Reggie chuckled. "By the way, Bill said growing up in cattle country, the shooting made total sense to him."

"I'm feeling better about this all the time," said Dusty.

"Besides, it's probably going to be less expensive to have two lawyers in the same firm.

They could share the load."

"That would be great," said Dusty. "We don't want cheap work. It's just kind of hard paying somebody a ton of money for something that you could do yourself."

"True, but remember that old adage: A lawyer who represents himself has a fool for a client," Reggie cautioned.

"Yes, I believe I've heard that plenty of times from my dad." Dusty settled back in his chair. "That's actually why I called you in the first place."

"Good man." Reggie rustled through some papers. "I've got his phone number right here." He rattled it off and Dusty wrote it down.

"Thanks a lot, Reggie. I really appreciate it."

"I told you before, Dusty, you haven't seen the last of me. I want to learn how to packhorses and you're going to help me."

"Any time."

They hung up and Dusty dialed the number of his new lawyer. *What a weird feeling.* He was able to get an appointment the next day for both of them. Hopefully Cassie could make it. He wasn't sure how her schedule was, but this was pretty high priority. And as luck would have it, Bill and Garth both had a matter in King County in the morning they had to appear in. Dusty was considering the meeting when the office bell jingled. Almost simultaneously the door to his office opened and Mike walked in.

"Please, feel free to walk right in," said Dusty, sarcastically.

"I came to find out where the fire was. I mean, when two pickups go screaming through downtown Eagleclaw, you figure there has got to be a fire. There's just no other explanation for it," concluded Mike.

"Is that so?" said Dusty innocently.

"Fill me in, Boss." Mike sat down across from him and focused his brown eyes on Dusty intently.

In spite of himself, Dusty could feel a shot of heat up his back. "Cassie and I just had, um, a little discussion. "He nervously picked up the files on his desk and straightened them.

"Oh," said Mike knowingly. "Anything to do with the discussion you had last night?"

"Might have had a little bit to do with that," relented Dusty, hoping that would end the line of questioning.

"Uh-huh," Mike grunted and continued to look at Dusty.

"Nothing else to it." said Dusty. "We're good." Then he paused and added, "I think."

Dusty sat back in his chair, "Oh, and by the way, I've got an appointment in downtown Seattle tomorrow on the 74th Floor of the Columbia Center. Danner & Grisham."

"Really?" Mike marveled. "Kind of top dollar, huh?"

"It's not every day you get a civil suit for wrongful death dropped on your doorstep. I figured I better get it taken care of right away."

Mike stood. "That ought to do it. If you need anything at all, let me know. I'm always happy to help."

"Thanks, Mike," Dusty said sincerely. "I really appreciate it."

He watched as his friend left the office. Turning back to his files, he tried not to think about the next day.

Traffic was the usual long snake of stop-and-go. Dusty and Cassie sat in his pickup truck. The sea of taillights blinked bright red in unison, then a pause, no taillights, and then the sea of red.

"What time did you say our appointment was?" Cassie asked.

"2 p.m. I figured if we left by 11 in the morning, we should be almost bulletproof."

"Yeah, well, it's Seattle. There's no guarantees. Ever." She flipped her hair back and stared out the window disgusted.

"I always hope for the best and prepare for the worst."

"Good policy," agreed Cassie.

The short jaunt from Eagleclaw to Seattle was going to take every bit of two hours by the way the traffic was going. And then parking after that. Dusty wished he was in the wilderness somewhere with his horses about now. He glanced over at Cassie. *It would be good if she came too.* He smiled. *Maybe with just the two of us out there it will cut down on some of the jealousy.* He could only hope.

The car behind him honked. It startled him and he slammed on the brakes to avoid hitting the person in front of him.

In true Seattle style the gray skies began with a mist and ended up in a torrential downpour as they swung around the corner from Renton and began the home stretch to downtown. Although it was late morning, it appeared almost evening with the dark clouds. Dusty's wipers were working full blast and it barely kept the windows clear. He turned on his defogger. The extreme moisture on the outside of the windows was fogging up the inside. *I hate this.* The weather only intensified his distaste for the meeting they were about to have.

Luckily, they found an opening in one of the parking spaces across the street from the big black Columbia Center. Going five stories below it into the cavernous parking garage with the extremely low ceilings made Dusty feel claustrophobic. He'd take the open area across the street anytime.

Dodging large puddles and water-spraying cars, they negotiated their way across the street. Dusty held Cassie's hand protectively. He was wearing his suit and raincoat. He wished he had an umbrella. Cassie also was dressed professionally. Her knee-high brown leather boots and tan raincoat had been a good choice. As they entered the Columbia Center, the reflection in the dark window surprised Dusty. They looked like downtown business people. *Looks are deceiving. If people only knew the reason they were there and where it happened. Horse packing deep in the Pasayten Wilderness.* He chuckled to himself.

Cassie looked up at him. "What?"

He opened the door for her. "Oh, just thinking about what brought us here. Such a contrast."

She smiled. "I'll say."

Dusty glanced at his watch. "We've got about an hour. You want to get something to eat first?"

"Good idea."

The bottom two floors of the Columbia Center was full of fast food restaurants.

"Thai food?" asked Cassie.

"Sure, I'll give it try," said Dusty.

Chapter Forty-Nine

Dusty lost his stomach, as always, as the elevator hurtled skyward. As his stomach felt light, he wished he hadn't eaten.

Cassie looked at him with concern. "Are you okay?"

"Yeah." His cheeks burned. "I...a...it's just a heights things." He looked away quickly.

Her eyes crinkled in a smile. "You're kidding, right? I mean, you ride Muley everywhere."

Dusty replied quickly. "That's different. He doesn't want to fall off any more than I do. This is a machine."

She squeezed his hand. "You're such a cowboy."

He smiled down at her. "Mountain Cowboy."

The doors opened and they got out and transferred to the next set of elevators to take them to the 74th floor. *My favorite part.* He quietly followed Cassie on, willing himself to be calm. The ensuing ride was surprisingly quick. The monotone voice announced the 74th floor and out he bounded, into the bright office lights and streaming sights of downtown Seattle all around them. Even the still pounding rain on the windows did little to diminish the awe-inspiring views.

The receptionist greeted them. "Mr. Grisham will be with you in a few minutes."

They sat in the plush conference room. Dusty immediately noticed Ranch & Home Magazine on the coffee table. *Reggie was right. This guy sounded like he was going to be okay.*

The attorney walked out a few minutes later. Dusty noticed that besides wearing slacks, a dress shirt and tie, he was wearing cowboy boots. He had blonde hair and intelligent blue eyes. He walked directly up to Dusty and Cassie. "Hi, I'm Bill. Nice to meet you." The attorney looked directly into his eyes and his firm grasp said he meant it.

"Thanks for seeing us on such short notice."

"No problem. Glad I could help." Bill then turned to Cassie and shook her hand. "I understand you're a lawyer as well?"

"Yes," she said simply.

"Well, come on back to the conference room. Let's see what we can do." He turned and Dusty and Cassie followed him down the long hallway. Downtown Seattle gleamed through a bank of windows on one side—western art on the other.

The conference room had a long table with Elliott Bay clearly visible from the windows at the end. "Garth should be in here in just a few minutes. He was finishing up a call."

Bill had no sooner said it than a man in his late 50s hurried into the conference room. He was heavyset and his head was shaved. "Hey, good to meet you guys." He set his file down on the table. The smell of Brute aftershave filled the room. "Bill talked to me about this. Sounds like the earlier the strategy, the better."

After discussing the case at length, Garth made a decision. "Due to your professional standing we can get it set before the regular motions calendar starts." Realizing he still had his earbuds in, Garth took them out and laid them on the table. "I'm going to get ahold of the police report and give Raleigh a call this afternoon. Might as well get this case out in the open. The big man smiled at Cassie. It's a pretty dark day when the defendant has to let the plaintiff know who to sue.

Cassie watched him intently. She flinched when he said "sue."

Garth didn't miss it, "Don't worry, this is going to be over before it gets started," he said gently, beaming like a giant Mr. Clean.

"That's a good idea, Garth," agreed Bill. "Once we've got the appearance out of the way, we can start to plan our timelines."

Dusty was impressed. The two attorneys worked well as a team. And he liked them. He felt a lot more optimistic.

"I think this is going to work out okay," said Cassie on the elevator as they plummeted earthward.

Dusty squeezed her hand. "I do too." He had managed to keep a professional distance from her in the conference room, but anywhere else he had a hard time staying away. *Crazy. It's like she's a magnet to me—but in a good way.*

"What?" Cassie looked at him puzzled.

"Oh, nothing. Just thinking it is all going to work out." The elevator doors opened and they evacuated with the crowd into the crush of humanity. "You want to get dinner? I think we are going to be in the midst of rush hour traffic now."

"Sounds good," she agreed. "How about the waterfront?"

"Lead the way," he gestured gallantly.

Friday came quickly. Dusty again found himself driving to Seattle with Cassie next to him in the truck. He sighed. At least it wasn't raining this time.

"They gave us a 1:30 setting. We will avoid the morning rush that way." Cassie said, trying to be optimistic.

"That's something," said Dusty.

"Well, it could be worse. It's Friday. At least the Seahawks aren't playing in Seattle tonight," said Cassie.

"I'll be glad when they're paying us to appear in court, instead of the other way around," said Dusty.

"Me too," agreed Cassie glumly.

They drove the rest of the way to Seattle in silence. The sun was breaking through the clouds as they looked for parking opposite the courthouse. Usually Dusty got pretty lucky on finding spots around the old courthouse building—but not today. They parked four blocks away and hurried down the sidewalk. Dusty glanced at his watch. 1:10. With any luck at all, they could make it through security and into the courtroom just in time. He had to check himself. He was just the client this time.

Bill and Garth were waiting outside the courtroom as they arrived. Bill wore a navy suit and light green tie with blue stripes, accenting the blue in his eyes. Cassie smiled at him approvingly. Garth was on his phone with an ear piece in. He smiled at them and nodded. Bill waved him off. "He's always on that thing. Let's go in. He'll catch up."

They followed the lawyer through the doors. The courtroom was moderately busy with Friday afternoon motions. Various attorneys sat in last-minute conferences with their clients. The clerk and court reporter were already seated, so the judge was going to be out any minute.

"This is going to be painless," assured Bill. "As you know."

Dusty nodded. He really didn't know. He'd never been a client before. The more he thought about it, the more he liked being the lawyer in situations like this.

Garth hurried into the courtroom and slid in next to Cassie. He smiled at her appreciatively. Dusty felt a slight tick in his cheek. *Let's just get going.* He sighed and looked down at the floor.

"All rise," the clerk called. The black-robed judge walked in and sat down at the bench. He was a middle-aged man with glasses. He glanced carefully at the docket.

"I see we have kind of an unusual case," he stated. "I'll call that one first and try to get these lawyers out of my courtroom and back to work. Stanton v. Rose and Martin."

For the first time Dusty saw Raleigh Higganbotham and his client. Raleigh was medium built, with an expensive suit, Dusty noted, as they exchanged a slight nod of recognition. Buster, seated at counsel table, was somewhat cleaned up. At least Dusty couldn't smell him from where he sat. The diminutive little man had a pronounced hump across his shoulders. His hair was slicked back and he had on an ill-fitting suit jacket. He and his counsel were seated in the front of the courtroom on one side, with Dusty, Cassie and their counsel on the other side.

"So we are here for a civil action in a wrongful death case?" The judge asked, looking at Raleigh.

"That's correct, Your Honor. My client, Buster Stanton, is suing on behalf of the estate of his brother, Clem Stanton and his nephew, Edward Stanton, also known as Pinto, for his loss."

"So let me just clarify. You are suing Ms. Martin on behalf of the estate of your brother, Clem Stanton, and you are suing Mr. Dustin Rose on behalf of the estate of your nephew, Edward Stanton." The judge looked directly at Raleigh.

"That's correct, Your Honor." Raleigh nodded his head emphatically.

"And Misters Grisham and Danner, what say you?" The judge turned to Dusty's table.

Bill stood. "I am here representing Dustin Rose. At this time we would like to file our motion to dismiss." Bill Grisham walked up and handed the clerk several papers. Then stepped back and added, "In addition, Your Honor, at this time we would like to present to the court our counterclaims for harassment, libel and slander. We would make a motion for setting an expedited summary judgment hearing for Mr. Rose, as this case is wholly without merit and is a highly burdensome imposition on his very busy law practice. And as Your Honor can see, he has taken time to personally appear to show his earnestness and desire to expeditiously resolve this matter." With that, Bill handed the second stack of papers to the clerk and sat down next to Dusty at counsel table.

Garth stood up.

"Mr. Danner?"

"I am representing Cassandra Martin. We are joining with Mr. Grisham in the motion to dismiss, the counterclaims and motion for an expedited setting for summary judgment motion."

"Mr. Higganbotham," said the Judge, "Your response?"

Raleigh stood up. "Your Honor, I was served just before the close of business last night with the paperwork. I haven't had time to review it, let alone prepare argument." The thin attorney gestured theatrically at Cassie, "In fact, we weren't even aware of Ms. Martin being a party until late yesterday afternoon."

"I see," said the judge. "So you would like some time to mull this over, I take it?"

"Yes, Your Honor."

"Granted. Talk to each other and set an expedited date for summary judgment." Addressing both sides, "Anything else today?"

"That should do it," said Bill.

"No, Your Honor," Garth chimed in.

The judge smiled, "Have a good day, gentlemen." And turning to Cassie, "and lady."

"Thank you," she said under her breath as she left.

Hearing the next matter being called in the background as she walked out the door, Cassie didn't even see Buster until she just about ran into him. He had planted himself in her path. The smell up close was unmistakable, even though she had only heard it described. He was a man in his early 60s. He had shoulder-length hair, which was slicked straight back. The hair grease he'd used didn't appear to be clean. The blue suit jacket was rumpled and strained to fit over his stooped shoulders.

She was unable to take her eyes off his face. It seemed to transform before her. His features melted and he bared his yellow teeth. His eyes became reptilian slits. He looked more snake than man. "It was you, you worthless whore. You took my brother away from me," he spat out. The fowl breath that followed made Cassie gag involuntarily, but still, she couldn't pull her eyes away from his face. He looked more like a little demon. He hissed, "You'll pay for this, bitch. You'll payyyyyy…"

Suddenly Cassie felt a strong arm close around her and pull her away from the evil tirade. Dusty whisked her down the court hallway. "D…did…did you see that?" She finally managed to get out.

"I saw him, the sicko. I always wondered where Pinto got that ugly face from," said Dusty. "You weren't supposed to talk to him. You know that."

"I know. But seriously?" Cassie stopped flat in the hallway. "He blocked my way out the door." She felt indignation raise up in her throat.

"Cassie, I'm sorry. That's all I saw," soothed Dusty. "I was talking to Bill."

"Okay." Her shoulders dropped in defeat.

"Let's just get out of the city. Two out of three days is too much," said Dusty.

"I agree."

"You want to ride tomorrow?" Dusty asked, hoping to change the subject onto a happier note.

"What time and where?" she asked.

"Let's do Buck Creek," said Dusty. "It's close. We may hit some snow, so be ready."

She smiled back at him. "Oh, I think I can handle it."

"Yeah, I guess you can." Shades of hypothermia and sleeping bags passed through his mind. He took her hand and they hurried across the street to his truck.

Chapter Fifty

Dusty pulled up to Cassie's house early the next morning. He had Muley in the trailer and Scout next to him. Sammy barked and ran alongside as they pulled into the driveway. Cassie was standing holding Prince, already saddled. She had her boots and coat on and her saddlebags nearby ready to go.

As Dusty opened the trailer door, she loaded her horse. "Glad you have the dividers," she commented, as Muley laid his ears back.

"Yeah," said Dusty ruefully. "Sorry about that. He's always a little alpha."

"No problem. Better than a wimp." Cassie tossed her stuff into the back seat and opened the front door. Scout stared at her, not giving up his seat by Dusty.

Dusty swung in the door. "Aren't you bringing Sammy?"

"Well, sure, I'd like to," she said hesitatingly.

"No problem." He smiled his white-toothed smile. "Scout, in the back." Amazingly, Scout obeyed. "Just put her in next to him. Don't worry. He'll be a gentleman."

Sure enough, Scout left room for Sammy. As she bounded into the truck, he greeted her like an old friend.

"That's quite a dog you've got," Cassie said, impressed.

"Best dog I've ever had."

They drove up to the parking area of Buck Creek. The small

farms and thickening of fir trees was comforting. Dusty felt the stress of Seattle and the courtroom drama slip down his back. They passed some sections of logged-out areas along the road and then the forest became tighter and green as the little two-lane highway wound its way up to Mount Rainier. Dusty glanced over at Cassie. She was silent gazing out the window with her little smile, the corners of her lips barely turned up on the sides. He reached over and squeezed her hand.

"What?" she said. But it was more of a statement than a question. She knew. Dusty felt his heart swell. *This was as good as it gets. I waited a long time to meet this woman.*

The parking lot held a few pickup trucks.

"It's modern rifle hunting season," said Dusty. "Neither one of our horses is brown, so that ought to help."

"I've got my orange vest. I figured better safe than sorry," said Cassie, as she pulled it out of the back.

The early morning sky was turning from gray to blue. It looked like it was going to be a beautiful late fall day. Dusty was thankful for that. He knew there was no control of the weather up here, but after the extreme temperatures he'd been in, crisp and sunny would be a pleasant change.

Cassie swung into the saddle on her big gray. She was dressed for the weather with a heavy coat, turtleneck, Sorel boots and her cowboy hat. Prince danced, eager to get going in the cold weather.

Dusty got on Muley and they headed out. "Let's go up to Ranger Creek," he suggested. "We can have lunch up at the shelter on top."

"Sounds good. I haven't been up there in ages," said Cassie.

Muley was walking out, and puffs of steam came from his nostrils. The fir trees were pungent. The smell of horse sweat, fir and fresh dirt made Dusty feel light for the first time in days.

Wherever the hunters were, they must not be seeing any animals. The only sounds were the hooves and jingles from their bridles and his spurs. The trail started low and began to climb in switchbacks. They paused for the horses occasionally. Scout and Sammy would stop with them, puffing, little wisps of steams rising from the dogs' bodies. As they began again, Dusty smiled watching the two Aussies. They would vary from trailing behind their owners, to both running in front. On occasion they were side-by-side on the trail, so close they touched. He glanced back and saw Cassie watching them, smiling.

They arrived at the wooden shelter in a couple of hours. Both the horses walked at a good clip, in spite of the altitude gain. Tying the horses up in the trees next to it, Dusty walked over to the enclosure. It was a three-sided shelter, open in the front. As far as Dusty was concerned, these things were just a good place to gather mice and bugs. He would never, by choice, sleep in one. The fire ring was in front, but just outside of the roof, so the smoke wouldn't fill the inside. Someone had left a few sticks of firewood next to the rock ring. Dusty set his lunch down and walked around picking up twigs.

As he bent down, the hair on the back of his neck stood up. Automatically he glanced down at Scout. His Aussie was looking past him. Sammy ran up to Scout and he turned to follow her. Dusty had gotten an armful of small sticks for the fire. He shook his head. He knew he was getting way too sensitive lately. Throwing the pile down by the ring, he squatted to start a fire.

Cassie walked up and put her lunch down. "A fire for lunch?" she asked, pleased.

"I figured it was a little nippy out today."

"I'd take a fire anytime."

"A woman after my own heart," he said. *Boy, was she!* He threw some more twigs on the fire. They snapped red and hot. Loading it up a stick at a time, the fire was blazing in no time. He sat down next to Cassie as they ate their sandwiches. Their dogs lay enjoying the fire by their feet. Dusty felt punch drunk with the proximity of Cassie, the warmth of the fire and caress of the fragrant outdoors. Then a shot whizzed by.

Dusty paused, stunned. At first he wondered if he imagined it.

Scout howled and ran for cover. He hated gunfire of any kind. Sammy began to bark.

Cassie had hesitated after the first gunshot, but on the second one she dropped down. At first Dusty wasn't sure if she was hit. He leaned over and grabbed her. "Are you okay?" he asked urgently.

"Yes. Let's get out of here."

Together they half crouched and half ran around to the side of the shelter. Dusty put himself between Cassie and the bullets. As they reached the side, a couple more pinged off the old logs.

As they tried to make sense of the attack, a voice roared from behind the trees.

"I ain't waitin' for the law. You kil't my kin, and now you's gonna die."

Not again. Shades of Roy and the gunfight at Cougar Lake flitted through Dusty's mind.

Cassie pulled her .38 Firestorm semi-automatic out of her holster.

"Just hold on for a second," Dusty said, pulling his Vaquero out of his belt. "Stay back here." Not waiting for an answer, he crouched along the wall, trying to get a location of Buster. The horses were restless after the first shot. Muley was straining at his tie. Prince was dancing around. Scout was nowhere to be seen, and Dusty knew he was hiding. *I only hope I can find him again.*

As Dusty neared the end of the logs, he felt warm breath on his leg. Looking down, Sammy smiled up at him. Stooping down, he carefully grabbed her collar and led her back to Cassie. "You better hang onto her. She's not afraid of bullets."

Alarmed, Cassie grabbed her dog, "No, I've shot too many times around her, I guess." She stroked Sammy to calm herself down as much as her dog.

"Stay here. I'm going to try to get a shot at him. If not that, at least a location. We can't stay in the open like sitting ducks. He could be anywhere."

As Dusty turned to go, Cassie put a light arm on him. "Be careful. I'll cover you."

Looking around the edge of the shelter, the fire danced in the ring. The trees were thick and he couldn't make out anybody. As he scanned the area, a shot split the wood next to his head. His ears rang. "Damn, that was close," he uttered involuntarily. It must have been louder than he thought.

A crazy laugh sounded from behind the trees on his right. "Gonna get closer all the time, you murderers!"

As Dusty pulled back, four more shots rang out. Two hit the wood and the others ricocheted off the small boulders next to him. The horses panicked. Muley sat down on his rope and broke his halter. He got up and bolted through the woods. Prince, not willing to be left behind, whinnied and, with enormous strength, broke his lead and galloped in pursuit of Muley.

Dusty watched with mixed emotions. He didn't want his horse to leave him, but he didn't want him to stay and get shot. *That's the toughest horse I've ever had.* He turned back to Buster.

It was hard to see, but looking intently where the shots had come from, Dusty could see a green parka. By the sounds of it, Buster was alone. He had to get around to the back side of him and hopefully get his gun.

"Cassie, can you cover me while I go around the back of him?"

She inched her way along the side. "Sure."

"I don't know how many bullets he's got, but it sounds like a lot, so be careful."

"Don't worry about me," she said.

"I will," Dusty said forcefully. He surprised himself by how much he meant it. Turning back to the corner, he tried one more time, "Buster, there's better ways to settle this than gunfire."

The crazy laugh came again from the green parka. "Sure, there is. Just hand the girl over." More shots rang against the shelter. Dusty gestured at Cassie and passed by her. She returned the gunfire, Sammy at her feet. Dusty dropped down and headed out the back of the shelter, slipping into the trees. The greenery was disorienting, but Dusty was able to find his way by the sounds of the gunfire at first. Then everything became quiet. Coming up from the back, he caught sight of the green parka again and slowly inched his way up on his stomach. It was uneven terrain and damp. By the time he got behind the parka, he was soaked and dirty. That was the least of his worries. When he got in clear view of the parka, he saw it hung out on a log with sticks propping it up. Buster was gone. His stomach turned cold. He'd left Cassie alone.

Chapter Fifty-One

Dusty ran as fast as he could. He heard the dog snarling before he saw her. As he rounded the corner of the shelter, the misshapen little man was leveling a gun at Cassie. "Drop it." He snarled, gesturing at her gun. As Cassie hesitated, an airborne ball of wet fur snarled its way toward Buster. He turned his gun toward the dog and Dusty plowed into the side of him, knocking him down. Buster's shot rang harmlessly into the ground.

"Sammy," she cried. Running over, she threw her arms around her dog.

Dusty grabbed Buster's gun and threw it away. The older man stopped fighting. He appeared to have all the wind knocked out of him. Dusty frisked him and found two boxes of ammo and a large hunting knife. Buster glared at him, his eyes slits and his yellow teeth exposed. Shades of Pinto went through Dusty's mind.

Cassie walked over to where the horses had been tied and reappeared with what was left of the lead ropes still tied to the trees. "I had to cut if off, it was pulled so tight around the tree. I think you'll still have enough to do the job."

Dusty tied Buster's hands together. "This works."

Once restrained, the old man began to cry. This was almost worse than the shooting. Dusty felt pity for Buster, watching the tears pour out and the yellow teeth contort. A body-racking sob shook him. "Th…they…they was all I had," he wailed.

"I'm truly sorry for you, sir. It's a terrible loss." Dusty stood up and brushed off. *Maybe he should have brought them up a little better. Abduction and rape wasn't a real good future plan.*

Cassie stood next to him, silently watching. Sammy, now quiet, sat at her feet.

"You ready for a walk?" asked Dusty.

"Sure. Let me just put out this fire real quick," she said, and threw dirt on it. "I hope we've got horses down at the trailer."

"So do I." Dusty got behind Buster and gestured when she had finished. "Lead on."

"So what happened to your animals?" Mike prompted. Dusty, Mike and Shelley sat in Maude's Mountain Café. Their eyes were riveted on Dusty. He paused and took a drink of coffee.

"Were the horses at the trailer?" urged Shelley, unable to contain herself.

"Weee'l," Dusty teased.

She pushed his arm, her big bracelets rattling. "Come on, Dusty, what happened?"

"Luckily, it wasn't that far back to the trailer. We made pretty good time and didn't even get any snowflakes until we hit bottom. Muley was right there and Prince a little ways from him."

"That is one smart horse," said Mike admiringly.

"He sure is," agreed Dusty.

"What about Scout?" Shelley urged. "Did you find him okay?"

Dusty frowned. "That was the tough part. Scout is so afraid of gunshot, I thought I'd lost him for sure this time. That's a pretty big forest to look through. And now they've got all those cougars." He ran his hand through his hair. "All I could think of was poor Scout getting disoriented and ending up dinner for a cougar in the middle of nowhere."

"Oh, Dusty, what happened?" said Shelley, bouncing up and down in her chair.

"I finally found him and you'll never guess where."

"I got a feeling we're going to find out," said Mike.

"After calling and shouting and just figuring the worst, guess who climbed out from underneath my pickup truck?"

"Scout," said Shelley joyfully.

"That's right," said Dusty. "And he was no less the wear from his wild run."

"Oh, thank goodness," Shelley said reverently, clasping her hands together, bright red fingernails intertwined.

Mike took a drink of his coffee. "Well, that's quite the story. Sorry I missed that ride."

"Sorry you did too." Dusty hesitated. "But I've got to say, Cassie's a pretty good partner in a gunfight."

The three of them laughed. "I bet she is," Mike agreed.

"What about that bad guy?" asked Shelley, having learned the animals were all safe. "What happened to him?"

"After we got the animals all rounded up, we took him down to the sheriff's department. Turns out he's got quite a record down here in the U.S., and Canada can't wait to get their hands on him when we're done."

"Why is that no surprise?" Mike commented.

"Well, good for you guys," said Shelley, clapping again.

"Yup. Just cleaning up the woods one bad guy at a time, I guess." Dusty stood up and threw some bills on the table.

"Or one family at a time," observed Mike, watching Dusty. "Where are you going?"

"I've got a dinner date with a beautiful mountain woman," said Dusty. "I don't want to be late."

"Hey, Dusty," Mike called to him as he walked away.

Dusty stopped and turned back. "What?"

"You did it. You saved her this time."

A huge white-toothed grin spread across Dusty's face. "Yes, I did." He turned and walked out the door whistling.

The ride continues in book 4…

Chapter One

Dusty sat at his desk and stared at the open file in front of him. His clients were coming in this afternoon and he needed to give them an update on their case. Once again, his mind slipped from the pages in front of him to the mountains.

"Here's your coffee, Mr. Dustin Rose." The gray-haired, slightly plump woman placed a steaming cup on his desk.

"Thank you, Mrs. Phillips," he said gratefully. He picked it up and took a drink. The hot liquid flowed down his throat and he felt better already.

A satisfied smile passed over her face, "Anything else this morning?" she asked brightly.

"Not at the moment. I think the Wilsons are coming in at 1:30?"

"Yes, they are. Let me know if you need anything." She turned and left his office, closing the door carefully behind her.

Armed with a cup of coffee, Dusty ran his fingers through his hair and concentrated on the file. Faintly in the background he heard the phone ring in the front office and Mrs. Phillips saying, "Just a moment, please." Almost simultaneously Dusty's phone buzzed on his desk.

"Mr. Bill Grisham is on line one."

Bill Grisham. I haven't heard that name for a while. Dusty felt a cold chill. *I wonder what he wants?* Hopefully it wasn't any more about the Stanton family. Bill was a Seattle attorney who had represented him in a wrongful death case. Dusty flashed back to last fall on the high hunt in the Pasayten with Pinto Stanton going ballistic at his Uncle Bob's outfit, and before that, Clem Stanton in the Pasayten and the abduction of the Ross family. Then the family patriarch Buster Stanton, who started a wrongful death suit as retribution for the death of his relatives. *Hopefully there weren't any more Stantons out there.* Buster had been the final straw. When Dusty had gotten back from the hunting trip, Buster had served him with a wrongful death suit for Pinto and Clem's deaths. But in the end, when Buster had tried to take justice in his own hands, he wound up in jail himself.

Dusty punched in the button and picked up the receiver, "Hey, Bill."

"Hey, Dusty. How are things out in the country?"

"Not so bad." Then Dusty couldn't help himself, "Is everything okay?"

Bill immediately caught the apprehension in Dusty's voice and chuckled, "Oh, don't worry, everything's fine. Buster is right where he needs to be."

Dusty's shoulders relaxed as he felt a weight lifting, "That's a relief." He took a drink of coffee. "To what do I owe the pleasure of this call?"

"I needed to ask you a little favor," began Bill. "I've got a client and honestly, Dusty, I'm swamped. I just got a call and I'm in on a big airline crash in the Bahamas. It's a huge class action suit." Bill warmed to his topic. "Tons of fatalities. They just drove the freaking thing right off the end of the airstrip."

Dusty flinched. Wrongful death cases weren't his favorite, but he could tell Bill was in his element. "How did you get a case like that in Seattle?"

"I've got friends," said Bill smugly.

"I guess."

Bill caught himself, "I could go on about that case all day, but I have a client down in Oregon, and I think he's right up your alley."

"Really," Dusty said, intrigued as to what Bill thought his "alley" was. He didn't have to wait long.

"He's a horseshoer and he lives on the outskirts of a little town called Joseph."

"I know where that is; the gateway to the Eagle Cap Wilderness," said Dusty.

Bill laughed, "I should have just said that. I forget most people go by cities, but you go by wildernesses."

"You got that right," agreed Dusty.

"He does some shoeing along with the outfitting business. In Joseph. If you want to live there and you're not a farmer, you pretty much do whatever it takes." Bill paused. "He's a hardworking guy. I met him in the service years ago. That's why he looked me up."

"So what's the case?" Dusty stared out the window, his full attention now on the call.

"He's getting hit with a wrongful death suit. He took a couple on a pack trip in the Eagle Cap on their anniversary. It was supposed to be a big celebration. Instead, the woman was killed in an accident with the horses."

"How did that happen?"

"I'll let Jim tell you, if you're interested."

"Oh, I'm interested," Dusty said firmly.

"Great. His name is Jim Murphy, and I'll give him your information. He's pretty shook up about this, so I know he's going to want to talk to you right away."

"I'm happy to be of service."

"Dusty, I owe you one," said Bill earnestly. "I told Jim I couldn't do it, but I'd get him the best—well, next best," he corrected himself.

Grinning, Dusty replied, "Thanks, Bill. I'll wait for his call."

After hanging up the phone, Dusty stared at it for a few minutes. The Eagle Cap Wilderness was one of the places he'd always wanted to visit. He'd read it was one of the most beautiful places in the Northwestern United States. It was first occupied by the ancestors of the Nez Perce tribe around AD 1400 and later by the Cayuse, the Shoshone and Bannocks. The wilderness was used as hunting grounds for big horn sheep, deer and to gather huckleberries. It was summer home to the Joseph Band of the Nez Perce tribe.

The front door bell jingled. Dusty's office door opened and Mike walked in.

"Hey, Dust," Mike greeted him and sat down.

"Make yourself at home," said Dusty sarcastically. He had long ago given up on trying to get Mike to knock first.

Mike smiled at him, undaunted. "You want to get some lunch?"

"Sure." Dusty stood up. "I was just thinking. Would you be interested in going on a pack trip with me?"

"Yes." Mike responded immediately.

Dusty paused, "Aren't you even going to ask me where?"

"It's all good, but okay. Where?" Mike said obligingly.

"The Eagle Cap Wilderness."

"Whoa! Heck, yeah!" It was Mike's turn to stop. "You're asking me now and not Cassie?"

"It's going to be business," said Dusty, walking toward the door.

"Huh. Packing in and business," Mike repeated, following Dusty out the door. "I love this job."

About The Author

Powerful new novelist, Susie Drougas, rides with her own Greek packer, husband Mike.

Susie has written a series of exciting new books set in the high country. She is a longtime court reporter in Eastern Washington and has been packing horses in the mountains for over 25 years. She is the mother of two grown daughters. She and her husband Mike are members of the Back Country Horsemen of Washington.

Susie is passionate about educating and sharing the beauty and the bounty of riding and packing horses. She has effectively put us in the saddle to experience firsthand a rugged backcountry pack trip in the Pasayten Wilderness in her first novel, "Pack Saddles & Gunpowder." She has carried on the ride in her second novel, "Mountain Cowboys." And has returned to a fall hunting trip in the Pasayten for her latest novel, "High Hunt."

www.SusieDrougas.com

To Vic & Shari
Love
Gram